Martyred

Alisha Perkins

For every woman who never asked for a halo…

CHAPTER 1

ELIZA

ELIZA ALWAYS THOUGHT OF CAMILLE when she saw blood. It brought her back to that claw-foot, peeling porcelain bathtub, the water a hazy pink from all the blood that had mixed in. Back then the sight of it made her nauseous and terrified. Now, years later, watching blood drip down her right pointer finger, she was annoyed, and slightly turned on. She got up off all fours and wiped the garden dirt from the back of her hand onto the top of her thigh, leaving a black streak across her worn overalls. She raised her finger to her mouth and slowly licked the copper-colored drops as if they were nothing more than tears that had fallen. Iron on her tongue was a taste she had acquired an appreciation for over the last few years. The blood was there, but she no longer felt any pain. Her eyes closed and she relished in the moment for only a second, any longer would've seemed monstrous. First flecks of the morning sunlight lit her strawberry blond hair, which was pulled back into a low pony under her large-brimmed gray-and-white hat. A gift from her two daughters for her thirty-fifth birthday, a big one. Too close to forty, too far from young.

It was that very birthday when the revelations started happening. Feeling less than, wanting to be more. Remembering blowing out thirty-five candles nestled in the dark chocolate mousse cake still held in Millie's arms as her friends' singing voices surrounded her. Their faces shimmering in the soft candlelight, making her feel safe among their glow. Safe enough to finally no longer ignore the nagging in her mind and pit in her stomach. The craving to change. Change herself. Change the world.

Early birthday–morning coffee had led to looking out over her acreage, the trees lying dormant under the blanket of winter that still hunkered heavy. A few plants had found their way through the most recent snowfall that had covered her world and left it white for a few hours before the dirt and grime fell on top and brought the purity back down to reality. Nothing stays that simple or beautiful for long. Thoughts started just like those plants, small but determined, longing to break through the tough exterior and be seen.

Her suburban mom friends were all older than her—*wiser* is what they would say if you asked. Age is an idea, not an exact, whatever that meant. That didn't seem to help the nagging that seemed to spider web in her mind, telling her that she had yet to do something meaningful, something more than being someone's wife and mother. *A good wife*, she liked to think, *and a better mother*. But that didn't leave her feeling complete. What was a life if it only led to being someone's support system? Where was the effect on society? Where was the change she was supposed to be in the world?

Thirty-five wasn't when it really started. The spiders had been there for a while, dormant, moving only when poked. Weaving little networks, small thoughts, tiny webs to catch the insecurities and inadequacies for her to return to at a moment's notice. Over time the webs had grown, the spiders working harder, weaving, catching, terrorizing. God, she hated spiders.

Being caught in a web forces a person into fight or flight mode. Eliza had two choices: fight her way out, leaving a mark behind her, or stay caught and quiet. No one would fault her—she had it pretty good out there in

Darlington, Maryland. Married to Rhett Kingfield, one of the owners of the Boston Reveres, the professional baseball team. Rhett made his money in farmland, which was pretty funny with his last name being Kingfield. It strangely fit baseball, as well. Most days, the land they lived on left much to be desired, but the other days it somehow suffocated Eliza.

Her throat was closing, chest tightening, spiders hanging between the white-washed and worn fence posts of the garden she was kneeling on. Her roses were in full bloom, their petals reaching toward the sky, and her fingers were still in her mouth, lingering too long. She had decided back then, on her birthday, not to fly under the radar; she had chosen to fight. The spiders no longer unnerved her like they did then. She wanted to be one of them now. Weaving, catching, terrorizing.

She tilted her face up toward the sun. Darkness may have been her comfort, but the warmth was renewing. Another day, another chance to make a difference. Her finger grazed her bottom lip as it dropped from her mouth. The blood was gone, but not for long.

CHAPTER 2

CAMILLE

THE PHONE RANG FOR THE THIRD TIME in the five minutes since Camille had walked into what her boss called an office and she called a glorified cubicle. The felt walls were littered with pictures of her three kids in different stages of life and play, her husband of seventeen years sprinkled in among them. He was always there, good ol' faithful Noel. Standing no taller than 5'10 on a good day, with shoulders not much broader than hers, he wasn't the type of man who turned heads, but he was reliable and kind with an odd sense of humor, one Camille found endearing. For the most part, parenting was his gig as a part-time stay-at-home dad while she climbed the ladder at PTSK for the last twenty-some years. Starting with a short stint as in intern to Bre O'Brien (only one "e" to set her apart from the other anchors, as if there were so many named Bree), Camille had worked her way through the ranks. Intern to production assistant, on to producer and now lead anchor. "A face for radio" her aunt had always joked just to bring her down a peg, but here she was, front and center at one of the largest TV stations in the country. She called the heart of Manhattan her work home, though they decided to call Williamsburg, New York, in Brooklyn their actual home. A small part of Camille died when they moved out of Manhattan, but it was for the kids. *The things we do for our kids.*

The phone rang a fourth time.

"What now?" she said under her breath before picking up the receiver.

And with her best Michigan manners, she muttered (with a smile of course), "Hello."

"Millie? Why do you sound so damn happy?" she heard Eliza say through the earpiece.

Only Eliza called her "Millie," a nickname she gave her back in middle school as part of their proving to others their they-only-needed-each-other phase. It turned out to not be a phase; they really only did need each other. "Millie" coming out of anyone else's mouth sounded contrived and forced, but not Eliza's.

"Oh E, it's you. My damn phone has rang off the hook since I got in. I've been trying to maintain my niceties while silently cussing everyone out."

"Quietly cussing isn't really your jam." Eliza chuckled a little. "That kind of day, huh? What's going on in the big word of important people?"

"Always something. You know New York."

"I miss New York." Eliza sighed into the speaker a little too loudly.

"Come visit. You know country life is slowly killing you, right?"

"Yeah, I know," Eliza lied. Deep down she had found a peace and quiet she never knew existed before they moved out here. Sure, she missed the chaos of NYC, but she also loved the serenity the wheat blowing in the wind brought her. Admitting that out loud to Millie was a nonstarter. She was a city lifer, certain those who outright chose the country or suburb life over the hustle and bustle must not be living their fullest life. Pieces of her belonged in the city, but most of her belonged here, in her garden, finding intention.

"Maybe I could sneak away for a night," Eliza said, not sure she was 100 percent on board with the idea.

"Oh my God, yes!" Millie chirped.

"Okay. I will chat with Rhett. I'll let you get back to saving the world or whatever you do in that fancy office of yours," Eliza said through a smile.

"Saving the world by sharing the depressing news one story at a time."

"At least you look good doing it."

"That's the worst of it. I don't. I haven't been to the gym in like two weeks with work and the kids. I am gaining a pound a day on average, which is like ten per day on TV. Shit. I can't even imagine what I must look like to the viewers." Millie exhaled as if there were no hope.

Millie was an anomaly in the news world. Blond, busty, bikini bod, and bubbly were the characteristics of most female news anchors. Millie was a black-haired, brazen bad ass with a large bust and a hell of a booty. She often wondered if she were part of the station's attempt to be more open minded in their outward portrayal. They wanted to appear as the station that didn't care about social norms or outward appearances. Tolerant, open minded, and barrier breaking. Millie didn't love the idea of being the barrier breaker, but sometimes to get what you want, you have to be a little uncomfortable. She was beginning to feel uncomfortable in her wardrobe on set, and it was starting to do things to her head.

Skipping the gym had been part of the problem. The other, and likely larger part, had been the lack of intimacy in her marriage. Noel was always too tired to get it up. Since he couldn't get it up, she was putting down the food. Comfort comes in many forms, and for Millie it came in late-night Cheetos at the office or a doughnut on the car ride in from Brooklyn. The residue on her fingers was a constant reminder of the person she was becoming. A person she didn't much care for. One who works too much, lacks any close connections other than with Eliza, and one who shoves her feelings down her throat.

She looked down at her fingers, seeing the sugar glaze from her morning doughnut (doughnuts) still sticking to the edges of her perfectly French-tipped fingernails.

"Okay, text me later after you talk to Rhett. I am going to find a way to get you here. It has been too long. Love you."

Millie ended their call with their standard ending since college. The handset slid back into the cradle as she brought her finger to her perfectly Kat Von D Misfit– covered red lips and licked the sweet, sugary, crystal doughnut residue.

CHAPTER 3

VERA

PAT'S COARSE TONGUE LICKED Vera's fingers awake. She rolled over in the bed, now face-to-face with the hairless cat that was treating her fingers like morning snack sticks. Pat was short for *Patanjali*, the father of modern yoga. Vera would, of course, never have had a cat, much less a hairless one, and especially not one named after some yoga guy. The cat, the name, and the lack of hair were all due to her live-in girlfriend, Spencer Morris. Spencer was one of those women whom *The Bachelor* always has unique job monikers for. Cologne connoisseur (sells perfume at Macy's), agricultural engineer (farmer), manscaper (waxer), or male model (dumb but pretty). Spencer didn't have an actual job, per se. She was a woman of many talents, or "passions" as she would say. "Organic faith healer" was the title she led with most often.

Spencer believed that cats were magical creatures in ancient Egypt who brought luck to the people they lived with, but Spencer had bad allergies. So hairless, lucky Pat was now face-to-face with Vera's morning breath.

Vera was less granola, more power suit. As the founder of Sutton PR, resurrecting careers and dodging bullets had become just another Tuesday for this ferocious female in a man's world.

Glass ceilings weren't just broken by Vera, they were obliterated, leaving tiny pieces scattered on the floor at her feet, where she would crush them even smaller with the red soles of her pumps. That was the only way she knew how to do it. The way her father modeled when they first came to America from Columbia a week before Vera's sixth birthday.

Jorge Suarez had wanted a better life for his precious little Vera and decided the only way that would happen was for him to take Vera and his wife, Clara, to the United States of America, away from their war-torn country. Several years, two trials, and many lawyers later, they were granted political asylum and then residency. Five years after that, they became American citizens. The process was hard but worth it for a better life for Vera, Jorge would say. Along with citizenship came a name change. Jorge feared things would be hard enough for them as it was, so he decided to lighten the load by taking on a traditional last name. Suarez became Sutton and Jorge became American. While Clara and Vera settled into their new American life, Jorge found odd jobs to keep them afloat. This landed him on the floor of a large computer software company as a janitor. Jorge held several degrees in Columbia, but none translated to the United States, so while he dragged the cloth mop across the floor, he took mental notes of the happenings around him. Over time he began to see things the engineers were missing, but he stayed silent so as not to squander his job and risk their family losing their small apartment in San Rafael, California. In his spare time, he coded a unique program and presented it to one of the company's CEOs. Jorge was called into his office later that day, and what Jorge thought was the end of his career became just the beginning.

Engineer money was enough to send Vera to college anywhere she wanted, but she hadn't needed any with her valedictorian grades, which earned her a scholarship to NYU. She was the first in her family to go to an American college, though her father wouldn't live to see it. As her mother smiled and cried in the crowd, Vera walked across the stage, looked toward the sky, smiled at her father, and made a promise to make him proud and break barriers the way he did. She lifted her tassel from the right to the left, accepted her degree, and scurried as quickly as she could into the arms of her best friends waiting for her offstage. In Eliza and Camille's arms, Vera cried, only for a minute, anymore and it would make a scene. Camille and Eliza held her tightly for that minute, Camille trying her best not to cry, as well. Then, with eyes wiped and backs straightened, the three headed off to the rest of their lives.

Eliza, now in middle of nowhere, Maryland; Camille in the heart of NYC (well, Brooklyn, but good luck getting her to admit it); and Vera in DC.

Vera pulled her fingers away from Pat, grabbed her cell phone, and saw the text from Eliza just checking in. She made a mental note to write back later and began to bite her fingernail as she opened Twitter on her phone, bracing herself for yet another man throwing his dick where it didn't belong, and knowing she would have to fix it. Sometimes she truly hated her job.

She spat a fingernail chunk on the floor and began to scroll.

CHAPTER 4

ELIZA

WHEN DID PEANUT BUTTER become a hard line in schools? Guns can enter our schools, but peanut butter, that was a hard-fought no. It is so hard to pack a lunch every day without incorporating a random peanut butter and jelly in the mix, Eliza thought as she stared into their Viking fridge, trying to come up with another fancy lunch to make the other moms talk. She grabbed the turkey, cream cheese, and pickles; pickle "sushi" it was. The other moms might not be wagging their tongues at her Pinterest-worthy lunch, but it was better than another turkey sandwich.

"The girls," as they had affectionately been called, were two light-haired beauties like their mother. Their father's wit and mother's expressions. The older one, Kinsley, the future chemist and rule follower. Eliza worked hard to show her that some lines are intended to be crossed and some rules meant to be broken. Glass ceilings don't just break on their own.

Piper, on the other hand, was one of those children who would grow up to be a strong leader, not allowing anyone to walk over her. In the meantime, though, she was skirting the line with her parents between strong willed and just being a dick. Most days she left her doting parents in stitches with her wittiness and sarcasm. Two kids, same parents, same household, same rules, two very different offspring.

Once the girls were off to school, she took a seat in her office (the one her in-laws never understood why she needed) in their gorgeous home she had designed. Of course, Rhett wanted to take some of the credit, and she let him, but they both knew she was the real visionary of this place. Convincing her to move to the country had taken more time than Rhett liked, but in the end he won. He usually did.

Mindlessly she began to scroll through Twitter, a morning ritual she was mildly aware of, not knowing if it was good or bad. Coffee in one hand, fingers scrolling the track pad with the other as she got caught up on the world's headlines (and gossip). Love–hate relationships are hard to break, and her social media habit was one of the worst. Every day something new to worry about, concern yourself with, or take a stance on. Twitter was flooded with #metoos, #futureisfemale, #blacklivesmatter, and #politics. The coffee was a little too hot this morning and burned her tongue as she took a sip. She swallowed, shook her head, and kept scrolling. Story after story of women being sexually assaulted by men, paid less than men, talked down to by men. It was exhausting and aggravating. Out here among the oak trees and hay, it seemed there was little she could do to change it. Her daughters were being told over and again that they could do anything, be anything, and take no shit from anyone, but deep in her stomach with the still-hot coffee sat a pit of feeling useless. Her children needed her less, and Rhett was gone more, which left Eliza with too much time on her hands and too many of the world's problems to fix. With no answer in sight, she kept scrolling, kept reading, kept sipping the coffee, though she could no longer taste it. She couldn't help but wonder if this is what her life had come to, drinking tasteless coffee and leaving no mark on the world she lived in.

A text from Millie lit up her cell phone screen and pulled her of out her temporary self-pity.

"NYC. This weekend. Boss man is having a company party to celebrate himself or some bullshit. Be here. I need a date."

A smile spread across Eliza's face. Millie clearly wasn't letting her get out of coming to visit. She might not have all the answers, but she now had plans, and that was something.

"Shouldn't you be taking Noel as your date?" she texted back.

She waited for Millie to write back

"Nah. He can watch the kids. I need a night out and I need my E."

Needed. It felt better than Eliza realized to be "needed." She bit her lower lip, felt her chest warm, and wrote back "Okay. I'll text Rhett, but count me in."

"YAY!! Wear something sexy. I want everyone to be jealous of my date. See you soon. Muah!"

"Sexy, huh? I will have to do some digging, but for you I think I can make it happen."

Sexy wasn't Eliza's go-to, but she was kidding herself to think she didn't have a wardrobe that most women would desire. Rhett made up for his trips in dresses, red-soled shoes, and diamonds. His guilt was all over her. Initially she didn't love it, but over time she realized it was more about him than her, and so she allowed herself to slowly and carefully skirt the edges of being a Stepford Wife. Being the owner of a baseball team meant that things in Rhett's life had to be and look a certain way, and while she pushed the limits, she never pushed too far. The last sip of coffee ran down her throat. She swallowed it down the same way she swallowed being subconsciously told how to act and who to be. It didn't sit right. It never had.

CHAPTER 5

CAMILLE

A TOAST TO #1

The invitation was practically a penned pat on the back for Connor Dixon, the head of PTSK ever since his father had been hit with early onset dementia and he had stepped in and "saved the day," or at least that was the way he told it.

Connor and Melia Dixon want to thank everyone for their support and productivity by inviting you to be a guest for a toast to being #1 in the rankings for the third year in a row.

The Dixons were millionaires several times over, owning more houses than she did shoes. Camille had never been to the Dixon mansion—or was it a complex? She wasn't sure. She just knew it was a big-ass house on the Upper East Side. Two Boots or Tanoshi were the only reasons Camille ever wandered over to that side of the city. Pizza and sushi were worth it, but otherwise she always felt too underdressed and tawdry in that part of town. If Connor needed a party to toot his own horn about the work that the people like her were actually doing to make him #1, then she sure as hell was going to drink her weight in underpaid wages at that party. Maybe when Connor was good and liquored up, she could finally broach the subject of getting paid as much as Brian Tannon, her cohost. For a station that thrived on being modern, equal, and all that, this was a black spot they needed to fix. *If not, it might make for a good exposé during the evening news,* Camille thought. At any given moment, she loved the idea that she could blow the lid off this whole thing and ruin the network. It was like a loaded gun she kept in her stockings. She didn't have a conceal and carry, though, so technically the gun was a liability for her too. One she needed to deal with before it went too far. Couple cups of courage, and this Friday she would tackle the problem head on—maybe even chat about the new online initiative she had heard rumbling about.

As if reading her mind, Connor popped his head into her "office."

"Hey there. How's my favorite anchor?" he said, smiling and revealing his veneers that looked more like Chiclets than actual teeth.

"Hey," Camille replied, mustering up a smile that could never match his level of douche. He was an asshat, but for the most part, he was a pretty good boss too.

"You see the invite? You will be there, right?"

"Yep." She peered at him over her computer screen, the electronic invite still playing classical music in the background.

"Great. Should be a terrific night."

"Sounds like it will be fun. I plan to take full advantage of the open bar," Camille said, bearing her real teeth.

"I wouldn't have it any other way," Connor replied. "I'll let you get back to making me the big bucks. See you Friday." He grinned again.

Camille smiled without showing her teeth this time.

As soon as he was gone, she shut the invite on her screen, took a sip of her coffee (through a straw, of course, as not to wreck her TV ready teeth or lipstick), and headed toward the set.

She rolled her eyes as she recalled her conversation with Connor. The guy reeked of arrogance and old money. He had been spoiled with it his whole life carrying himself as if he were entitled to it instead of earned it. All of that was true, of course, but such an unflattering look, acting as if the world was yours for the taking. She hated that deep down she actually liked the guy, arrogance and all.

CHAPTER 6

VERA

TODAY WAS SUPPOSED TO BE different; easy. Well maybe not easy, but easier than her days usually go. Vera had already blocked off her calendar for the entire day and told her staff not to disturb.

The first vibration from her cell came as she was sitting in the hard, clear plastic chairs of Dr. Whitman's office. Her hand was over the armrest holding onto Spencer's in the space between their weirdly comfortable, yet odd-looking, seats. Spencer couldn't stop talking about how Dr. Whitman was the very best in the field, over thousands of successful procedures have been performed, and how with the yoga and an all-natural diet, this would be an easy feat. Vera felt the vibrations again in the back pocket of her jeans. The sound of the vibrating against the plastic eerily reminded her of a fart that someone was tried to keep in but had somehow escaped. She hoped Spencer couldn't hear it, though she didn't know what would've upset her more—knowing it was her cell phone or thinking she was being inappropriate.

Dr. Whitman knocked on the door before opening it only a fraction and peeked her petite face into the room, her sleek blond ponytail falling gently over her shoulder as she leaned in.

"All right to come in?" she queried.

What a strange thing to ask, Vera thought. No one was undressed or indecent, so why did this woman feel like she needed to ask before entering her own office? Was she being polite or submissive? Either way, Vera was strangely endeared to her, though she wished she would've walked in like she owned the place; she did, after all.

"Of course," Spencer cooed, obviously impressed with the good doctor for her manners and not her gall.

"Great, great," she said with a smile as she entered the room and took a seat behind the desk, *her* desk. Vera was glad that at least she didn't ask to sit, as well.

"Spencer and Vera," Dr. Whitman said in a manner that didn't imply whether it was a question or a statement.

"Yep!" Spencer chimed in.

Dr. Whitman looked up and locked eyes with Vera. Vera's phone buzzed again. She shifted her legs, crossing them, allowing the phone in her back pocket to lift off the seat enough to no longer make a noise.

"Yes," Vera responded and looked back at the back of her computer.

This whole thing had been Spencer's idea from the start. Vera, for her part, could have gone her whole life without having kids. A mother was not something she ever thought would be on her tombstone. *Mom* was a word reserved for the women like Eliza and Camille, women who were in tune with others' needs and went out of their way to meet them. It wasn't that Vera was cold; she was hardened. Life had given her many things, but it had also taken. She had her freedom, her career, and her Spencer, but she lacked a mother and father. Colon cancer had taken her father, and Clara died of a broken heart not long after. Seven months later, to be exact, and it wasn't a broken heart as much as it was a failing one. Clara liked to sugar coat the story by saying that her heart was too broken without Jorge to go on. Vera liked the idea, too, so she let it stick. That hardening had started before all of that though. Back in middle school and high school when God started gifting her with the goods that got her noticed—not that she needed them—her newfound curves only escalated her already creamy, olive skin and straight, long, dark hair.

"Boys will be boys" is what her mother had said when Vera came home crying because of the things the boys would taunt her with at school. The catcalls and comments felt degrading and disgusting to Vera, but no one around her seemed to stop it. She already knew that she wasn't interested in boys, which made the entire exchange extra vile. She would feel a hand slap her ass on her way to organic chemistry or someone holler out "Chica, you are like a piñata cuz I wanna hit that" as she twisted the lock on her locker. *Keep quiet, head down, keep going*—the words her father had lived by when they got to America. She repeated them in her head, but it took everything in her not to make noise, fight back, and stop them. Being passive had gotten her through high school, but fighting back had given her the chance to own her own company. This piñata was done taking a beating.

"Vera!" she heard Spencer say out of the fog.

Spencer's head was cocked to the side, awaiting her response to a question Vera hadn't even heard.

"I'm so sorry. What did you say?" Vera asked the doctor again and caught Spencer huff a little under her breath.

"I asked if you're ready to talk about the results?" the doctor repeated, not looking half as irritated as Spencer.

Vera felt her phone buzz again, raising her anxiety level even higher.

"Yes, of course." She smiled and looked at Spencer, who didn't meet her gaze.

"Well, it seems there is good news and bad news," the doctor began as she scrolled through the computer screen, waiting for them to tell her which way to go, yet never asking out loud

Breaking the uncomfortable silence, "The challenging news is that it seems Spencer's uterus is a hostile environment and not ideally suited to carry a child." She went on.

Spencer's mouth opened, her jaw dropping slightly, eyes welling with tears as she turned to Vera.

Buzz.

Vera mouthed "I'm sorry" back to her, knowing it wouldn't make a difference.

"The good news, however..." the doctor continued, not acknowledging or noticing the exchange. "Vera, your uterus is healthy and should handle a pregnancy fairly well" She stopped scrolling, looked up, and smiled as though this somehow fixed the situation.

Vera shook her head side to side rapidly.

Buzz.

"I'm sorry. What?" Vera's voice cracked.

"You are a perfect candidate to carry the fetus. In fact, we can start you on hormones today and get the process underway. You can even look through our sperm sample book today if you like." Dr. Whitmore was still smiling.

Buzz.

It was beginning to feel like the phone was buzzing in unison with the buzz in her ears.

Spencer reached out and squeezed her hand, making Vera realize she had let go once she heard Vera's uterus was better than hers. Vera's eyes met hers. In them she could see part excitement, part grudge—Spencer holding Vera's healthy uterus against her.

Choking back tears, Spencer said, "V, what do you think?"

Her lungs suddenly felt like they were collapsing as her breathing somehow quickened. *Me, carry a baby? Me, a mother? Me, pregnant? Me, stuffed like someone's piñata?* Vera's mind was swirling.

The back of her neck started to feel clammy as she looked between Spencer and the doctor.

"I . . . I just . . . I . . ."

Her phone buzzed again.

"I gotta get this," Vera said as she pulled her damp hand out of Spencer's and reached for her back pocket.

"V, you promised!" Spencer called after her, and Vera wasn't sure whether she meant about the baby or the phone. Phone in hand, she walked swiftly through the lobby of excited, hopeful parents-to-be and into the elevator, franticly pushing the door close button before anyone (namely Spencer) could get in.

She finally felt the breath catch in her lungs once the doors shut. In the corner of the fake mahogany-walled elevator, Vera slowly slunk down into a ball on the marble floor. As the elevator jumped to a start and began its slow descent from the thirty-fourth floor where the Whitman Clinic resided, Vera squeezed her eyes shut for only second, regained her composure, and by floor twenty-eight was standing back up with her back rest against the wall.

Buzz.

She brought the phone to her screen and saw a slew of texts from Dash, her assistant.

"Sorry to bug you, but . . ."

"I know you have the day off . . ."

She slid the screen open and immediately saw the six missed calls and fourteen texts. The most recent one she opened read: *CALL IMMEDIATELY. CONNOR DIXON IS HERE WITH HIS WIFE. HE WANTS TO RUN FOR MAYOR OF NEW YORK.*

So, it was going to be that kind of a day.

CHAPTER 7

ELIZA

ELIZA COULD FEEL HER FINGERS beginning to prune in the dirty sink water when Kinsley called to get her attention. "Did you know that the female black widow spiders eat the males after they make babies with them?" she asked as she gripped the edges of her book and her mouth half full of pretzels.

"Kinsley, don't talk with your mouth full," Eliza requested from her sink, her hands covered in soapy water.

"And that only the female spiders are the ones who bite people and kill them?" she kept going, finally swallowing the pretzel remains. "That means that the girls are in charge, right? They are the ones who people fear? And the boys are scared of them too? That would be so awesome!" Kinsley smiled.

"Yeah, it is rather different than people, huh?" Eliza responded, her back still to Kinsley. Deep down the whole thing unnerved her more than she would care to admit. Spiders, eight-legged femme fatales, and here we were two-legged doormats for men on their way up. Rhett was always incredibly supportive of her and the girls, always the first to tell her daughters that they could be and do anything a boy could. The ideal feminist male. Her father was also a patron believer in women and their infinite capabilities. Truth be told, it was mainly only Eliza's internal thoughts and fears that kept her from going all "pussy hat" in on this feminist movement.

Too extreme. Too loud. Too callous. Too much. She didn't want to be one of those women. Sign wielding, curse throwing, angry, bra-burning gals who assumed this was the only way. Maybe it was; maybe she was wrong. What she desperately wanted in herself she pushed onto her girls.

"I want to be a black widow," Kinsley declared as she shoved more pretzel sticks into her mouth.

"I think you just might be, honey." Eliza smiled over her shoulder at the bright little girl seated at the counter. She was going to change the world, but first Eliza had to start that change for her. It was one thing to preach; it was another to act.

Action. Battle. Combat. Fight.

Her hands balled into fists under the water. She wasn't sure what it was yet, but she knew it was time to do something. Finding it may be hard, but her eyes were more open than they had ever been.

Water dripped off her hands as she pulled them out of the sink and dried them with a towel. She grabbed her phone and texted Rhett, "Hey. Is it okay if I go to see Millie in NYC this weekend? She has an event she wants me to be her date for." He would say yes; he always said yes. He was one of the good ones. Back when they married, she wasn't aware of how rare that was. He was her corndog in a world of plain wieners.

Phone back on the counter, hands back in the water. Back to being the good wife and mother. She could hear Kinsley's pencil scribbling down notes behind her, small strokes on her way to a better future. One where the women and their hourglass figures are in charge, and men fear them. Oh what a wonderful world it would be.

CHAPTER 8

CAMILLE

SHE HAD JUST SLIPPED INTO the soft, worn sheets of her marital bed, which had recently felt more like a battleground, when her phone buzzed. "Okay. I am in. Shopping may have to be involved. I will see what I can come up with here. I have one more request though . . . invite Vera. It's been too long, and this thing between you guys needs to get resolved."

Camille's smile turned to a grimace as she read the end of Eliza's text. Invite Vera. Why? Why did she have to go there? Eliza was a lot of things, and stubborn was at the very top. If Camille didn't get Vera to come, then E wasn't coming, and that Camille couldn't stand for. God forbid she would have to make Noel get dressed up. His idea of fancy involved a V-neck sweater and Dockers khakis. You could wear that kind of thing when you spent your entire day teaching math to middle-school kids, but in the real world, one where no one talks about Fortnite, you needed to own a suit. Camille had tried for years to get him to buy one, but he always stayed strong in his convictions that there wasn't anywhere that his sweater wouldn't do. It had become just one of the many things she had given up on.

Sweaters. Kids' schedules. Dinner plans. Sex. All the fights she had stopped trying to fight. Her life felt like a series of concessions. Partially because of her mom guilt and partially because she was too tired to fight him anymore. It became easier to say yes than to stand up for what she wanted. No one at the office would ever believe she was a woman who got walked over.

"Strong," "confident," "powerful" were words she would hear whispered about her (or "bitch," too, if she were being candid with herself). As much as she would like to believe those were true, they were just fallacies, as well. The only part of her that was strong was her coffee (she was up to four cups a day). She was confident that she was failing at life. And the most powerful thing she did everyday was take a Xanax to fall asleep at night. It was nice to be revered and looked up to, but it was exhausting, as well. Her self-confidence was somewhere at the bottom of that bag of Cheetos she would eat on the ride home from work. No matter how many she ate, she was always left still digging for more with cheese-residue fingers, an orange coat of shame.

Her headboard shook as she struck her head back at it, probably the most action it had gotten in years. *Vera*, she thought as her head hit it again. What to say to her. Things had been tense between them ever since the Risner scandal last year. For a long time, Vera had been Camille's greatest asset in the media world. A real, live gossip stream in her back pocket. Vera had the scoop on everyone and everything that would make the headlines. Of course, the dirt came with a catch. Vera needed Camille just as much as Camille needed her. Camille was her spin agent. A bloodline straight to the American public. Vera could tell them what to think and how to feel about a person or situation just by the way she worded it to Camille. For her part, Camille was no idiot; she knew she was being fed a certain story for specific reasons, but the dish was too good not to use, so she played Vera's puppet.

Sam Risner was where the marionette broke. Sam had been a longtime client of Vera's, asking her to help him raise money and investors in a start-up company he was building that would give back half of its profits to charity. Long story short, PSTK got wind that they weren't donating half of their profits, in fact they were not donating anything. Camille reached out to Vera for a comment, and Vera had asked her to hold the story until they got their ducks in a row. The ducks were never given a chance to fall in line as Camille broke the story an hour later on the six p.m. news.

"I am sorry. I had no choice. The boss said we had to be the first to break the story. I hope you understand," Camille had texted Vera in the first commercial break. Vera never responded. That was four months ago.

"Why are you banging your head against the wall?" Noel asked, looking at Camille like she was going crazy. He was reading *Alexander Hamilton* by Ron Chernow in the spot next to her on their queen bed. It wasn't that they couldn't afford a king, money wasn't tight, but they had promised when they got married that they would always have a queen bed so they could stay close to one another. Idealistic views of the young and in love. What Camille wouldn't do now to get a little more space and a little farther from his snoring at night.

"E won't come to the party unless I get Vera to come," she said through gritted teeth.

Noel looked at her but didn't say anything, waiting for her to continue. He did this sometimes, a trick he had learned in marriage therapy the few times they had gone. Stay quiet, people will talk if you just stay quiet.

Camille continued, "And so now I have to figure out what to say. How do I get her to come? She hasn't spoken a word to me in four months, and I just up and invite her to a party?"

Noel stared silently.

"I mean . . . I was doing my job. She of all people should get that, right? She puts her job before everyone and everything." Camille exhaled loudly.

Noel kept quiet.

"Damn, E. Why does she do this to me? She is such a fixer." She banged her head again. Then turned to Noel.

Noel's lips stayed shut.

"Oh that's just fucking great, Noel. Sit there and silently judge me. Whatever." Camille flung the covers off of her and got out of bed.

"No, I just—"

"Don't bother!" she called as she slammed the door and padded down the stairs.

She took a seat on the davenport in the once-formal living room that had become a toy room for her kids. Deep breath, she picked up the phone.

"Hey, V. Long time, I know. I realize this may seem out of the blue, but I have missed you, missed us, missed all of us, and I have a work party this weekend that E is coming in for, and I wondered if there was a possibility we could put this thing behind us and get drunk together. You know that is something we are all good at. What do you say?"

Camille reread the text once more, and though it was a little clunkier than she would normally write, she hoped it was enough gloss to entice Vera back to NYC and back to her. She hit Send.

CHAPTER 9

VERA

THE DAMN CAT WAS MEOWING loudly in the background, begging to be fed yet again as Spencer, too, was whining. "You need to fricking think about it? What is there to think about, Vera?" Spencer yelled at her. "Yelled" might not be the right word. Spencer didn't believe in raising her voice. She also didn't believe in swearing. Sometimes Vera was not sure how they even ended up together. The Latina in her loved to raise her voice, and she had obtained the mouth of a sailor at the hands of her father. Jorge was a good man with a bad mouth. Some of the best men are. He would always say "Mi hija, the real swear words are the unkind words we call each other. The rest are just bold adjectives." She smiled, thinking of that now.

"What are you smiling about?" Spencer "yelled."

"Nothing. I just . . . I don't know, Spence. I am not sure I am the one who can carry this baby. I don't even know if I ever fully wanted a baby." The words slipped out before Vera even realized she said them.

"Oh! Oh! Now you don't even want a baby? What happened to all those conversations where we talked about baby names and what preschool we would enroll him/her in? Was it all a lie? Is *this* all a lie? Were you just spinning things like you always do? Trying to pacify me?" This was the angriest Vera had ever seen Spencer. Crimson red warmed Spencer's cheeks through her makeup free skin, making it appear as though she actually had used blush, when in reality it was only the application on anger.

"No, of course it wasn't a lie. I just didn't think it would all fall on me. Don't act like this isn't a shock to you too. You know we both were planning on you carrying the baby." Vera was beginning to raise her voice.

"Oh! So, it is MY fault now that I can't carry the child? I am the one who screwed up?" Now Spencer was the one spinning.

"Spence, you know that's not what I mean. . . . I just—"

"Whatever, Vera. I am sick and tired of our life revolving around you and your job. It's Vera this and Sutton and Associates that. You never think about me anymore. After six years, you would think my thoughts and feelings would at least register."

She took a breath and continued. "I wanted to get married. 'You said' Let's wait. I want a baby. 'You say,' Let's wait." She used air quotes incorrectly around the wrong parts of the sentence. "I am done waiting. You figure out what you want, Vera, because I know what I want, and it isn't what you are giving me right now. So unless you can change . . ." she drifted off, but didn't need to finish. They both knew what she was going to say.

"Spence," Vera said sadly.

"No. No, Vera. You need to get right with your soul. Maybe see someone. But you need to do something!" Spencer said as she walked toward the door.

Vera realized for the first time that Spencer already had a bag packed and waiting. She had all day to think about this. All day she sat at home, stewing and blaming. Part of this was her disappoint was in herself, her uterus to be exact, but the other was the fact that she had to rely on someone else to meet her needs. That shouldn't have been out of her comfort zone, though, since Vera had been the breadwinner and provided for the both of them since the beginning of their relationship. This was different. Vera was one hell of a breadwinner, but was she a baby maker?

One hand lifted Spencer's bag and the other grabbed the door.

"I am going to stay at Shawn's until you get this sorted out," she said as she turned back to look at a sullen Vera.

"Spence, is that really nesse—" was all she got out before the door slammed shut louder than any yelling Spencer could ever do. The sound was deafening.

THUD-THUD. THUD-THUD.

Heartbeats pounded the inside of Vera's chest. She could hear it in her ears and feel it in her feet. She didn't know if the deep breaths that followed were from her anger or heartbreak. It wasn't until Vera hung her head that she realized she was still wearing her Ted Baker floral print satin pumps from work. The fight had begun the moment she walked in from her day off-turned-workday. Usually being barefoot with a glass of wine was how she ended her day, Spencer curled up next to her on the couch like a little puppy anxiously awaiting her attention. Every relationship has a dog and a cat, Spencer was definitely the dog, Vera the cat, well . . . and Pat.

Slowly, she pulled one foot out of the shoe, then the other. Normally she would pick them up and place them on one of the shelves in her closet, but not today. Energy was no longer her friend, and apparently, she was Spencer's enemy. Her closet was a thing of beauty though. When they were first looking for a place, Spencer had been adamant that they live in Columbia Heights—the best "gayborhood" in DC, she had called it. Vera truly didn't care where they lived as long as she had good space, nice views, and a huge closet. Spencer wanted to be close to the vegan grocery store. They settled on the art deco penthouse apartment.

The cork of The Snitch chardonnay slid out with ease. She couldn't help but wonder what it said about her that her three favorite wines were call The Snitch, Blindfold, and Prisoner. Dark soul, she supposed, and right now Spencer would agree. She watched the buttery liquid splash into her oversized wine glass and felt the tension in her shoulders ease ever so slightly. The big wine glass made her feel like less of a heavy drinker when she only had one glass. She brought the glass to her lips and took a sip. (Okay . . . a gulp). Chardonnay cascaded down her throat and into to her bloodstream, releasing her stress and cares.

The glass felt heavy in her hand as she walked over to the dark-blue, crushed-velvet davenport, the piece that the entire space was styled after. Vera had seen it in a client's summer home in the Hamptons, and the air of elegance met with comfort never left her. She sunk into that comfort now, a heavy glass for a heavy day.

Leaden eyelids forced her to close her eyes, and instantly she leaned her head back and curled her legs up to her left side. Another sip. Gulp. Spencer had hit her so hard when she walked in the door with her questions and accusations that she had immediately forgotten about her meeting with Connor Dixon and his wife.

Elevator to executive room. Pulling on the sleeve of her ivory Theory blazer, she walked in the room, teeth gleaming through her glossy, nude-lipped smile, and extended her hand out to Connor Dixon. He didn't stand when she entered the room, a concession she found odd for someone of his caliber. However, his wife did and shook Vera's hand without making direct eye contact. Vera stood back up after bending down to shake his hand, putting her shoulders back, eluding the power they both knew she possessed. She loved the power she felt in the walls of this office. Here she didn't have to waiver on decisions about babies or her uterus. Here she had the world at her fingertips and never thought twice about a decision she made.

"Mr. Dixon, Mrs. Dixon, how can I help you?" Vera got straight to the point as she took a seat next to her associate.

"Well . . ." Mr. Dixon began, "I want to run for mayor of New York City," he said with an obnoxiously large smile as he turned to his wife for approval. She kept her lips together as she looked back at him. Another move Vera found confusing.

"And I hear you are the best," he continued, now veering his smile back at Vera.

"Wow. Mayor . . ." Vera said, trying to sound less surprised and more impressed. She felt her lips press firmly together, as well, as he began to tell her all about his policies and plans. How he was bored just running the TV station and wanted to see what he was capable of. He mentioned how much money he had a number of times and that funding the campaign shouldn't be a problem. All he was missing was her. His words, not hers.

While he spoke, Vera stole glances at the wife from time to time. Every time her eyes would dart in her direction, Connor's eyes would look at his wife, as well. No smile, no nodding, no talking. Her hand in his, she sat there, playing a part. The part of the happy wife. Vera couldn't help but feel a little unsettled by her empty eyes.

"Well, Mr. Dixon, let me think about it, and I will get back to you." Vera finally cut of his ramblings.

"Great," he said. "Cost is not an issue, though. So, whatever I need to get you on staff, I can pay." He smiled again.

That was how they left it. Vera didn't stand, only reached her hand across the table this time to shake his hand. Only willing to give up power once in a dynamic, this time he was meeting her halfway. The wife, however, smiled slightly and nodded at Vera as her husband escorted her out, his hand on her lower back leading the way.

Another gulp. What was she going to do about Connor Dixon?

BUZZ-BUZZ.

Her phone caught her off guard more than it should have, considering how often it went off. Expecting it to be Spencer wanting to talk or say sorry, she quickly set her wine down on the coffee table, splashing a little out of the glass that quickly soaked into the reclaimed wood of the table. She picked up her phone and saw that not only was it not Spencer, it was Camille.

They hadn't spoken in months. Vera slightly hated herself for the pit she immediately felt in her stomach at the hope that nothing was wrong. Why should she care? Instead, she read a different sorry message followed by an invite to a party. Normally this kind of thing would've pissed her off, but after the day she had, it seemed almost like a blessing.

She typed *I am in* and hit Send.

CHAPTER 10

ELIZA

GOING FROM SEVENTY TO THIRTY degrees always made Eliza feel a little light-headed every time she entered an ice arena. "SHOOT!" Eliza yelled immediately, wishing she hadn't. Time and again, she had told herself that she wouldn't be one of those parents who gets crazy wrapped up in their child's sports and hollers things from the stands. She wasn't really *in* the stands, though. She was standing by the glass because, truth be told, she couldn't handle the other parents and their yelling.

Hockey season seemed to be year-round for their youngest at this point. There was the regular season, which lasted October to March, then a short break, followed by the spring season that ran April to August. Piper liked it that way. Hockey was her thing. Sometimes Eliza wondered if it was harder on the parents than the kids. All these early-morning practices and freezing arenas were beginning to wear down more than just her tires. Yet here she stood, flannel shirt and Sorel boots under a large Canada Goose down jacket at another random ice arena. Really, though, she wouldn't have it any other way. Watching her girls do something that made them inimitable raised her pride meter up higher than she would ever admit out loud. She was always telling them to "do more of what makes you awesome."

Rhett wasn't here. It killed him more than it did her how much he missed, but it broke her significantly. As Eliza cheered, he was landing from a ten day–long series in Chicago, Cleveland, and New York. In her heart she knew he would rather be here with them, but in her head, it was hard not to be envious of the life he led. Flitting here and there, fancy dinners, special events. A lot of woo-ing and a lot of glitz. Tonight was another one of those fancy events. Straight from the airport he was going to head home and change, pick her up, and whisk her off to some celebrity or senator or someone's something ball. In the beginning of their marriage, she would have been thrilled to attend. Designer name brands, perfect hair, the right mannerisms. Eliza played the part and assumed she was happy. Happy was really just a show. The entire thing never sat right with her. She would never be pretty enough, smart enough, accomplished enough, enough. Rich, white, privileged people swarmed these events, wanting nothing more than to stroke their own ego and maybe have others stroke something else. It was a who's who, and she didn't care. She would shake hands, smile, fake conversation, all the while dying inside. Roaring at the smugness, the arrogance, the fog of bullshit in the air. None of these people were real; they didn't even know what *real* looked like. If it wasn't green or didn't elevate their status, it didn't matter; therefore, she didn't matter. Eliza wanted to matter.

Slowly, with time and age, she stopped playing the game. Stopped smiling through an internal scream, stopped feigning her interest. Quietly drinking champagne in the corners of the room, watching the dogs fight for alpha position. All the while she sipped her drink, weaving a web in her mind.

For the most part, Rhett no longer made her come to the events after many conversations regarding her feelings about the places and those people. He only asked now if it was of the utmost importance for him or the team. Eliza respected him for that, and so she would play the part when needed. Tonight would be show time. The new Elie Saab dress would zip up the back, and she would zip up her mouth. She knew deep down she would likely still not have the courage to speak her mind even if she felt so inclined, but she was getting there; she could feel it. Female designers were the majority of brands in her closet, a few men too . . mainly the gay ones. Over time she had started to feel a strong distrust of men who became powerful. There were good ones, of course, Rhett being one of them, but it seemed everywhere she turned there was yet another story of a man abusing his power, so she was protesting in small ways. Ways she felt made a small difference since she was scared of really pushing the limits, fighting back against the patriarchy. The strange part was that she never had a negative encounter with a man herself. Sure, there was the catcalling, the inappropriate come-ons, but no man had ever disrespected her saying no. No one had ever forced themselves on her or threatened her. This, she was realizing, was not most women's story. And though she wasn't a victim, she was beginning to realize that she had still feared men her whole life. Never walking alone at night, always questioning the motives of a man approaching her. She may not have been a victim, but she was still being held captive. The threat of what a man was capable of was enough to scare her, but her fear was slowly growing into resentment. As Eliza's daughters were getting older, she wanted a better existence for them. One where men and women were truly on equal ground. There was a stirring in her stomach she was having a hard time ignoring. She was on the cusp of fighting back. She may be late to the party, but it was time to get messed up.

CHAPTER 11

CAMILLE

THE TV IN THE BACKGROUND was filling the air with SpongeBob's voice as Camille scooted her kids out the door. "Have a wonderful day at school. Don't forget who you are and what you stand for!" Camille said each day as she kissed each kid and scooted them out the door. Leaning her shoulder against the doorway, she waved goodbye to their backs and tried to ignore the mom guilt pang in her stomach. She always tried to be home to get the kids off to school; it was one of those things she wanted her kids to remember about her. "She always got us ready for school and kissed us on the way to the bus," she hoped they would say when she was gone. Sometimes she wished she was gone. Sometimes she got that dark.

Depression and anxiety had been a part of her life since she was a child. All these years later, she had a much better handle on it, but the struggle was still real. Camille didn't have to look far to get down on herself. Everyone else in her industry was "perfect." The face, the body, the voice. Most days she was proud to be the glitch, but then there were days like today when she woke up and was disgusted by the imperfect in the mirror. Her hands would pull her skin down and back trying to smooth the wrinkles, and she would fixate on the bags under her eyes that were exacerbated by her fair skin, a gift from her father. She never tanned, either was pasty white or burned, no in-between, no golden glow for this gal. Put that face with this body and she really enjoyed beating the shit out of herself. Every day she would get tweets and emails about her yo-yoing weight. People could be so cruel, and it was so easy from behind a computer. Certain days she ignored them, others she fired off fierce, but well-worded, passive-aggressive emails back, and then days like this she let it hit her, allowed herself to believe it.

Once the yellow school bus was out of her periphery, she turned and closed the door to their brownstone. Steam rose from her coffee on the side table near the door. Next to it was a framed picture of her family. She picked up her coffee and took a sip, staring too long at the photo. *Were we happy then?* she wondered. When was the last time she and Noel were happy? Was he happy? She knew she wasn't. Camille had begun to convince herself that he was no longer turned on by her because of her weight gain and lack of gym time. The truth was that, though she was ballooning in her head, to the outside would, Noel included, she looked no different. Maybe she knew that deep down and liked the excuse better than the truth, that maybe he just didn't love her anymore. At her core she felt very unlovable—but Noel, he would always love her. He had stood there with her and took those vows. It had to be the weight. She took another sip of coffee.

BUZZ-BUZZ.

Fluff from her robe caught on the edges of her phone case as she pulled it out of her pocket, making her realize for the first time that she was still in a robe. She looked at the time on the screen before the text and felt a twinge of stress, realizing she still had to get ready for work. Without reading the message or removing the fuzz, she threw her phone back into her robe pocket. How did she always manage to run out of time? Coffee sloshed back and forth in her cup as she tried not to spill it while hurrying up the stairs and into the shower, coffee still in hand.

•• •• ••

Rubbing the towel back and forth over her damp hair and looking at herself in the mirror, she realized she was lacking something. That thing that used to make her *someone*. That pizzazz she held onto deep inside as the thing that made her stand out. Camille had never been the smartest or the prettiest girl in the room, but yet people were drawn to her. Swiping mascara across her eyes, knowing the makeup team at the station would wipe it off and start anew, made her feel slightly less frumpy. It took every part of her not to put her robe back on to head to the office, also knowing the wardrobe people would make her change when she got there anyway.

Paparazzi were rarely interested in her, partly because she was a woman anchor, but mainly because she wasn't that interesting. Her life was very mainstream, no highs or lows to report, or so they thought. Wouldn't they have a field day if they found out that a few nights ago she had tried to roll over and put her hand down Noel's pants, only for him to take it out and tell her he was too tired for that tonight. Wouldn't the country love to see that their perfect misfit anchor's life wasn't so perfect? She exhaled a deep sigh as she passed the robe still on the bed and threw on some yoga pants that had never actually been to yoga and a "cute for workout gear" top. Camille was halfway down the stairs before she realized she didn't know where her phone was. Back up the stairs and reaching into the robe that she thought again about putting on, part of her wanted to just give up. Instead, she pulled the fuzz off the corner of the phone and headed down the stairs and out the door, raising her hand in the air almost habitually.

Once she slid into the back seat of the cab, trying her best not to touch anything (God only knew what happened in this taxi before her), she pulled out her phone and read the text.

"Any word from V?" Eliza's text read.

Realizing in that moment that Camille had one other unread message, she swiped out of Eliza's text to see that the other text she missed was indeed from Vera.

Camille felt her jaw drop slightly.

"I am in."

She shifted on the broken plastic leather of the cab, trying to decide what or if she should write back. She *should* write back, of course. But what? Never in a million years did Camille think that Vera would respond, much less agree to come to the party. Staring at the text, she couldn't decide if these three words made her more excited or tense. They hadn't spoken in months, and now they were going to attend a very public event together. Maybe this was a bad idea. But she didn't have a choice. It seemed her life was becoming less and less about being able to make her own choices.

CHAPTER 12

VERA

THE SILENCE WAS DEAFENING in the condo alone. "What self-respecting person doesn't respond to someone after twelve hours?" Vera said out loud to no one as she checked her phone for the fourth time since she had gotten up. Spencer never came home last night, and though Vera had tried to call and text, they hadn't connected. Truthfully, Vera wasn't 100 percent sure how she felt about it. Was it wrong that she enjoyed being alone last night? Was it wrong that she didn't know if she had the mothering gene? Why couldn't she just be a strong woman? Why did she have to be someone's mother? Did that make her more of a woman? Or less?

Spencer's lack of communication wasn't what Vera was mumbling about though. She still hadn't heard back from Camille after agreeing to attend her party last night. Immediately after sending it, she regretted it and drank the rest of her wine alone. Then she slept on the couch and woke up to no cat licking her face. Apparently, Spencer had taken Pat with her, something Vera hadn't noticed until this morning. Dawn's early light brought a splitting headache and a hope that the party could be a good thing. She needed this, needed her girls, needed something in her life to be simple. Nothing seemed simple anymore, not Spencer, not babies, and not work. Remembering Dixon's meeting yesterday made her head pound even more.

Vera had checked her phone as she plugged it in and turned on the shower. Endless emails and texts littered her screen, but none from Camille or Spencer.

While her battery juiced up for another busy day, she hopped in the shower, hoping the steam would help her sweat some of the leftover wine out. She hated herself for checking the phone again after stepping out of the shower. One towel wrapped around her hair, another around her bust, she stood on her heated floor and touched the screen to no avail. Another designer suit, a sleek ponytail (because she didn't have the energy to put into doing her hair), and three Motrin later, she grabbed her phone off the charger, peeking one more time, threw her briefcase over her shoulder, and pulled on her pumps as she shut the door behind her.

Walking to work each morning was one of the things Vera loved most about their condo. Watching the seasons change in DC was something she never grew tired of. Her job didn't allow much time for the gym, and outside of her infrequent runs through the National Mall or National Arboretum, her only form of workout was the walks she took to and from work, along with the stairs she climbed at work. Her office was located on the fifteenth floor of one of the older buildings in DC, and though she had set up shop seven years ago, she had yet to take their elevator. Part principle, part exercise. Running through some of the most historic parts of DC left her feeling even more American, and after each jog, she vowed to do it more often, but she was not a person who often had time for this. Stairs in heels was no joke, and she could probably outrun any one to her office in her Louboutins, so she let that be enough.

Summer season in DC was hard to beat. Weather fluctuated in the seventies and eighties with occasional rain, though Vera rarely carried an umbrella. Phone still in her hand, willing it to buzz so she could relinquish this ridiculous anxiety around Camille or Spencer texting her back, Vera popped into Cakes and Beans, her local coffee shop. She breezed right past everyone in line, over to the pickup counter, where a black cup with "V" was scribbled on it in silver Sharpie sat. With her free hand, she grabbed her latte and smiled and winked to Leo, the barista who had it waiting for her every day, even weekends. Leo covered the mic that ran over his newly dyed ombre bun and whispered "muah" followed by an actual kiss. He was her coffee god. Glorious hair, gay, and superb espresso machine skills. What more could a woman want in a man?

Sunlight warmed the top of her ponytail as she briskly walked through the busy streets of DC. She slipped her phone into her back pocket as she began her daily stair climb. Her assistant, Dash, met her at the door of her office. Vera loved and hated that she got there before her.

"Morning, V!" she said with a smile, also wearing the same sleek pony.

When had she started allowing her to call her V? *Is that a thing?* Vera wondered.

"Morning," Vera mumbled while lifting her latte to her lips and her sunglasses onto her hair. She wanted to give the cheerful lady more, but couldn't muster it. She needed that damn Motrin to kick in. Or maybe she just needed to eat something.

"Mr. Dixon called this morning wondering if you have *quote* 'made the right decision and decided to work with him,'" Dash said, trying to use air quotes while still holding files in her arms.

"Right," Vera responded, both reiterating the word he used and responding to Dash's underlying request to respond to Dixon.

"That is all I have at the moment. Do you need anything?" Dash asked, looking at her earnestly.

"Actually, could you go get me something for breakfast? Something greasy?" Vera responded and pulled her sunglasses off her head carefully, as not to wreck her hair.

Dash smiled but didn't dare ask her boss if she had a rough night. They both knew she did. "Of course," she said.

"Thanks, Dash," Vera said as she headed into her office and set her briefcase on the dresser against the wall, next to her awards for her PR achievements. She pulled out a few files and paperwork and latched the bag shut. Setting her latte and files on her clear glass desk, she pulled her phone out of her back pocket and laid it facedown next to her computer. Slinking into her cognac-colored Columbian leather chair, a gift to herself when she opened the firm to remember where she came from, but also because the very best leather truly came from Columbia, she vowed not to turn her phone over until it buzzed. Instead, she pulled up Google on her computer, typed in "Connor Dixon," and began to take notes.

CHAPTER 13

ELIZA

DIAMONDS CAUGHT AND THREW the light all over the walls as Eliza slid her heavy, dangling earrings out of her ears and set them on the counter in her closet. When they built the house, the closet designer had suggested these counters, and while at the time it seemed like a waste of space, it was one of the few things she was willing to admit she was wrong about. Admitting oversights was one of the benefits of getting older, no longer needing to prove as much. Vulnerability was never her strong suit, and making a wrong decision her downfall. Hours and hours spent in therapy talking about her fear of failure, of disappointing people, making the wrong decision. Some may call it perfection, but she thought it felt more like a fear of being vulnerable or appearing weak. Over time she realized her life was a series of attempts to prove herself to others. With a successful husband like Rhett and a beautiful life, she felt pressure to be the perfect wife and mother to complete the picture. Screw up and people would see the cracks in the Michelangelo.

People assumed because she was "just a homemaker," it meant a lack of education and ability, so she did her best to prove them wrong on that front, as well. As if the pressure to be smart, perfect, wife, mother, and look the part wasn't enough, there was the physical side too. Eliza had always been an active person, even as a child. Never struggling with weight or an eating disorder. Somehow managing to stay between the two. That didn't mean it was always easy, and that was becoming even more apparent as she got older. Like many women approaching or in their forties, things were beginning to fall, sag, flab, and rub. She had to work twice as hard for half the success. God forbid she not look like the girl he married. Not because he would ever say that, but because she couldn't live with herself if she didn't. What would people say if she let herself go? Would Rhett think about trading her in for a younger model? Her heart told her no, of course he wouldn't, but was he really ready to deal with menopause and her body changing no matter how many burpees she did?

Tilting her head to the opposite side and removing her other earring, she caught Rhett staring at her from behind, his smile breaking her. The corner of her mouth rose a little as he walked up behind her and wrapped his arms around her bare shoulders. She had chosen a strapless high-low royal blue dress, paired with her diamond and sapphire earrings and multicolor floral pumps. "Good woman. Wild soul." Was written between her shoulder blades, only appearing when she bore her shoulders freely. Rhett leaned down and kissed the words. Not even a year old, the tattoo had been a freeing moment for her. A middle finger to the person she thought she was supposed to be. A permanent reminder of the one she wanted to be. He loved her for it.

Rhett withdrew his hands from her collarbone and began to slowly unzip her dress. He took his time, as though he wanted to savor every vertebrae that made up her strong backbone, the one holding their family together. He kissed the side of her neck as the zipper came to a stop and the dress fell to the floor. Eliza turned to face him, standing in her La Perla lace thong and high heels. Rhett placed his hands on her hip bones and took his time looking her over, and then he ran his hands up her body, over her breasts, and to her face. As his hands cupped her soft cheeks, the ones she wondered if she should have enhanced, he leaned in close to her and whispered, "You get more beautiful with each passing day."

Eliza's shoulders fell as her hand raised to his salt-and-pepper beard. More salt than pepper these days, but she was a salt girl anyways. Pulling him close, she kissed him long and hard, allowing his tongue to explore her mouth the way his eyes had done with her body. This man was one of the good ones. *Why couldn't they all be this good?* she thought.

As she held his face, he began to unbutton his shirt, grazing her breasts as he fumbled with the buttons. Sex wasn't always like this for them. After many years of marriage, most of the time it was a quickie while the girls were at school or before she and Rhett were too exhausted to keep their eyes open. Rare moments like this were something Eliza looked forward to. The past few months she had become increasingly aware that she had a good man on her hands and looked at him in a new light. A light that had lit a fire in her. While he finished the shirt, she reached for his buckle and felt the smooth leather run through her fingers as she pulled it off and unbuttoned his pants. Shirt and pants fell to the floor in unison and they followed, making love on the carpet in their closet. Thank God she had decided not to put hardwood in there.

CHAPTER 14

CAMILLE

THE STREETS OUTSIDE THE TAXI were already alive with chaos as Camille typed "Vera is in" while the cab came to a quick stop in front of the tall skyscraper that housed PTSK. She whisked two twenties over the seat to cover the $34 fare and shut the door behind her. Her hand started to vibrate as she swiped her badge and put her phone on the belt, walking through security. She picked it up and saw a message back from Eliza.

"She is in. That is really all you wrote? WTF?"

Texting left a lot of mistakes to be made, especially when it came to context. Eliza had thought she was being cheeky and short like it was no surprise that Vera was coming, but in reality, Camille was trying to get her ass out of a taxi.

"Sorry. Was in a hurry heading to work. Yes. She is in. That is all I know. I haven't figured out what to say back yet. I was shocked actually," she wrote, knowing that punctuation was no longer cool when teenagers texted and not able help herself from doing things the old-fashioned way.

"Well . . . I, for one, am excited," Eliza responded.

Excited. There was a little of that, Camille supposed, but a lot of uncertainty, as well. Stepping into the elevator, she threw her phone back into her purse and closed her eyes, her last moment of quiet for the day.

Elevator doors opened to reveal a flurry of people running in different directions, some on the phone, others leaving to go on assignment, and producers yelling things through their headsets. The media world was a messy one. Camille put her head down, trying her best not to make any eye contact until she was able to get to the coffee machine. Everyone in the office knew that Camille was brought to you by coffee. Her eyes darted around as she filled a mug with her face on it, a novelty she both loved and distained. Holding her mug felt like holding a gun to her, strangely comforting in a way it wasn't supposed to be. Locked and loaded, she headed to her desk, shoving yesterday's transcripts out of the way to make room for her mug.

She wanted desperately to be one of those people who threw their phone into their purse only to forget where it is hours later when they needed to Google how to get red wine out of carpet. Instead, she sat down and immediately fished it out of her purse. This was her other weapon. Staring at the screen, she willed Vera to send a follow-up text, one that explained her reasoning or apologized for her part in the Risner scandal; instead her screen only lit with more unanswered emails that she needed to respond to. Camille put her phone "apple up" (as her kids called it) and opened her computer, vowing to respond to Vera once she went through some of these emails.

Twenty minutes and thirty-two emails later, she felt her eyes glance over to her phone, knowing that she needed to be the bigger person. She was the "bigger" person. She lifted the coffee mug to her lips, spun her phone over, and pulled her texts open with her thumb.

"Vera [old school again using someone's name to start a text], I just wanted you to know that I am very glad that you are willing to join E and me for the party. I know things happened. I want to say again that I am sorry for my part in it. I truly have missed you and am excited to see you. If Spencer wants to come stay with Noel and the kids, she is more than welcome. Hope you are well."

Camille reread the text four times, erasing parts, changing verbiage, until finally deciding that she needed to move on.

SEND.

Impulsive power and excitement ran through her body. Forgiveness does that to a person. Frees something you didn't know you were holding. A little bird had just been given flight. Camille was feeling brave and strong, so she scrolled down and clicked on Noel's name.

She typed "What are you going to do to me later?" and smiled, lifting her coffee and watching for him to reply.

Coffee flew out of her cup when one of the production assistants peeked his head around the corner and said, "Hair and makeup in ten, Cami!" startling the shit out of her.

"Geez, girl," he said, covering his headset. "You watching porn or something?" He giggled and walked away.

Porn. Maybe that would help get Noel in the mood, she thought.

After an agonizing five minutes of staring at her phone, pretending to care about what her Twitter feed was saying, and with no response from Noel, she grabbed her coffee. Armed with both her weapons, she headed down to put on her war paint. Even on a bad day there is always lipstick.

CHAPTER 15

VERA

VERA WIPED THE LIPSTICK STAIN off the lid of her latte, shaking the cup and realizing she was close to needing another. Some days were two-cup days and others were grab two beers and jump days. Camille had written her back and Vera was fighting the urge to respond like an excited schoolgirl and had decided to play hard to get, at least a little. The better half of the last two hours she had spent reading articles and interviews on Connor Dixon. His assistant had followed up every hour on the hour to see if she had made a decision. Vera wasn't sure yet if this flattered or unnerved her. Everything she was reading looked clean. On paper he was a businessman with an impressive portfolio, though arrogant and rich . . . the kind of white privileged motherfucker that Vera hated. Never had to work too hard, never thought twice about money or power, never wondered what if the answer was "no." Her mind wanted her to take him on, make him shine, make a good mayor out of a shitty man. Her heart was speaking a different language though. He unsettled her. Something about his smile, his smugness, and his "I get my way" vibe.

"Dash?" she called into the phone intercom.

"Yes, Vera?" Dash said with a smile she could hear even through the intercom.

"Set up another meeting with Connor Dixon. I want his wife there again too. But I want her to talk. Give them a heads up that I will be wanting to hear from her. Oh, and make it for when I get back in town. Monday."

"On it!" Dash clicked off and Vera could see her
punching numbers into the phone outside her office.

Crumbles fell onto her perfectly clean desk from
the breakfast sandwich Dash had brought her a while
earlier, the biscuit and bacon working wonders on her
hangover. While she chewed, she brushed the crumbs onto
the floor and shut her computer. No more Connor Dixon.
She wasn't going to find the answers online anyhow. She
needed to hear from Melia, see her speak about her
husband. The truth was always in the woman's eyes. For
years men had fooled people, using their power as a
weapon, throwing their weight and wealth around.
Women, on the contrary, had spent years on the sidelines,
observing, keeping their mouths shut but taking it all in.
Most still didn't know how to wield their power
effectively, so they only told the truth. Even if they
couldn't speak it, their faces showed it. The power in their
eyes was stronger to Vera than any amount of money or
status.

Vera was one of the few women who had learned
how to employ her power. "Boss bitch" was a term that
had been coined because of women like her. She didn't
mean for it to overlap into her personal life, but at times it
did. Sneaking in, branding her no longer a "badass boss
bitch," but instead just a "bitch," a trait she didn't love but
was working on. Spencer took the brunt of it. Vera
subconsciously demanded perfection and submission from
her family and friends. Leader was a role Vera was born
for, and she didn't know how to turn it off. Over the years,
it had cost her girlfriends, friends, jobs, and it had taken
her too many years to realize that she would never be able
to work under someone. Much later she had whittled her
life down to her company, Spencer, Eliza, and Camille.
Maybe Dash, too, on a good day.

For the last few months, though, one of the four pillars that kept her table upright had been missing. Her fallout with Camille hit her harder than she would ever admit out loud. Not to Spencer, not Eliza, not Camille, and especially not to herself. Missing Camille didn't make her wrong in the situation, but it did make her feel incomplete. They had both made missteps in the Risner fiasco, but Vera was too stubborn to admit fault. Camille, for her part, apologized over and over again for months until she stopped. Vera didn't blame her for ceasing. She was more steadfast than most, but Vera had let her anger cloud her ability to acknowledge culpability.

Washing the bacon bits down with another swig of her almost empty latte, she picked up her cell phone, reading and rereading the text from Cami. She was sorry, she always had been, and knowing Cami, she truly meant it. Vera was used to the hard decisions that jobs forced people to make. Decisions that went outside of normal moral and ethical opinions. Lying to herself that she was doing the right thing was something she had perfected. Wading through tough shit to get to the right shit. Sacrificing things along the way she wasn't even sure she factored into the equation. Camille had been one of those sacrifices when the Risner scandal broke. Vera did everything to help out a client, though her gut told her to drop him. In the end, it was Camille who broke the story to the nation and ruined Risner's career. Fear spread throughout Vera's office about the blowback they would face. Swift moves by Vera saved them and they distanced themselves from a man who had been playing them along. If Vera was being 100 percent honest with herself, she would admit she was never actually mad at Camille. She understood she didn't have a choice in the matter and was just doing her job. No, Vera was mad at herself for being made a fool. She could reconcile a lot about herself, but being made to look like a fool was not one of them. Not an option in this profession when your wile was what people paid for. Camille might have been the one apologizing, but it was Vera who was too busy avenging herself to allow for forgiveness. She needed to forgive herself first. Her lack of self-reconciliation left Camille in purgatory.

"Looking forward to seeing you guys. I am sorry. I know that isn't enough, but I hope it is a start. I owe you more than that and I will work on it. I will see you soon."

SEND.

CHAPTER 16

ELIZA

STILL NAKED FROM THE NIGHT BEFORE, Eliza woke up in her bed, thankful they made their way from the closet floor and into the bed or Rhett's back would've been a mess this morning. She slid her legs slowly over the soft cotton sheets, enjoying the feeling and last night's moments one more time before the real world tightened its grip. Soft snoring told her Rhett was still in bed, and that meant it was still early or he had overslept. She hoped it was the latter; he rarely allowed himself that luxury. People might assume with that kind of money and power one would come and go as he pleased, but Rhett kept things on a tight schedule and was more involved than anyone would ever give him credit for. It was harder to hate him and his money if you saw him as a hard worker, and people love to hate.

Naked feet padded across the floor as Eliza crossed her arms over her bare chest and tiptoed into the closet, throwing on her Lululemon capris, sports bra, and tank top. She tried to convince herself that she chose the brand because it was the best for running, but that wasn't true, and she knew it. Labels still mattered a little to her. Obscure designers were her jam, but Lululemon was her go-to.

She pulled her post-sex hair through a baseball cap worn with sweat lines crusted into it. Rhett had been telling her for months to throw it out or wash it, and though she knew it probably wasn't the best to push that old sweat onto her forehead, she didn't care. Motivation and accomplishment had chafed through that hat. Medals and times meant nothing to Eliza. She truly loved running, had since she was a little girl. Sometimes she wondered if it was because all her early memories with Millie were them running around in their make-believe worlds right there in the heart of Beverly Hills, Michigan. Hours were spent running between the two houses, over moats, jumping on hippos' backs, running from bears, and sidestepping explosives or bubbling tar. Running felt more freeing than anything else ever did. Warm summer air blowing through their let-down hair. Unaware of time or place, just being in the moment with your best friend escaping anything and everything that came your way. How couldn't someone love that feeling?

Lacing up her On Cloud shoes, Eliza noticed for the first time that they were beginning to wear on the bottom. Mileage never occurred to her. It wasn't something she clocked or kept track of. Everything was about feel. But shoes, those you needed to change before you felt like you needed new ones. Push them too far, and they rebelled, causing injury. She needed to order new ones before the insurgence hit. Her phone slid into her pocket, but not before she checked the time, it was 5:17 a.m. . . . Rhett hadn't pampered himself. She slid one AirPod into her ear and the other into her crop pocket. When she ran in town and on bike paths with lots of people, she would put both headphones in, but still keep the volume low, staying aware of her surroundings. Out here, though, with few people and even fewer houses, it was best to stay alert. She wasn't sure when or how she had become overly aware that she was to be afraid. Not all men were bad, of course, and she knew that, but there was a voice telling her that the good ones weren't the ones lurking down gravel roads, watching and waiting for you to run by. The good ones were still in bed, awaiting their alarm clocks to start their day after having sex with their wives. "Better to be safe than sorry" was what she would tell people when they would question her neuroses that surrounded the safety of her and her daughters. It was much more than that, though. It was an unfounded fear.

Locking the deadbolt as she left the house was another part of that fear. The odds that someone would break into their house, through their gate, in a town where that never happens is practically unheard of. But she always locked the door, always. Taking the steps one by one, she headed off their porch, down their long driveway, and onto the gravel road. *Do men ever think twice about putting both earbuds in?* she wondered. *Do they ever fear running alone as dawn is rising? Do they ever think they should wait until the sun is up? Do they incessantly lock the door? Do they question the motives of every other man they come in contact with?*

Running was usually where she found peace, mental clarity, and exultation. With every piece of gravel getting wedged in her shoe treads and thrown out by each kick, her mind was cycling through thoughts. In with the good, out with the bad. When the runs weren't as illustrious as the ones she ventured on as a child, that was the mantra she would repeat to herself over and again, "In with the good shit, out with the bullshit." Today, though, she could feel the bullshit nestling. That same spot in her stomach where the feeling had settled yesterday before the gala was materializing again. *This is bullshit,* she thought. *Why in the hell do men get to feel as free as I did running as a little girl? No cares, no worries, no precautions. Nothing to lose.* She wanted that autonomy back. Wanted it for her girls. Imagine growing up in a world where you blasted the music in your headphones and ran without looking over your shoulder. Never acknowledging or even noticing who else was out on the roads with you. Just running. Running limitless. Living uninhibited.

Miles and miles flew by as her thoughts churned. With each footstep into the ground, she swore change. Revolution for herself, her girls, every girl. Each arm swing moving with more conviction. No longer powered by the release, she was now fueled by anger. An anger she didn't know could exist. Indignation powerful enough to spark revolt in the most demure and benevolent of women.

Gravel roads weren't her preferred running paths, but this was where she turned up the most dirt. The quiet that used to make her uneasy, she was growing accustomed to, possibly loving the space that allowed her to think. Tomorrow would be different, though. She would be back among the masses running in Central Park. Comfort among the masses, less looking over her shoulder, but feeling constricted, trapped. Maybe she couldn't win. Maybe, right now, no woman could.

Stopping only when she arrived back at their gate, she tried but failed to catch her breath, wondering if she would ever again feel like she could breathe easy.

CHAPTER 17

CAMILLE

"LIVE IN 3 . . . 2 . . . 1 . . ." the producer called and pointed to Camille.

"Hello. I am Camille Givens." She paused to allow for her cohost Brian Tannon to introduce himself. She surreptitiously loved that her station believed in the "women-first" philosophy and always let her open the show. It chapped Brian's ass, and Camille fancied that. Brian's relationship with Camille was mix of compassion and contention. He loved her as much as he didn't want to see her star outshine his. They were living in a time when it was good to be a woman in power. Camille was that woman. The one telling other women about all the things in life they needed to know. She was their best friend and their sister. Everyone instantly wanted to know her, be around her. People, mainly women, were drawn to her.

"And I am Brian Tannon," he said with the fakest grin he could muster.

"Tonight on PTSK . . ." Camille went on to give the headlines. It was never lost on her how depressing her job was. Every night she flooded into people homes and told them about the worst things happening in the world around them. She invoked fear, rage, and stress. Many meetings had begun with her pitching that they throw in a happy segment, something uplifting each night. She was told in no uncertain terms that "she was to give people the information they needed to know. She was not a fairy godmother and this wasn't Canada." Still she thought it couldn't hurt to spread a little joy in a country where suicide was on the rise.

That was the top story today on their broadcast. People were attempting to kill themselves in record numbers. Baby boomers would say it is was because millennials couldn't handle a world where their parents didn't do everything for them, millennials would say it is because of the pressures put on them because of social media, and Camille would say it is because shit is hard. A lump caught in her throat, but only for a second while she read off the teleprompter. She hated when stories hit too close to home. Pills would have been an easier option, but it was still cutting that she tried. Movies had told her the more dramatic way was to slit her wrists and then try to drown in the bathtub.

Blood dripped all over the white ceramic tile of her parents' house as she moved from the sink to the tub. Red stained her clothes as she removed them, a step she had overlooked before beginning her endeavor. The water began to turn pink as drops of blood fell from her wrists as she lowered herself into the warm tub. Weirdly she had wanted to make sure the tub felt comfortable, worrying that if it was too cold she would change her mind and get out. She lay there, her wrists propped on the edges of the porcelain tub walls, watching the blood fall slowly into the tub and dissipate into the water, leaving behind a rosy trail.

Lowering her head below the water had been harder than she assumed. Trying to fight the natural defense to rise out of the water and gasp for air was something she hadn't anticipated. How could she have thought the whole thing through—she was only seventeen. Bobbing up and down, she kept trying to stay below the water, let the air escape her lungs completely, but her body was fighting her. The water was beginning to have the faintest salt tang from the blood mixing in, and every time she went under, she would taste it on her tongue.

Time came and went. She wasn't sure how long she was into her attempt, but she was starting to tire, either from fighting her breath or the blood loss. Hopeful this would make it harder to fight the fight-or-flight response, she kept her efforts up, though the water had become lukewarm. She exhaled and went under one last time, feeling herself becoming dizzy. Reflex kept her eyes open, watching the last few bubbles float up to the water above her, but she refrained from floating up, as well. Darkness crept in from the edges of her eyes, making the water begin to appear magenta. Moments before everything faded to black, she saw something dance in the water above her.

Camille heard her before she felt her. Eliza was screaming.

"Millie!!! Oh my God, Millie!" she yelled over and again, holding her above the water, shaking her back and forth.

Color began to flood back into Camille's peripheral vision. Slowly, she began to see Eliza holding her, her shirt soaking wet and slick hair stuck to her shoulders. Camille felt her chest rise and fall faster than she was comfortable with, and she began to gasp and spit out the iron-tasting water. She made eye contact with Eliza for the first time, seeing the fear in her eyes, wondering if it was a reflection of her own eyes. She hadn't realized she was holding onto Eliza's arm wrapped around her chest until she saw the blood running down Eliza's forearms, dropping slowly into the water. The two girls stayed motionless, holding on to each other for dear life. No one spoke. They just breathed in unison—Eliza thankful that Millie's chest was rising and falling with hers and Camille just trying to catch her breath, not sure how she got here. The two girls never spoke of the incident again. Camille never asked how Eliza knew to come; Eliza never asked what the hell she was thinking. That moment had broken them both. They were too young and too scared to realize the gravity of what had just happened to their psyches, but they were wise enough to realize they needed each other in ways they could never explain to the outside world. Camille would start seeing the campus therapist when they entered NYU, though Eliza never pushed. Eliza would start running when Camille was in session. Both were working on their issues, so they could be free of judgment for one another. Their love was one that the storybooks rarely wrote about, the love of two friends with broken foundations who together built an indestructible one. It wouldn't be the last time they would save each other's lives.

Camille swallowed the lump down. She was a damn professional. "When we come back, we will tell you about the concerns surrounding a new strain of flu virus sweeping the south. Stay tuned."

CHAPTER 18

VERA

OPENING THE FRONT DOOR TO SILENCE, Vera couldn't decide if she enjoyed or resented it. As she threw her briefcase on the bench and slid each of her pumps off, she didn't realize she was waiting for Pat to come slinking around the corner. Pat was always excited to see her when she got home but would never let on, his slow, methodical walk an attempt at saying, "You are home. Whatever."

Vera had spent the walk home from the office texting back and forth with Eliza about this weekend and the party. E was always a plethora of knowledge on what to wear, expect, and know going into an event. Sometimes Vera wondered if she had some kind of inside line to all the best party planners. The party was yet another celebration of Connor Dixon's success, a gathering to throw his money and power around. His ego needed a constant reason to remind people that he was, in fact, a bigger deal than they were. He always chose his words carefully in public, doing his best to come off as the charitable good boy, but everyone knew he had ulterior motives to everything he did. E told her to bring a gown, something that would look good on Instagram because there was no doubt this party would be thrown all over social media. *When did "Instagram-worthy attire" become a thing?* Vera wondered.

Walking toward the kitchen, finally willing to meet Pat halfway, Vera remembered Pat wasn't coming and Spencer wasn't home. *What does it say about me that I thought of the cat before Spencer?* she reflected. Throwing last night's bottle into the trash, she then reached into the wine fridge and grabbed another. This morning's headache should have advised her differently, but after her meeting with Connor and Melia before she finally left the office close to seven, she needed something to numb his voice. *If you can't be happy, at least you can be drunk,* she thought. Uncorking the wine, she thought back to her attempt at a conversation with Melia Dixon. "Conversation" wasn't really what she would've called it, more of a "nod and look for approval" session. The woman barely said more than two words to Vera, but her eyes and smile said a lot. She may not have said say much, but the eyes were never quiet.

The meeting was supposed to happen when she got back from New York, but when Dash reached out to Connor, he was insistent it happen right away and wouldn't stop pestering until Vera agreed to today. Which was why at five o'clock p.m., Connor and Melia were taking their seats in front of Vera's desk. Every question Vera asked her was met with Melia saying something scripted, turning to Connor, meeting his mock smile, generating a huge smile of her own, and then turning back to Vera. Every second of the exchange felt forced, choreographed, or maybe it was in Vera's head. *Maybe,* Vera thought, *the love is lost, but the money pays the difference. She is his puppet for a price.* It certainly wouldn't look good for a man entering a political race to also be entering a divorce.

They had been together longer than they had been apart, and at Melia's age, that meant something. Most of the women in the circles she ran were two or three times divorced, never able to keep a man or a steady income. When Melia met Connor, she knew she had found the one, but she didn't let him know it. He fawned over her, begging her constantly to give him the time of day. An arm's reach, that's how far she kept him for months, some of the most painstaking months of her life, or so she thought.

Once she finally gave in, things went hard and fast. They were married in Martha's Vineyard at one of his family's many homes a mere four months after their first date. The first few years were storybook. Long vacations to exotic locations, endless spoiling, countless compliments, and hours of lovemaking. When she mentioned having children, his smile spread farther past his cheeks than she ever thought it could. This, of course, was before he had them redone in those awful veneers, back when his smile was a genuine as the rest of him.

Months bled into years, and Melia never became with child. They went to countless doctors and clinics trying to diagnose the problem. Not one could figure out what was going on and encouraged them to just keep trying. Melia was a healthy, young woman, though Connor refused to be checked, assuring her good swimmers were one of the Dixon men's best traits. The light in her eyes, the glow he had not been able to look away from lost a little of its luster every year she went without being pregnant. She did her best to keep up appearances, but there were so many of them and not enough left of her.

While Melia's hopes were crashing, Connor was on the rise in his father's company. Talks were beginning to arise that his father's health was on a secret decline and Connor would inherit the company. Power was Connor's baby and fertility was good. It wouldn't be long until that baby was born and Connor's interests in furthering his bottom line would shadow his interest in wiping bottoms. That's how the next several years would go for the once-happy couple, now resorted to a broken woman and a man trying to fix it with money and power. She was rewarded with whatever she wanted or needed, except the thing she desired most. She breached the topic of adoption, and Connor's response destroyed her: "I don't want all my family's money to go to some black or Asian kid. I mean, I am not racist, but I just want our money to stay in the blood. You get that, right?"

Before Vera today had sat a woman who was broken but strong. Strong women don't play the victim, don't make themselves look pathetic, and they don't point fingers. They simply stand and they deal. He had broken her, but she was still standing, strangely still standing with him, looking at him like a woman in love, but yet heartbroken. Vera wasn't sure whether to feel sad for her or impressed by her.

During her time at NYU, Eliza and Camille had helped Vera fall in love with local New York legend, Billy Joel. It was the Piano Man himself who once said, "She can kill with her smile and wound with her eyes." Something about that quote always stuck with Vera. She knew women were capable of more than anyone would ever give them credit for. She had a sense that Melia was once one of those women with a killer instinct and scrappy sensibility, but time and misogyny had frayed her edges and darkened her eyes.

Vera grabbed Melia's arm before she left the room after her husband, Melia flinching in return, jumping more than most people would in that situation. Neither woman said a word. Melia just nodded at Vera, pulled her arm gently free, and turned and followed her husband down the hall. Vera was unsure if the nod was telling her to work for Connor or permission to say no. Before Mr. Dixon left the room (in front of Melia, which Vera didn't miss) Vera had asked for the weekend to make her final decision, knowing full well she was going to get to see him in action at the party and get a final feel on this whole endeavor. She still wasn't sure he was the type of client she would ever take on, harkening her back to Risner, forcing the muscles around her mouth to tighten. But something in Melia's eyes made her want to save her. None of their conversation had led her to believe this woman needed saving, but Vera was in the mood to be a hero. If working for Connor was the only way to get closer to Melia, then maybe she had to take the lesser of two evils, something Vera never liked to do. She wasn't one to shy away from a challenge, but she was very careful not to be someone's patsy again.

Mindlessly, she twisted the corkscrew deeper and deeper as Vera went over that meeting in her head, looking for anything she missed. When she pulled the cork out, she grabbed a glass and was about to pour, but instead took the whole bottle and glass over to the couch. The bottle was probably more than she needed to drink, but it was better to be safe than sober.

CHAPTER 19

ELIZA

THE BREEZE AT DAWN HAS SECRETS to tell you, if you only wake up for them. It has been said that the darkest hour of the night is right before dawn. Eliza was up before dawn many times, and while the darkness definitely hung heavy, she never saw it as a bad thing. Everyone had secrets; everyone had darkness in them. Sometimes you never knew what would bring it out; others searched for a reason to let it go.

The wind this morning smelled of lavender and tobacco, still lingering from its strong night scent. Eliza had never been a smoker, even when Camille had decided to take it up in college, but she certainly loved the smell of the tobacco plant. Anything labeled "tobacco scent" smelled of an artificial attempt to her, compared to the darkness-lingering aroma of the tobacco plant at dawn. It would only be appropriate that the tobacco plants would more fragrant at night, the darkness of the sky mixing with the malevolent smell of a toxic plant.

Rays of sun had barely flirted with the horizon and Eliza had already fed the baby kittens, who were now old enough to eat solid food, thrown hay out for the horses, and let the chickens out of the little red coop in their side yard. Kingfield Farm had started with one dog, two barn cats, and ideas. It had grown into two dogs, too many cats, and countless other animals. Multicolored eggs were left behind in the nests for Eliza to grab as the hens scattered out to peck at the ground, no longer restricted. She placed each egg gently into a basket and headed toward the garden, basket of eggs in one hand, empty basket for any and all produce ripe for the picking in the other.

The plastic of her blue Hunter galoshes helped to gently push one of the fatter farm cats away from her cozy perch in front of the garden gate. Cats came and went at the farm. At times there was a dozen, other times they were down to two. Procreate, venture out, don't make it back, or do make it back, procreate some more. Farm cat's circle of life.

Eliza's boots sunk ever so slightly into the dirt between the rows of meticulously planted produce. She headed to the far row and made her way forward. Collecting the same way every morning as the sun rose was peaceful and satisfying for her.

Basket full, she let the gate latch behind her and headed back to the house. Placing the plentiful baskets on the front porch, she picked up the pail of leftovers and headed toward the pigs. Eliza never wanted pigs. They were disgusting, filthy animals that tended to carry disease, but Rhett sold her on the idea of bacon and pork chops, so they were giving the pig thing a go. Pigs have been known to eat anything, literally anything. This was a characteristic of theirs that Eliza had endeared. She never had to think twice about what to do with a leftover casserole about to go bad, or the fatty parts of meat that she and the girls mentally couldn't eat. Everything that didn't go in their mouths went to the pigs. Nature's garbage disposal. They kept a pail in the garage and would throw all their scraps into it each day, and every morning Eliza would haul it out and dump it into their pen. Of course, this wasn't enough for the eight sows they were housing, so she would mix in grain and near rotten vegetables from her garden. Eliza had named the pigs, though she knew she shouldn't. They were going to slaughter soon, friend to feed. It felt inhumane for her not to acknowledge them while they were here though, so she named them and spoke to them when she fed them.

Kevin Bacon, Porkchop, Wilbur, Babe, Hogwarts, Hamlet, Amy Swinehouse, and Alexander Hamilton all stirred from their muddy slumber and began to squeal when they saw her approach. Feeding the animals was supposed to be the girls' chores but somehow had become Eliza's. She would be lying if she said she didn't secretly like it. Creature appreciation was at times the only validation Eliza found in a day. She had succumb to the praise of pigs.

Her family's rubbish poured over the fence posts and into the slop bin for the waiting pigs. One man's trash, a pig's treasure. No complaining, no whining, no picking through what they did and didn't want. Every pig in the pen fighting each other to get access to her throwaways. *What a strange and simple life,* Eliza thought. Swine have to be some of the greediest of animals. They simply take and take. They provide nothing until they are dead. Their only worth lies in their mortality. Isn't it odd that we use the word "pig" to describe humans who are dirty and worthless? Are we implying they are worthless unless dead? Just selfish, filthy whiners until slaughtered, giving nothing to the world and only taking up space and air. Surviving on others' scraps and lying in your own filth. Pigs. There were plenty of them out there and not just on Eliza's farm.

CHAPTER 20

CAMILLE

GOOSEBUMPS BEGAN TO PRICK Camille's skin as she ran her hand slowly over Noel's shoulder under the comforter. Early morning light had just begun to sneak in around the edges of their black-out blinds, and Camille was hoping she would catch Noel off guard before his alarm clock—her hand rising and falling on the side of his ribcage as she veered her fingertips farther south. He had lost weight recently, not that he needed to, and though she was proud of him, she tried to swallow the resentment that lurked in the back of her mouth. Men say the words "diet" or "lose weight" and immediately drop fifteen pounds. Meanwhile, even if Camille was trying, it would be a struggle to drop half a pound.

The crease between his stomach and upper thigh led her right to his good morning, and a good one she hoped it would be. He was ready, morning was still a natural primer for Noel. She began to caress and move her hand around as Noel groaned and grunted himself awake. Camille moved her body a little closer, only to feel him pull away and pull her hand out of his boxers.

"Are you serious?" he snapped, his back to her so she wouldn't smell his morning breath.

"Yes. Very," she said through a smile and tried to guide her hand back over his hip.

"The kids could come in at any second," he retorted and grabbed her hand.

"Noel, it is before dawn. The kids are not going to just walk in here." She moved her body closer, trying to nestle her breasts against his bare back.

"Jesus, Camille, are you some horny teenager? We can't do this right now," he said as he forcefully threw her hand back toward her and pulled the covers off his body and left the bed. Camille rolled over on her back, closing her eyes so she didn't see if he was going to shower it off or go back to bed on the couch. Tears burned behind her eyelids as she caressed the hand he held just a little too tightly. She wasn't sure what hurt most—the stinging tears she was holding back, the hand she was grasping, or her heart that was breaking.

Marriage was hard. Camille knew that going into it, but for years it had been so good that she assumed they would be the anomaly. Camille was half the person she was now when she met Noel. Half her physical size, that is, but likely twice the self-esteem. Not the type of girl who needed to join a sorority, because she had all she needed in Eliza and Vera, the three of them would attend the NYU frat parties as some of the only people in the house without any Greek letter tattooed on their body.

Zeta Beta Tau was butt to balls deep with people for one of their well-known keggers. Eliza and Vera had been hesitant to attend another frat party after a rape drug in a drink attempt at another frat the week prior. Luckily, Eliza's beer had been intercepted by a high-school friend who advised her not to drink it and proceeded to return the drink to his frat brother with such force that most of the liquid ended up on his shirt. Camille, though, was feeling the best she had since the incident in high school. Shortly after she and Eliza held onto each other in a tub of her blood, she began to eat her feelings. She had never been a chubby kid, never struggled with weight, but she found herself trying to fix trauma with food. During her senior year and into entering NYU, Camille had gained over forty pounds. Eliza noticed, everyone noticed, but E was careful not to say anything, realizing that the two events were likely interlinked, and she didn't want to go for another bloody swim. Camille was the only one who wasn't aware of how bad it had gotten. She wasn't blind to the fact that she was making poor choices and her body was paying for it, but she was numb to the emotions surrounding it. Adding to the numbing effect, Camille had taken up sitting on anything she could. Not chairs, but guys. Food and sex had become her coping mechanisms. It pained Eliza to watch the destructive path Camille was on but, instead of speaking up, she ran out. Pounding out her disappointment and fear for her friend with each footstep. She invited Millie with every time she went. The answer always the same: "Maybe next time."

A positive home test two months into their freshman year at NYU sent Camille into the free clinic with Eliza holding her hand in the waiting room. Eight days late and trying to decide if her boobs hurt because she was pregnant or from her late period finally arriving. Camille took a sip of the Frappuccino she made Eliza stop for on the way and wondered if she even knew who the father was.

"Camille?" a nursing student in light pink scrubs called from the door leading to the exam rooms as she looked down at the file, making sure she read the name correctly.

Camille and Eliza rose in unison as if they were both the person she was calling. One and the same. Hands still linked, they headed toward the nurse, sullen and with fear strewn across their faces.

"Oh. I thought this was for a pregnancy test," the nurse said, looking at Camille, slightly bemused.

She continued before Camille could pull the Starbucks straw out of her mouth to respond, "They must have screwed it up in the system. How far along are you?" The nurse smiled.

Camille left that appointment with a negative blood test and a positive assurance that it was time to get her shit together. That was six months before the ZBT party. Camille had joined Eliza on some runs, eaten better, and looked great. She knew it, felt it, and wanted to show it. So now Eliza and Vera stood begrudgingly with red solo cups of cheap beer as Camille scanned the room until her eyes fell and settled on Noel.

Camille and Noel were together from the minute they met at that party. It took time for them to get around to the marrying part, but it was inevitable. They were the type of couple everyone aspired to be, the ones who made being married look like a constant sleepover with your best friend. You couldn't help getting the commitment bug just being around them.

Kids. That was the turning point. It was for most people. Everything is hunky dory when it is just the two of you, a constant honeymoon of meeting each other's needs. Parents aren't allowed to have needs. Camille loved her children passionately. There was no denying that. Somehow, though, they left her feeling like she was back in that frat house. Everything was broken, no one slept, and someone was always throwing up. Except this time, she wasn't falling in love—she was falling out of it. What she wouldn't do for a roofie in this frat house of life.

CHAPTER 21

VERA

SWOLLEN, PUFFY, HAGGARD BAGS rested on top of sullen cheekbones in the reflection on Vera's computer screen. Luckily, she had decided yesterday not to go into the office today and just work from home before she headed to NYC. The woman staring back at her from the screen looked less hungover, more weathered. Age made wine weather her face more than it had in her college days, when one could drink all night and still look fresh faced for eight a.m. chemistry. Now she looked like a woman on a bender in her best years. It wasn't a good look.

Fingers pounded on the keyboard, matching the pounding in her head. Drinking was always an activity Vera enjoyed, but rarely to excess. Her mother was always reminding her that she needed to keep her wits about her.

"Things happen when you aren't of clear mind," her mother would say.

So Vera was always the designated driver, voice of reason, and babysitter when Eliza and Camille went overboard. The freedoms that applied to two white girls being raised in the suburbs with middle-class families and privileges—they weren't even aware they had didn't apply to Vera. Her parents would never say it out loud, but she knew that they were different, she was different, and so different rules applied. Life would never be a careless, worry-free existence for her. Every step, every move was thought out, calculated, overprocessed. A wrong step, and it would be scrutinized more than most. Vera wanted to make her parents proud, but more than anything, she wanted to make a name for herself in a country they beseeched to get into. Being a citizen wasn't enough; she wanted to be a legend.

No one fails upward unless you are a rich, white male, so she worked harder, sacrificed more, and pushed limits. Staying clear-headed was the least of her worries. But for the last few nights, her worries had gotten the worst of her clear head.

Emails didn't wait for her to drain the haziness out, so she mixed Motrin and her homemade coffee and tried to manufacture some semblance of a boss. Mixed in with the fuzz were thoughts of Connor Dixon, Melia, and, of course, Spencer. They hadn't spoken since she slammed the door shut two days ago. Vera's texts and calls went unanswered. At night when the wine set in, Vera wasn't even sure what she would say if Spencer were to answer. "Sorry" was of course where she would start, but she wasn't sure where it would end. Connor Dixon had been a great distraction to a relationship problem she wasn't sure she wanted to fix. Love wasn't the problem, and truly neither was Spencer. It was Vera.

Before Spencer, Vera was happy being single. "Married to her work" was what Eliza and Camille would say, because good friends don't ever call you a slut. "Slut" was such a harsh word for a female with no marrying gene who looked at sex as sport. When men acted like that, they were called "player" or "stallion"; women were "sluts." Vera never thought of herself that way, instead feeling more like a goddess in tune with her needs than a whore looking for her needs to be met elsewhere. She had a good head on her shoulders, a successful job, a powerful position, and a life most would envy. Why couldn't she have sex when she wanted it with no strings attached? But then she met Spencer.

DC girls' trip to see Jack Causewell in concert at Lyla Addison Pavilion had brought Eliza and Camille in to stay with Vera for the weekend. Large crowds were not Vera's scene, but Camille was hell bent on seeing Jack, so she literally dragged Vera by the hand to the concert. Music floated through the warm summer air as the three ladies entered in among the trees of Symphony Woods arm in arm. Rain from the night before had left the ground soppy. Cans of Michelob Ultra (Camille was trying to lose the baby weight) in their hands, bodies swaying to the music. While Camille bellowed the lyrics and thrust her beer in the air, Vera was suddenly lurched forward. Quick reflexes were the only thing that stopped her face from landing in the sludge as she turned her head from all fours to see the girl who was on top of her.

Sun-kissed blond hair flew forward, covering her face, but already Vera could feel the warmth of her smile. Slender frame covered in fringe and leather. An unmanicured hand revealed green eyes as it brushed the hair away from her face. Vera was right about the smile, even in the most awkward of situations, Spencer's grin was captivating. Spencer didn't immediately get off of Vera, and Vera didn't mind.

Once back on their feet, they spent the rest of the concert making small talk—Vera not sure how she had become so knock-kneed simply by someone's smile, and Spencer obliviously unaware that Vera had fallen for her back when she was on her knees.

Never the type of woman to show her hand, reveal too much, or fall too easily, Vera was caught off guard by her immediate draw to this woman. Toward the end of the concert when Spencer entangled her fingers in Vera's, she felt her heart leap into her throat. A woman with this kind of power was rarely rendered powerless, but somehow those willowy, nail-bitten fingers had rattled the perfectly manicured Vera.

Looking down at her fingers now as she hastily returned emails, Vera realized that she was in desperate need of a manicure. Spencer, Connor, and Camille had sent her from perfection to consumption. This person wouldn't do and couldn't last. She wasn't sure where she was with Spencer, or who she was going to be to Connor, but she sure as shit knew what she was, and that girl needed to get her shit together before she showed face in the city that never sleeps.

CHAPTER 22

ELIZA

IF LOOKS COULD KILL, then Piper was a murderer. Her woeful eyes left Eliza with a strong pang of guilt still an hour into her three-hour drive into the city. That girl had some kind of ability to make her mother feel bad about leaving, even though Eliza basically never left. She was always there. Maybe that was the problem. The girls had gotten so used to her being the constant that they threw that much more of a fit when she left. She couldn't blame them; she hated when schedules were thrown out of whack, hated not knowing what was around the corner. Her daughters had followed her lead on this. They liked routine, thrived on schedule. So when the scheduler went on the fritz, they, too, felt strained.

Kinsley, now in the throes of adolescence and more worried about friends and her phone, had hugged Eliza and kissed her goodbye, tapping on her screen before her back was even fully turned. Piper, on the other hand, no longer a child but not yet a preteen, was stuck in that limbo age right before hormones set in when everything feels off, but for no good reason. Her arms wrapped around Eliza and wouldn't let go. Over and over again, she asked why she had to go. Couldn't she just stay here? Couldn't Millie come here? When would she be back? The questions peppered one after the other, barely allowing Eliza time to answer. When Eliza had answered every question at least twice, she unlatched Piper's arms from her neck and took her face in her hands.

"Piper, you will be okay. I will be back before you know it. You will have so much fun with Daddy. You can call me and text me. I promise everything will be okay. I love you."

Then Eliza leaned in and kissed the space right above her glaring eyes and finally released Piper to her father standing behind her, patiently waiting for a girl who only wanted her mother. It killed and pleased Eliza, that girl's love for her. A long kiss and quick goodbye with Rhett and she was on her way.

"I promise." Those were the words that she was spiraling around as the clouds began to float in and out of an otherwise sunny day. In the background, someone was talking politics on the radio, but she had the volume so low she had no idea what they were even discussing. Volume wouldn't have mattered. The voices in her head were far louder.

I promise. The words made her scrunch her face up in disgust. She hated using them, but somehow, they would slide out from time to time. Being a mother was much tougher than she could have ever imagined. When they were little and it was hard to take them places or deal with tantrums, she thought it couldn't get any more demanding. She was wrong. Little kids are physically demanding, but big kids are mentally exhausting. Her mother-in-law used to say, "Little kids, little problems. Big kids, big problems," and boy was she right, though of course Eliza would never admit that to her.

Simply keeping the children fed, clothed, educated, and alive was hard enough, but then every night when she lay in bed in her perfect house with her perfect husband and perfect children, she couldn't stop the negative thoughts that would creep in. When the rest of the world lay dormant enjoying the quiet respite, Eliza lay awake, wrestling with her feared shortcomings.

In the dark of night she wondered if other mothers felt insufficient. Did they feel they were failing their children? Did they fret over not having the right answers or messing them up beyond repair? Eliza had heard other mothers talk about the "mom guilt," but it always seem to be said in an afterthought sort of way. Her guilt was not an afterthought; it was top of mind. Every decision she made, every step she took, she first thought of her children. *What kind of example am I setting? Am I strong enough? Am I feminine enough? Do they know I am educated? Do they see that I have dreams? Am I helping to raise their self-esteem? Am I doing enough to make the world a better place for them?*

Eliza rarely left, rarely allowed time for herself when the girls were home. She knew her time with them was limited, and she was blessed enough to be able to make them her number-one priority, and so they were. She was their mother, chauffer, cook, therapist, tutor, friend, coach, cheerleader, security blanket, and hopefully their role model. School hours were hers, her time to do whatever she needed to make herself a better mother and wife. Outside of eight to three, those hours weren't for her; they belonged to the young women she was raising to be better than she was.

Millie was a mother, too, and though Eliza knew she would understand if she were to tell her why she always said no to trips and outings, they weren't the same. Mothers are a funny breed. There are so many ways to do it, and yet no one truly feels like they are doing it right. Millie was a great mother. She was far more relaxed than Eliza, and she envied her for it. Millie did many things Eliza would never do, but instead of judging her, Eliza embraced her for it. They decided long ago that they beat themselves up enough, so they didn't need to judge each other's parenting. And Vera had never owned so much as a goldfish, so there was no way Eliza could even begin to explain her guilt to her. Sometimes her life appealed to Eliza, fantasizing what it would be like to worry about no one other than yourself. Truthfully, that was what had forced Eliza to agree to this trip, Vera's life. If Vera would go, then she would. Allowing herself time to be Eliza, the woman (not Eliza, the wife and mother) was good for her soul but hard on her heart.

The girls would be fine. Rhett was a great dad. There was nothing to worry about. She had promised, against her better judgment. Nothing in this world was for sure. You couldn't promise safety, endless love, financial stability, or tomorrow. So Eliza hated to promise things, knowing she didn't know if she could deliver. Children, however, are black-and-white characters. Things are either good or bad, right or wrong, broken or promised. So Eliza promised. . . . In a world of gray, she swallowed her fears and she promised everything would be all right.

CHAPTER 23

CAMILLE

THE ONLY THING THAT MADE waking up alone in a bed for two tolerable was the knowledge that her other better half was on her way. Camille spent most of the night staring out her bedroom window, wondering what had gone so wrong. It had started simply enough, thinking maybe it was just work and their lack of time alone, but it had quickly spiraled into every other facet of their lives that led up to this moment.

It was him. It had to be. He was having trouble sexually and didn't want to tell her. She understood; it would be embarrassing for a man to have to admit the thing that make him a man was no longer manning up. But it was her. It was them. Why wouldn't he tell her? They used to tell each other everything. Staying up hours on end talking about nothing and everything. Solving all the world's problems before falling asleep naked next to each other after consummating out their last bits of energy.

The crème fabric of her pillowcase stuck to her cheek as they willed herself to sit. Tears that had slowly and quietly fallen all night long had turned the fabric into a tacky film. She should wash them, hide the fact that she had spent the night crying, but he likely didn't care, and she no longer had the energy.

Warm beads of sunlight were coming in at the perfect angle to warm her raw cheek skin and bring her back to life. Dawn brings our morning secrets to life, and the lies she had been telling herself could no longer stick.

It wasn't him. It was her. He had either fallen out of love or lost the attraction to her. It wasn't a lack of drive, it was a lack of desire. Being alone at night with your thoughts can put your true insecurities on display. The ugliness that hides in the light feels most comfortable in the dark. Dancing, twirling, spinning. All the things they used to do before she became "someone" and he watched her consume everything.

As newlyweds, the world felt as though it were their oyster. They could do anything, become anyone. Camille wanted to be Katie Couric. Noel wanted her to be Katie "Cooks," Katie "Cleans," Katie "Children." It wasn't that they didn't discuss it before marriage; it was just that Camille hoped she would change him. Women have a tendency to do that, find a man, plan to change him. Sometimes it worked. Some women were worth changing for—unfortunately Camille wasn't one of those women. She was pregnant with their first after the honeymoon.

Pregnancy was something a majority of America (especially women) could understand and felt enamored with. So with her big belly came a big promotion. Turns out that women love seeing themselves onscreen. A baby meant a boost in ratings, and so Camille became a headliner right before she became a mother.

The twins followed soon after a miscarriage that shook the marriage for the first time. Emotionally she was rock bottom, but sharing her journey with the viewers made ratings rocket. Her disappointments became their TV gold. Making TV gold had left her feeling like a bronze-medal parent. Missing more events than she attended, feeling like she was the mother on the sidelines, never in the game, and Noel was keeping score.

Her bare feet padded to the shower as it dawned on her that while she had hoped to fix him, instead *he* was trying to fix *her*. Every time she fell short, disappointed, or had to make a choice . . . it was always the wrong one, and she hoped he would understand. Instead, he never forgot.

She splashed some water on her face and looked at herself in the mirror as the water droplets fell and splashed on the bathroom counter, realizing she didn't know if it was the water or the tears. This was the lowest she had felt in years. Until then, she had been able to rationalize away their problems, assume things would get better, and hope for change. This was the moment, though, the moment she knew it was over. Things weren't going to get better; they weren't going to change. This was the end. She gasped as she felt her chest tighten, and she fell into the bathroom counter. She knew he would never say it. He never had the balls to be the man she needed him to be, so it would have to be her.

Separation. Or divorce. What was the difference? Which do you lead with in these kinds of conversations? Both words felt like a one–two gut-punch as she tried to say them to herself in the mirror. This time she knew the water falling was tears. So she stood, gripping the edges of sink and repeating the words over and over again as the tears streamed. It wasn't until she heard the echoes of the twins yelling her name rattling off the walls below that she remembered she didn't have time to lose it. She had to be a mother, and an anchor. *God*, she thought, *this will be great for ratings.*

CHAPTER 24

VERA

VERA COULDN'T HELP BUT ADMIRE how good her freshly manicured nails looked as she typed out another email on the iPhone from her seat on the private jet headed to NYC. She made great money and could afford her own private jet, but she would never allow herself that kind of luxury, and luckily for her it wasn't needed when she represented clients with even more liquidity in their bank account who were willing to share.

Today's flight was supplied by Tad McDaniels, a plastic surgeon with an innate ability of discretion that allowed DC's top politicians to have work done without the public knowing. People paid for discretion, and that tact paid for her flight.

"Ms. Sutton, we are ready to take off," the pilot said as she peeked through the curtain to inform her.

Her cell phone would continue to work the whole ride to NYC, but she wanted to take the time clear her mind. So, with champagne in hand, refilled twice since she had stepped on the flight, she put her phone on airplane mode and shut her eyes as they taxied down the runway heading toward a reunion that made her equally nervous and excited. Not to mention a party that had the potential to change her professional career forever. She downed the champagne and refilled it as the wheels left the ground.

•• •• ••

One hour and an entire bottle of Taittinger later, Vera was further from clarity and closer to drunk as she stepped onto the New York runway and into a waiting town car, taking her to Lower Manhattan, home of the Blacksmith hotel, site of the party and her suite, thanks to Melia. Somehow, unbeknownst to Vera, Melia had found out she was coming to the party and insisted that she book her a nice room at the hotel—the Dixons did own the place, after all and usually kept a few of the nicer rooms open at all time for friends and family. That and a large part of Manhattan real estate that most weren't even aware of. Pretending to fight the invitation was something Vera usually would have done, but she didn't have the energy to do it this time. Plus, she considered it research into who the Dixons were, which could only prove to be fruitful for her.

When she had mentioned to Eliza that she had the potential for them to drag their drunk asses no farther than up a few flights in an elevator at the end of the night, her squeal of excitement had sealed the deal. Cabs were plentiful in NYC, so there was no fear of drinking and driving, which was a nonstarter for Eliza since her cousin had been killed by a drunk driver in college, a funeral the three of them would never forget. Poor decisions aside, riding all the way to Brooklyn at the end of the night sounded less than appealing. So, without a fight, Vera accepted Melia's offer outright, to which she saw Melia smile genuinely for the first time.

Leaning into the space where the door met the seat, Vera wondered if she should have headed to Camille's first before going into the city. Should they hash it out alone in the comforts of Camille's two-story mock Manhattan abode? *Probably* was the answer, but instead she let the car continue to Manhattan. Camille had to work anyway, so surely she wouldn't have time to have a proper conversation. And, honestly, what was there to say? I am sorry? She said that already—in a text, yes, but she did say it. And she was truly sorry. She was sorry all along, but stubborn pride forced her to swallow it down. Sorry was for the weak, and she wasn't weak. She was strong. She had an appearance to keep up. Manicures and all. And she was not the type of woman to be sorry. That would mean you made a mistake, and Vera Sutton made none of those. Or at least she faked perfection. She had been faking for so long she had almost believed it. Nothing was her fault. Not Camille. Not Spencer. Not Risner. Not Abuela. Her grandmother was someone she never spoke of, not since she died. The ol' witch had managed to outlive her parents, which only managed to make Vera hate her more. She had tried to blame her death on Vera.

"You are a sinner, Vera. You have managed to kill your abuela with your deceit. God doesn't accept the gays. You have condemned our family" was what her final letter to Vera had said.

She should have thrown it out, but the letter stayed nestled in the back corner of her bedroom nightstand, next to her dental dam. Where some keep a bible, she kept another form of condemnation, her grandmother's dying declaration of blame on Vera alone. Forget eternal damnation, accusations like that fuck way more with your soul.

In a hidden corner was blame she couldn't shake but tried to ignore, much like the fallout with Camille. One huge difference, though, was that Camille loved her and wanted to make it right; it was Vera who was doing the condemning.

She was not her abuela. Forgiveness wasn't easy, but losing Camille was harder. Reaching for one of the mini bottles of vodka in the town car cooler, she unscrewed the cap and swallowed down the burning liquid along with her pride. She was here now, she was sorry, and she was going to do whatever it took to make it right with Cami again. She was going to do it all, after one more little bottle of liquor and a nap.

CHAPTER 25

ELIZA

SMALL VIBRATIONS GENTLY SHOOK Eliza's Audi Q7, a familiar buzz of the city she loved and loathed. It might have been the long way around, but she loved driving through the heart of Manhattan and across the Williamsburg Bridge on her way to Millie's house. The bridge's unsettling, yet comforting, tremors from the many cars in all different directions excited Eliza. There were no vibrations in the country, not much to buzz about. She rode the high all the way across the bridge and into Millie's neighborhood, where her buzz led to good fortune as she parked right in front of Millie's place. Usually she couldn't even find a spot on this block, much less directly in front of the brownstone. This was going to be a good night, she was sure.

Unable to make her own decision on an outfit, she had two dresses hanging in the back covered in black garment bags to protect them from the sun and smut. New York may have her heart, but it didn't have a filter.

Eliza closed the car door with her hip, hoping the dust that lay on the door panels from the gravel roads back home didn't leave a mark on her black capris. She hadn't bothered to change after feeding the animals, knowing she would have to go through the entire dress-up process later this evening. And honestly, she may try to sneak in a run in the city while Millie was at work. So, with the hair slicked back into a tight pony, country dust on her hip, and couture dresses hanging in the car, she bounded up Millie's Italianate brownstone. And then as the soles of her running shoes hit the top step, Millie swung open the heavy oak door, baring a smile that looked heavier than the door.

"E! You made it!" Millie said through a faux smile that Eliza immediately recognized from angst-y high school days and it made her heart sink a little.

Eliza leaned forward, engulfing her in a tight embrace. Millie's shoulders fell forward as she exhaled all the air from her lungs and began to sob. The convulsing of her body forced the zippers on Eliza's purse still on her shoulder to jingle a sad little melody.

"Mil, what is going on?" Eliza asked, not daring to release her friend from her uncomfortably awkward embrace. And Eliza wondered why her arms didn't fit around Millie like they did before. Was she gaining weight? Was she falling into the habits of old following the suicide attempt?

Millie didn't answer. She just kept sobbing, and Eliza just kept standing, holding, her hands growing tingly and her mind swirling. Then, as if on cue, or just like Clay Callihan, PTSK's early morning meteorologist, had predicted, raindrops began to fall from an already cloudy sky. The two women still didn't move—they stood, holding each other just as they had all those years ago, as the wetness seeped into their skin. A few drops hit the brownstone roof before trickling down and landing on Eliza's arm, a pink-brown hue sending her back to that tub, and instantly she squeezed Millie tighter as her tears mixed in with the rain.

••   ••   ••

Neither of them was sure who made the first move or how they ended up sitting across from each other in Camille's living room, but as their wet clothes clung to their skin, Millie tried to collect herself enough to tell Eliza what had been going on. Noel was already at work, and the children were already at school, or she would've kept her secret closer to the breast. But alone in this house that they had turned into a home with the only other person in the world who fully understood her, the secret was out.

"So . . ." Camille said, staring down at the floor and swallowing back another round of tears, "I think I need ask him for a divorce, or a separation, or I don't know . . . fuck!" She looked up, allowing her eyes to meet Eliza's, but she quickly averted them back to the aged wood floor, marked with the scuffs of their lives together, the rug her feet rested on unraveling on the ends just like them.

"Millie," Eliza began, not sure if she was addressing her or questioning. She started to rise, walking across the creaking floorboards, bending down in front of Camille's downcast head, placing her hands on her moist cheeks, and lifting her face to meet hers, as you would a child.

"Millie, I am going to make you some coffee. Then we are going to get you ready for work. We will figure this out. I am here for you."

Eliza maintained eye contact with Camille as the tears kept welling in the corners of her eyes. She was going to get her friend through this. They had been through worse; they could do it again. Coffee may not be the cure, but right now her relationship with Eliza and Coffee were the only ones that didn't fail her.

CHAPTER 26

CAMILLE

THERE WAS FAR TOO MUCH moisture in the shower. Camille could feel the wet air choking her. Between the water falling from the shower head, the tears falling from her eyes, and the steam rising from the cup of coffee sitting next to her shampoo, it was too much. She coughed over and again as she shut the shower off and opened the door, trying to regain her breath, leaving her coffee behind.

It was real now. She had said the words out loud to Eliza, solidifying their content. She was going to be a divorcée, a single mom, a hot mess. All of this was going to happen regardless, so as her chest began to slow her breathing back down, she decided that tonight she would set it all aside. Tonight she was going to let loose. Her two best friends were here to support her and her success, and she wasn't going to be this woman tonight. Standing naked in front of the mirror, she swiped away the dew, bringing her blurry figure to life. This would possibly be one of the last few nights before the world always looked at her with a twinge of pity in their eyes. Once the news broke, every person she ran into or appeared on their TV would do the lip purse, head tilt, sad eye thing when they saw her. There was no stopping that, but for one last night, people would smile, nod, and reach out their hand to shake hers in awe instead of to stroke it in comfort. So she brushed her hair and walked naked into her room, where Eliza was sitting on her bed, aimlessly flipping through a magazine. She looked up, and the pity in her eyes was already creeping in from the edges, the look Camille was going to avoid for as long as possible.

"No," Camille said, pointing her finger at Eliza, "we aren't going to do that tonight."

"Do what?" Eliza retorted, knowing full well that benevolence was written all over her face.

"That face. That look," Camille snapped, immediately regretting it. "Tonight we are going to have fun. I earned this. I deserve this. And I will be fine." She placed her hands on her hips, remembering now that she was still standing in front of Eliza full bush.

"Millie, I . . ."

"No. Not tonight. Tomorrow. Tomorrow we come up with a plan. But tonight . . . tonight, we party," Camille said, moving from her power stance into her closet.

"Oh . . ." she called, her back still to Eliza, the words "sine qua non" sitting just above her hip bone. It was a tattoo they had gotten together in college, Eliza's only other tattoo, which she only agreed to because it could always be tastefully hidden. A Latin phrase, translated literally, it means something like "without which not" because without each other, they couldn't exist.

"Don't mention anything to Vera, please," she said as she pulled a tee over her head. "I am not ready to go there yet."

"Okay" was all Eliza could say. There was a lot more she wanted to say, but it wasn't going to happen today.

Eliza went back to flipping magazine pages as Camille got dressed and appeared in the doorway of the closet, silently waiting for Eliza to look up and see her, really see her.

It only took a few seconds. Camille knew it would. When Eliza's eyes met hers, she choked back the tears she felt welling in her heart, ready to flow out her eyes, and said, "You are coming to work with me, right?"

Eliza smiled. She nodded, though they both knew the answer without the gesture. She stood up, went over to Millie, wrapped her arms around her, and nuzzled her face into her wet, black hair. They stood there for one more minute before they went out into the world to be the brave girls they needed to be. Just two best friends, one finally being seen, and the other finally feeling needed.

CHAPTER 27

VERA

CRYING BOUNCED OFF THE WALLS of Vera's condo. She grabbed the baby monitor off her nightstand and frantically ran into the baby's room. Leaning over the edge of the crib, she saw the bed was empty, but the crying continued. As her eyes darted around the gray room, the monitor began to beep. Vera couldn't decide if it was dying or leading her to the baby. The beeping continued as she ran out into the hallway, down the steps, and into the street. More beeping came as she turned behind her to see a car coming straight toward her, the monitor still in her hand.

Vera jolted awake, sending the small bottle of champagne that Melia had included in the welcome basket rattling onto the floor. Her cell phone beeping beside her had forced its way into her dream, or nightmare, depending on how you looked at it.

The glass bottle stopped with clang against the ornate metal railing detailed with gothic spindles adjacent the bed as Vera squinted and looked at her phone.

A message from Eliza: "Heading in to watch Millie work, then heading to the hotel to get ready in your fancy suite. See you soon." She ended it with a kissy face emoji.

Vera wasn't sure whether it was the emoji or the champagne, but she immediately felt nauseous. Unaware of the fact that she had fallen asleep, sitting up in the bed, she realized she wasn't even sure how she had gotten into the hotel room. Running the back of her hand over her clammy forehead, she leaned against the bed, rested her back on the tufted leather headboard, and stared out the angled skylights in the slanted ceiling across her bed. The penthouse was a sight to behold. Two-level living with a private entrance, wrought-iron architecture mixed with the dark, cigar-lounge feel of old Cuba. Right now the best part of all was the free-standing claw-foot tub situated ten feet from her bed. A drink, a soak, and Aleve, and she would be a new lady. One ready to take on NYC, not fall victim to it.

Swinging her legs over the side of the bed, she plugged her phone into the cord already provided on the nightstand and willed herself to stand. She was sure she could feel all the alcohol swirling in her stomach, and she took a few slow steps over to the edge of the tub. The cool porcelain on her thighs reminded her that somehow not only had she gotten into the hotel and up to her room, but she had managed to strip down to her bra and underwear before climbing into bed. What would her mother say about her lack of wherewithal now?

As the water splashed into the tub, she fiddled with the knobs, trying to get the temperature just right, a feat she found near impossible in a tub. Even if you could manage to find the perfect temp, it would only last for a few minutes before it began to cool. This was largely the reason she didn't take baths, that and she hated the idea of sitting in your own filth. But in this moment, the shower seemed too far, and she felt like maybe she needed to let the filth soak in before she got too comfortable with who she had been these last few days.

Her bare feet padded across the smooth wooden floor as she made her way over to the basket Melia had left on the dresser for her. The clear cellophane wrap lay next to it, draped half on the dresser, half on the floor. The basket was a dark-woven wicker, not the Pier 1 kind, more the Tommy Bahama kind. The basket was big enough for several people, but the note was just to her. Nestled in between a few bottles of Taittinger, some elegant bath oils, dried lavender, dark chocolate truffles, and a slim, tasteful tennis bracelet lined with rubies, sapphires, and yellow diamonds was a note from Melia.

It was on thick, crème cardstock lined with gold foil edges with a simple, glossy M on top, matching the color of the paper, only shown by tilting the matte card to see the gloss catch the light. Handwritten below it in red pen was cursive penmanship that was somehow grandma charming yet modern. Vera had always appreciated people who still practiced the art of cursive, a dying skill among modern emoji conversations.

Dear Vera,

Welcome to your home away from home. I truly hope you will enjoy your time here and that it will be a memorable experience. Hope you like my choices in treats. I had the bracelet made to resemble the colors of the Colombian flag. I hope it makes you feel even closer to home.

Yours,
Melia

Vera set the card back on the dresser and lifted the bracelet in her fingers. Light from the window made the already beautiful stones glitter. She slowly placed it on top of her wrist, letting the ends dangle down before reaching under to clasp it. Unzipping a dress and putting on a bracelet were two things that could make you feel so alone. Jobs built for two, but you were only one. She fiddled for a few minutes before she heard the click and finally released her fingers from the clasp.

It fit perfectly. She tilted her wrist back and forth, watching the stones glint and glow, marveling at the meticulous craftsmanship and the ornate, yet not gaudy, design. But truly what she was most in awe of was the incredible thought. She knew she should question the motives, wonder if this was a ploy to get her to sign on with Connor, but her gut told her this wasn't about that. Connor was nowhere on that card or in the basket. Everything about this had a woman's touch. And though Melia seemed to play the perfect wife in public, she didn't seem the type to fake it behind the scenes to get ahead. Her eyes seemed empty when she looked at him, but alive when they looked at Vera. She wasn't sure if what she was seeing in the office was true, but this basket, this bracelet, seemed to clarify it a little further. Melia wasn't playing the game to get Vera on her husband's side—she was playing to win.

Gold foil from the wrapper lay in a curl on the floor as Vera popped the top off another of the bottles Melia had left. She was sure there were real crystal champagne flutes downstairs, but she was too lazy to get them. She took a swig off the top and wiped her mouth on the back of the arm that wasn't dripping in jewels. Then with the white-labeled bottle in hand, she tiptoed across the floor (something she always did when excited as a child), slid her caramel-colored silk panties off with the hand not holding the bottle, and slid into the tub.

Leaning back, she turned the antique faucet knob off with her foot, something she had always wanted to do since watching The Notebook, all the while rolling her wrist to watch the bracelet glisten. She rarely allowed herself moments of indulgence, but this gesture had seized her. No work, no Spencer, no stress . . . just a girl tipsy in the tub and a wrist of rocks weighing her down body and mind. She couldn't help but think that this was going to be a good night.

CHAPTER 28

ELIZA

THE SELECTION OF TEA BAGS at PTSK was dismal. Eliza usually didn't like to drink coffee after ten a.m., but with the morning it had been, and the tea selection presented, she decided a little caffeine might not be the worst idea. On the cab ride to the station, Millie had transformed from a mess of a woman on the edge to a happy-go-lucky gal ready to hit the town. Eliza couldn't help but think it was miraculous, really, her ability to set something so profound aside and become someone else entirely. She wasn't sure whether she envied it or was frightened by it.

She dumped the hot water into the stainless steel office kitchen sink and filled her mug with Millie's face on it with hot coffee. Liking coffee had become a learned effort for her, and as much as she knew it made it her look weak to the "real" coffee drinkers, she still needed cream or sugar, or anything to make it taste less like coffee. Today that meant a little sugar from a glass dispenser, and as it poured in, she hoped it would sweeten this dark day. Grabbing a stirrer, she turned, swirling her coffee with the stick, and walked out to the set, where Millie was still getting makeup touch-ups and scanning the teleprompter notes.

It wasn't lost on Eliza how out of place she looked her in her workout clothes, sweaty, slicked-back hair, and makeup-free face. Not to mention her calm demeanor among the chaos of everyone around her. She stirred and watched. A spider in the corner, taking it in, watching the world unfold.

She had hoped to get another run in before the party, but when this morning hadn't unfolded as expected, she felt she couldn't leave Millie. Really, she was scared too. Every small moment that Millie was remotely sad triggered a fear in Eliza she couldn't put words to. She could survive without her run, but she knew she would die without Millie. So instead of lacing up, she was sitting down to watch her friend fake it for the world.

One of the PAs brought out a chair from Connor's office for Eliza to sit in. She had heard many things about this Connor fellow, mainly from the tabloids and Millie's annoyed texts, but he did have great taste in furniture. Her body felt like it was melting into the chair. She ran her hands over the incredibly soft tartan flannel, wondering where someone even acquired a chair this lovely. Almost, as if he were reading her mind, Connor appeared behind her.

"I had it brought back from a trip to Ireland," his voice boomed from behind her, somehow authoritative with an undertone of smut.

"Holy shit!" she squealed, jumping up from the chair. His presence was usually felt before heard, but he had scared the shit out of her.

Now standing face-to-face, to break eye contact, she quietly looked down to make sure she hadn't spilled coffee on the decadent chair, but she then felt the need to meet his gaze again.

"Sorry, dear, I didn't mean to scare you," Connor said with a toothy smile.

"Oh. I . . ." Eliza started, then caught her breath, trying to slow her heartbeat. "I am sorry. I don't know why it startled me so."

"That chair can whisk you away to places you didn't even know existed. Places deep in your mind." He smiled again. "Or at least that is what the covey in Westport told me—that the chair was so comfortable it can bring you to corners in your mind that calm you beyond belief." Then he smiled again, all teeth.

"Wow. Well, that must be true because I was blissfully unaware." Eliza felt her lips curve up to match his. She knew who he was; he didn't even need to say, but like a good businessman, he did of course.

"Connor Dixon." He stuck his hand out. "You are friends with Camille?"

She met his hand, noticing how cold it felt on a hot day.

"Yes. I am Eliza," she replied, purposely leaving out her last name so he wouldn't make the connection to Rhett, which usually brought on a whole slew of questions about baseball that she had no interest in answering. "I have known Millie since we were kids. I am actually in town to be her date for your party tonight." She realized he was still holding her hand and so she gently pulled it back.

"Millie, huh?" His smile turned slightly sinister.

"Oh right. Camille. I have called her Millie since we were kids. Force of habit, I guess."

"I like it." Smile again. "You are her date tonight, huh? No Noel?" He closed his lips but kept the smile as he slightly tilted his head.

"Um. No." She was suddenly more frazzled than she expected. "We decided to make it a girls' night. We have another friend coming in from DC too. Vera. Vera Sutton." She stopped, wondering why she was suddenly telling him so much.

"Ah yes, Vera. I know Vera." His smile faded a bit, confusing Eliza.

They both stood silent after that. Him not wanting to show his disappointment in Vera not taking his campaign yet and Eliza wanting to end this strange interaction with her friend's boss. He was a good-looking man, but something about him didn't sit right with her. Call it women's intuition or just a general distrust of men, but she wasn't loving what Connor was putting out.

Finally, after what felt like hours, one of the camera operators called out, "Live in ten."

"Well," Connor began, "I look forward to seeing you all tonight. Enjoy the chair." The toothy smile spread across his face as he turned and walked off into the dark.

Resting her hand on the back of the chair, she shook off the odd encounter and turned back to watch Millie onstage. The two women locked eyes and in unison mouthed, "Are you okay?" which made them both smile.

"Three . . . two . . . one . . ."

"Hello, I am Camille . . ."

Eliza smiled, watching her friend set her world aside and rise to the occasion. She was a strong woman, stronger than Eliza gave her credit for. Millie was the type of woman who entered the room as an apology. But as she watched her friend project confidence, Eliza recognized she knew that in her heart she would always feel the need to protect her. Camille could easily take Eliza in a fight, but Eliza still felt it was her duty to defend. She peeled her eyes away from the shiny Millie in front of her and snuck one more peak over her should into the dark behind her, not sure what she thought might be there. Darkness was all she could see, so she turned back to keep an eye on her friend and slowly took a seat on the armrest of the chair. Something about allowing the chair to engulf her again felt disturbing now. Not wanting to be rude, she figured sitting on the armrest was enough to seem polite but not fall victim. God forbid she stand up to a man, especially one with power. She was too polite for that, after all. She was the woman who silently took a stand by sitting on an armrest.

CHAPTER 29

CAMILLE

"AND BEFORE WE GO, we want to take a moment and thank all of you for helping make PTSK your favorite news station for the third year in a row. Getting you the news is our top priority, but we like to do it with a little something extra, and we are glad you are enjoying it. So, thank you again and have a wonderful evening."

Camille smirked as she turned to Bill and began to have a fake conversation behind a pretentious smile, not as fake as his, but not much about him was real anyways.

"And we are out . . ." the producer called from behind her headpiece. "Great job, team. Let's wrap up, and we will see you all at the party this evening." Then she scurried off back into the darkness behind the cameras.

Camille stood, pushed her chair in, unhooked her microphone from her lapel and then the pack from her waist, handing it over to a PA. She smiled and thanked the crew like she did after every production, stepping off stage and immediately looking for Eliza, her lifeboat. She was sitting on the edge of a chair typing away on her phone, but she looked up as if she felt Camille needing her.

"You were awesome!" Eliza beamed, putting her phone back on the armrest and standing to hug Camille.

"Don't flatter me." Camille smiled, her face nestled in Eliza's hair that still smelled a little of sweat, but mostly of home.

"Seriously, you are a badass," Eliza reiterated as she pulled back from the hug and gripped Camille's shoulders, forcing eye contact.

"Right. Right." Camille shook her shoulders free. "You ready to go?"

"Yes, ma'am." Eliza bounced like an excited teenage girl, grabbing her phone and practically skipping to follow Camille out the door.

"See you ladies tonight." A call came from behind them, forcing the women to turn, and as the Camille pushed the heavy metal handle opening the door, enough light flooded in and lit Connor Dixon, standing back in the dark, his teeth glowing in the light.

Camille smiled, and Eliza flexed her hand up into a flat palm, her attempt at a polite wave to a person she didn't know. Then both turned and headed out into the light.

Camille felt Eliza shiver a little as her arm brushed against hers outside, though it was a warm summer evening. Something unsettled her. She didn't mention it, though, even when Eliza wrapped her arms around her torso and rubbed them, trying to warm herself.

Breaking the uneasiness, Eliza said, "Vera is already at the hotel and had a pretty amazing room, so I will just drive us over there and we can get ready there. Sounds like there is plenty of room."

"Okay. Sounds good," Camille replied, though the thought of seeing Vera turned her stomach again. She was going to have to do it, obviously, but somehow the thought of seeing Vera, the all-powerful, kick-ass entrepreneur, while her life was on the verge of falling apart made her want to hurl.

Competition was something the three never spoke of but knew existed between them. It did in any friendship, like it or not. Eliza was the one with the money and perfect kids. Vera was the one with the great single life and amazing practice that led her to break barriers, and Camille was the one with the high-profile job, but mainly the perfect marriage. It was one thing to admit the truth to Eliza, the one who would never judge and who maybe wasn't aware of everyone's place in their friend hierarchy, but to let Vera in on her secret was going to break her. Who was she if she wasn't part of "Camille and Noel"?

She swallowed back the urge to cry again as she climbed into the passenger seat of Eliza's Audi. She set her purse on the floor and turned to look out the window. There was nothing of note out there, but if she looked at Eliza, she would cry. She felt Eliza's hand on her thigh, which only made it harder to hold it in. The connection running through them allowed her to be the person she hid from everyone else. Camille let the tears well up as she stared at the brick wall, but didn't let them fall. She took a deep breath, put her hand on top of Eliza's, and squeezed it three times, their signal for "I love you," letting her know she could release it and start the car.

As Eliza started the car and put it in reverse, Camille suppressed her sadness, left her safe space, buckled her seatbelt, and braced for impact.

CHAPTER 30

VERA

COLD. THAT WAS THE ONLY WAY you could explain the water that surrounded Vera. Edges of the label on the bottle of champagne in her hand were beginning to peel from being immersed in the water. She had started by holding it out on the edge, but as the bottle and her mood got lighter, she had begun to let it float upside down in the water, her hand still wrapped around the neck, so none spilled out. She had turned the hot water on a few times with her toes, hoping to warm the water, but it still felt frigid. Turning the knob had become more of a game than a means. Before she had climbed in the bath, she had been adamant about the temperature, but now as she lay there, she wished she felt anything at all. She had been so busy building a career for herself that she forgot to feel, only think.

No one could argue that Vera was brilliant, cunning, a shark. But there was also no denying that with that came a lack of heart. She had once heard that sharks can hear their prey's heartbeat, and that is how they know where to attack, which to Vera meant that your heart was your weak spot, the part that gives you away. And she felt like a shark in the water now, trying to feel but lacking the wherewithal. The only glimmer of hope on the edge of the water was her bracelet, this confusing piece of jewelry that had warmed her heart. She didn't know what it meant or why it made her feel something, but there it was, sparkling in the light of the room, making her feel things.

She shifted in the tub, trying to drop her arm farther down the edge of the tub so she wouldn't have to look at it. With her free arm she lifted the almost empty bottle to her lips and thought about the text she had gotten from Eliza earlier this week: "I think you might be a black widow spider." She had ended it with a smiling emoji to make it feel less abrasive, Vera had assumed.

Initially she wanted to ignore it, but she couldn't help inquiring.

"Why do you say that?"

"Well . . . Kinsely is doing a report on them, and you have a lot of the female characteristics. It isn't a bad thing. It makes you tough!" Followed by the flexing-arm emoji.

"Such as?"

"Women are the dominant sex and can kill the males easily. They are fiercely protective, and their webs are as strong as steel. Just made me think of you, I guess." Winking smile with tongue sticking out.

Vera thought on this for a while, never actually responding to Eliza's text, but taking it in. She had spent the next twenty minutes at work Googling "black widow spiders," trying to understand if she was more spider than shark. "Shark" was a term she was comfortable with, something the world at large used for people who didn't rest and attacked what they wanted. But a spider—did anyone want to be seen as a tiny, eight-legged, black nuisance?

The more she read about the black widow, the more she identified with it. Not all are black; some are brown, light brown, dark gray. The male spiders try hard to wreck the webs that the females have spent hours building, and as a woman who had to claw her way to the top, she knew firsthand how men can try to wreck your success. Other women can, too, though. Regardless, she liked the idea of being seen as a black widow to her friends and in her mind's eye, but to the world, she wanted to remain a shark, a cold-hearted, rarely sleeping creature who didn't like the taste of humans, usually taking one bite and swimming away disinterested. People were meant to be controlled, not coddled. Most sharks are loners, though the ones who are social tend to live longer, so Vera was hoping Camille and Eliza were enough to keep her afloat.

As if on cue, there was a knock at her door below. And for the first time since getting to the hotel, she was going to be without a bottle in her hand, but with a friend to lean on. Her pack was here to help her hunt prey.

CHAPTER 31

ELIZA

ELIZA WISHED SHE HAD A KEY as she knocked again on Vera's hotel door, watching Millie type away on her phone through watery eyes. She had tried her best to compose herself, Eliza even waiting with her in the car for a few extra moments in the parking lot, but she still looked a mess. Eliza was too good a friend to tell her that, so instead she told her she was strong, took her hand, and walked with her into the hotel.

As Eliza lifted her fist to knock for the third time, the door opened to reveal a stunning old-world-meets-industrial suite mixing with a wet-meets-disheveled Vera standing before them, wrapped in a white fluffy towel and with black circles under her eyes.

Trying not to say the wrong thing, Eliza paused longer than she should, allowing too much time for Millie to jump in.

"Wow," Millie said, "this place is amazing. And you are a mess." She lifted her eyebrow in a concerned/joking fashion, her phone still held between her hands.

"Millie!" Eliza gasped.

"No, I didn't mean it in a bad way . . . I just . . ." Camille began, but Vera put her hand up, halting her in her tracks.

"Stop. You are right. I am a mess." Vera looked down, staring at the water pooling on the floor. "I just . . . I don't know . . . It's Spencer . . . It's work . . . It's Melia . . ."

"Melia?" Eliza turned her head quizzically.

Without bothering to answer, Vera continued, "And I have been drinking . . ." She looked up at them, making eye contact only with Eliza. "On and off for days," she finished, feeling the color drain from her face.

For most people this would just be a bender, a difficult phase in life that you needed to feel a little less, so you drink a little more, but most people didn't have an alcoholic for a mother. They rarely talked about it because Vera rarely talked about anything, but all three had watched her mother die from the disease. Vera had called it a broken heart; the world would call it a problem. Her grandfather was an alcoholic, and so her mother never drank, not a drop, until her dad died. Wine after the funeral led to vodka for lunch, and eventually gin all the time.

Watching her mother's demise had changed the once wild-drinking Vera into a mostly sober, very casual party drinker. She usually only drank in the presence of people who knew her mother, so basically only when Eliza and Camille were around to hold her accountable. But she had broken the last few days and wasn't sure if she could go back. The numbing feeling became something she craved, even in her bones.

Before Eliza could react, Camille stepped forward, embracing Vera in a tight hug, "We got this. We are here now. Everything is going to be okay." Eliza watched as Vera's shoulders loosened into Millie's enfolding arms, watching all of their past melt away. Eliza leaned forward and wrapped her arms around the two women, creating a web of security for their very own badass black widow.

The only water on the floor was what had fallen from Vera's beautiful, wet hair. Vera had never been a crier, and she was too tipsy to feel strong enough to warrant tears, but not drunk enough to know that this embrace meant everything. When the three finally released, it was Eliza, ever the good mother, to shoo everyone inside and start a pot of coffee and call for some room service to sober Vera up, as the three ladies sat in the aged, mahogany-walled living room on an emerald green crushed velvet couch and listened to Vera recount everything that had happened over the last week.

By the time the food arrived, they were on their second pot of coffee and had gotten Vera into a robe, and as the evening sky had begun to glow orange with the first glints of sunset, Eliza had started to the fire in the antique stone living room fireplace. It was still seventy plus degrees out, but all the women couldn't shake the chill of their lives. The devil doesn't always come in horns and a red cape; he comes as everything you ever wished for, but nothing being as it would seem. Each woman sat quietly in the warmth of the fire, eating fries and sipping coffee, surrounded by a love that not many knew. And yet each silently grappled with a negative shit storm in their minds, ones that couldn't be fixed by coffee and love, ones that only the strong survive.

Eliza knew that of the three of them, she was the one who was going to have to be the strongest. She usually was. Vera may be a tough cookie, but what she held in trade she lacked in emotional strength. And Millie put on one hell of a strong facade, but Eliza knew she could break at any second. So, Eliza took one more sip of the coffee she knew wasn't near strong enough for the courage she needed to muster and commanded that everyone get up. It was time to party.

CHAPTER 32

CAMILLE

SEEING VERA GETTING KNOCKED DOWN a peg delighted Camille more than it should have, definitely more than she would ever admit out loud. Showing up at her fancy hotel suite as the embarrassed, estranged, marriage failure she was, it was strangely comforting to see her long lost friend was equal parts as messy.

After lots of coffee, some honest discussion, and showers, the three women were now spread out among the bathroom: Eliza, in her tank and underwear, up on her tiptoes, applied mascara to her perfectly lined eyes. Vera, never one to shy away from nudity, stood in only her thong, straightening her beautiful dark hair. And Camille, in full sweats, on the floor, legs straight out but crossed one over the other, drinking a glass of vodka on the rocks, watching her beautiful friends. It had taken a team of professionals to make her look even half as beautiful as these two women looked naturally. Camille took another sip of her drink, letting the vodka sting her throat. It was better than letting more tears sting her eyes.

Once all three were bronzed, curled, highlighted, and liquored up, they slipped into the three stunning dresses that Eliza had hung in the hall during her many mothering duties she had performed while Vera sobered up and Camille drank up. Always one to love things clean and perfect, Eliza even traveled with her own bedding to switch out at every hotel she visited. Even the five-star accommodations didn't have enough class to wipe away the blue light evidence she had seen on Dateline. So as not to seem like a psychotic germophobe she would tell people that it was so she could enjoy the comforts of home even when away, but Camille knew her too well to buy that bull shit.

Eliza was in an emerald green, high-neck lace dress, bringing attention to her matching eyes and highlighting strawberry blond locks she left down in beachy waves that fell perfectly over her shoulders—just like it seemed her life did, Camille thought. Vera was in nude, ruched chiffon Alexander McQueen gown with a sweetheart neckline. No necklace so you couldn't help but notice her sexy collarbone, above which she wore her hair in a slicked-back straight ponytail. The only jewelry on her body was a tennis bracelet she seemed to keep fidgeting with. Camille couldn't help but notice that without the bracelet, she looked almost naked.

And as Camille turned to look at herself in the mirror, she was left feeling crestfallen. When she had bought the long black dress, it was two years and likely twenty pounds ago. The plunging neckline stilled showed off her ample chest, and the matching high slit showed off her curvy upper left thigh. But the dress overall was tighter than Camille was comfortable with. Couple that with her overall shitty outlook on her life and she was not deep enough into that vodka for tonight to be a success. Yet. She sucked in her gut, already made moderately smaller by her Spanx, and headed back to the liquor cart in the dining room. The black satin of her dress tail dragged on the floor behind her bare feet.

Messy fingernails dug into the ice bucket as she gripped the cold cubes and threw them quickly into her glass, shaking the excess water off her fingers. She used to take such pride in her appearance, but over the last few days, her fingernail polish had chipped (something she tried to hide in the papers on the desk as she read the news), adding to her haggard appearance. As she poured the clear liquid to the top of the glass, spilling over the edge slightly, she leaned forward, sipped the drink down, and picked the glass up.

"You look incredible!"

Camille jumped a little at the sound of Eliza's voice. She turned around and saw both women standing behind her, and she wished for only a moment that she could feel about herself the way she looked in their eyes right now. A sausage stuffed into a fancy black casing was how she felt, but the way they looked at her made her feel like a lean prime rib. Food analogies seemed best to Camille. Food being her biggest antidepressant, it only seemed fair that she use it as a gauge on life.

Never comfortable with compliments, Camille quickly raised her glass to the women to change the subject. "Well . . . I will drink for both of us." She tipped her glass back into her mouth after winking at Vera. Well on her way to being the Camille of lore, she was beginning to understand the numbing pleasure at the bottom of the bottle.

Vera smirked, half envious of her friend, the other half sad for her. Camille watched Vera's eyes turn from admiration to pity. She was having none of that tonight. They were here together to celebrate her, after all. The station may have been the host, but the ratings were from her. There would be no pity, no sadness, no pain, and certainly no divorce. But there would be alcohol.

Before Camille could throw back another sip, Vera slipped her fingers in between hers. They were perfectly manicured, which made the tears behind Camille's fake eyelashes begin to burn again. Even in the midst of a drunk episode, the woman managed to maintain her appearances.

Still staring at Vera's nails, Eliza gently took the glass out of Camille's other hand, setting it on a coaster she had slyly placed on the bar, and grabbed her other hand. Camille didn't have to look because she knew Eliza's nails wouldn't be done, but that wasn't the point. She had always been the type of woman who could pull off perfection with simplicity. Everyone knew those women, the ones who didn't have to try as hard. Eliza was one of them, and usually this would be the sort of thing that Camille would hold against her, but not her Eliza. There was nothing Camille would hold against her.

Hand in hand, the three women left the safety of their old-world suite, out their private entrance, through the lobby, into the elevator, and down into the lower level, where the party was already in full effect.

CHAPTER 33

VERA

AMBER-COLORED LIGHTING flooded the old brick walls, glinting in the polished marble floors. Antique chandeliers hung from exposed brick and beam ceilings, romanticizing an already stunning space. Vera had to hand it to Connor—this place was incredible. The man clearly had an eye for beautiful things, one had to look no further than his wife to see that.

People flitted around the room, weaving seamlessly in and out of their jovial conversations, patting themselves on the back or faking interest in their latest business venture or family trip. Vera had sobered up more than she was ready for at an event like this. She knew she needed to take notes and keep tabs on the Dixons to better gage her feelings about them as clients but being around artificial folks had a way of making Vera feel edgy.

She hadn't been aware that she was still holding Camille's hand until a waiter came around with a tray of sparkling champagne flutes and Camille released her hand to grab a glass. Eliza also extended her hand for a glass, still keeping her other hand tightly in Camille's. This sort of thing used to bother Vera, their closeness, their bond, but with time and tale, she had grown to like her view from the outside looking in. Theirs was a friendship most would long for, but it was also messy and codependent, two things Vera was not fully equipped to handle. The gesture between the two was meant more for Eliza than Camille, though Vera knew Eliza would assume it was the other way around. Eliza liked to pretend she was strong, and though she usually was, the fact that her hand was still nestled in Camille's with the other maintaining death grip around her champagne flute told Vera that this crowd made her feel a little off balance, as well.

High-end designer gowns, pseudo-celebrities, and those in the "industry" spanned the room. Vera had heard of or come into contact with many of these folks in her business, but somehow, she still felt off. Without thinking twice, she reached for a glass of champagne before the waiter left. Both Camille and Eliza turned and stared at her, the look in their eyes a mix of confusions and frustration.

"It's for looks," Vera half-lied. "I can't walk around here looking all 'sober'?" She tried to air quote with the glass in one hand.

Neither of them looked convinced, much less impressed, but they didn't say anything. They knew Vera was a big girl and that knew what she was doing, or at least they hoped.

As if on cue, Connor Dixon appeared from around a corner, his suit a navy crushed velvet, highlighting his impeccable physique. Vera wasn't even straight, but it was hard not to notice a body like that. The suit hung well on him, hitting all the right places, but the pièce de résistance was the woman hanging on his arm, Melia. She was a vision in a Donna Karan Atelier black-and white-silk gazar and sheer organza panel gown with high-neck crisscross straps that exposed her back when she turned to say hello to another incoming guest while her arm still stayed tucked in Connor's. Vera couldn't help but notice that her cool-toned blond hair that usually flowed freely framing her face was upswept into a side-angled, simple low ponytail, somehow making her emerge stronger than she usually appeared.

"Ladies," Connor's voice broke Vera's train of thought, "so glad you could make it." He smiled, revealing those teeth.

"Yes," Camille began, breaking her lips away from the edge of the already empty champagne glass, "great party." She smiled back and waved down another waiter.

Connor seemed to take her in, looking her up and down before turning his attention to Eliza.

"Hello again," he uttered, extending his hand to her. And as Eliza reached and shook his hand, Vera wondered if she had mentioned Eliza, or Camille had, or maybe he had just done his research on both of them and instantly knew they tended to travel in a pack. Vera looked to Camille to see if she looked surprised, but she was too busy still trying to flag a waiter.

"And Vera..." She heard Connor turn to her, forcing her to make eye contact. "It is great to see you here. I hope you find everything to your liking." Smile. "Feel free to chat with anyone here. It is like having a live reference party." Smile again followed by a mellow laugh.

He turned back to Camille, who finally looked relieved to have a waiter heading toward her. "And Millie," he waited for her to look at him, which she did rather quizzically since no one called her Millie outside of Eliza, "you are a huge part of the success of this station. This party is for you. I hope this is a night you enjoy. Let's chat later about the future we see for you at the station. Good things are in store for you, I believe." Smile.

Camille nodded as she reached over Eliza to grab two more glasses from the waiter. Connor placed his hand on Melia's arm, still wrapped through his, as he smiled and led her away. It was in that moment that Vera noticed the bracelet wrapped around Melia's delicate wrist. A tennis bracelet almost matching hers, but instead of

Columbian colors, it was red, white, and blue. Vera felt the space between her eyebrows scrunch in confusion as she looked from the bracelet and met Melia's eyes for a second before Connor turned her fully away from them. It was just long enough for Vera to catch it: Melia's wink as her eyes turned from Vera.

CHAPTER 34

ELIZA

CHAMPAGNE SPLASHED UP, nearing spilling over the edge. "I am not near drunk enough to party with my coworkers," Millie stated as she walked away from Eliza with a glass of champagne in each hand. Eliza wasn't sure whether she was to follow or let her mingle. The party was for her, after all. Better to let her do her thing, she supposed. She looked over toward Vera, who had also left, following behind Connor and Melia, attempting to get intel, Eliza assumed. That left Eliza alone in a room of strangers.

She had been used to this kind of thing, Rhett asking her to attend these things from time to time, the difference being she could look across the room and see him, be reminded of who she was, and feel confident enough to stand on her own two feet in a room of sharks. Without him, she felt like she was drowning in the water. She equally loved and hated that he had this effect on her. She was thankful after her afternoon with Millie that she had a man who loved her this much, but annoyed that she was a woman who couldn't stand without his approval or presence. But here in this room, she was going to sink or swim; she had to decide. He wasn't here, wasn't going to be coming, and she was a fish out of water. She was no shark, but it was time to swim with them. No more lifejacket—it was time to jump into the deep. She had to wade out of the shallow, no better time to try than around people who were too shallow to care if she were drowning.

The only good part about these kind of events was that the bars were everywhere and the liquor was top shelf. So, Eliza headed to the nearest bartender in a crisp, button-down white shirt behind another unique antique brick countertop and ordered herself an Old Fashioned. She usually stuck to wine, but tonight she was going to drink like a man. And if she had learned anything from watching *Mad Men,* it was that real men make real business deals with a dirty martini or an old-fashioned. Since she wasn't quite feeling like Bond yet, she was going to start with an old-fashioned. As the bartender went about stirring the whiskey, bitters, and sugar cube, she turned her back and rested it against the bar ledge. She had lost Millie and Vera, the mother part in her wanted to panic, realizing that they never made a plan. No meeting place, no safe word, no exit strategy. But the shark in her fought against the panic, willing her not to care. They would find their way, things would figure themselves out, and she was here to be anyone she wanted. In a room where no one knew her, she could be anyone.

"Ma'am?" she heard the bartender behind her.

She turned, grabbed her old-fashioned, tipped the young gen-Z boy looking at her with woeful eyes, and walked into the cocktail area, ready to grab the room by the balls.

•• •• ••

Eliza quickly realized that without Rhett she was damn near unrecognizable, a superpower she welcomes in these situations. She flitted from group to group, giving her two cents into each conversation, hoping to walk away and leave them wondering who that (insert amazing adjective here) woman was. At times she was smart, others she was quippy, and sometimes she was even politically sound. She was usually an arm piece, much like Melia looked when she saw her with Connor, but tonight she was an enigma. There were a few moments when people tried to place her.

"Do I know you?"

"Have we met?"

"You look familiar."

Eliza had a response to every question. No, they hadn't met, didn't know each other, and she had one of those faces. Tonight she wasn't Eliza Kingfield, she was Willa Morgan, visiting from an international affiliate station. Double first name as a first and last name made it difficult for people to remember you because they could never remember if your name was the first or last name. She was high up over there, across the pond. CEO seemed too high, so she settled on vice president of international marketing. Seemed vague enough, something people could relate to but wouldn't call her out on. Business was good overseas, and they were looking at a closer partnership with their American counterparts.

Of course, she had yet to tell anyone any of this. She had concocted the disguise on another trip to a different bar at the party. This time the bartender was female, and she ordered a vodka martini, never fully consuming the drink, merely using it as a tool for her identity. And as she used the metal olive skewer as a thought-processing chew device, she created a new persona while looking out over the crowd. The bits and pieces of her many cocktails were mixing in her veins, providing liquid courage and killer wits. Willa was a woman who enjoyed a good buzz, a break from the rigor of her daily life. She had no husband, no kids, just a job that consumed all her time. She would love to have kids, of course, but when you work eighty hours a week, there is simply no time. She had settled for a cat and a top-level apartment overlooking the Eiffel Tower. Born and raised in the Midwest, but now a Parisian. Eliza hated olives, but Willa never let any part of a drink go to waste, so she chewed both olives off her skewer and headed back into the crowd. She wasn't looking for anyone in particular, and that of course is when you run into someone noteworthy. Nina Park.

CHAPTER 35

CAMILLE

LIQUOR BEFORE BEER, you are in the clear. Liquor before champagne you are ... ? How did that go again? Camille thought as she sauntered over to the bar, trying to decide if she should stick with champagne or go back to the vodka she was drinking in the suite. She had to shove a little more than she was comfortable with to get to the bar. People were everywhere in this part of the venue. One could barely breathe, much less get a drink.

Camille had spent the last few minutes trying to act interested in Roger's story about how he and his partner adopted two rescue dogs last week. She stood there as he scrolled through pictures of Rover and Fido, or whatever their names were, and listened to him tell the assembled crowd about how they have started to warm up to him and Tim. Roger was a good guy, one of the video camera operators on her set, and had been married to his partner for just over a year. "We want kids, but we thought we should start with dog." He smiled while he said it. Camille had to swallow every instinct to tell him that marriages fall apart, and no amount of kids, or dogs, or whatever good deeds he and Tim were going to do would save it. So she stood, smiled, nodded, sipped her champagne faster than one should, and let Roger think the world was a happy place. Camille knew it wasn't, but she had vowed not to let her shit creep into her success.

"Vodka tonic," she said as she slapped her hand on the bar ledge, finally making her way. The slap made the bartender jump a little, making Camille wonder if everyone was turned off by her presence. But he quickly gained his composure and turned to grab the vodka. With a keen eye, Camille made sure he didn't cheat her on the pour when she felt a hand on her lower back. She thought she could feel his smile before she turned. But instead of a navy blue suit, before her stood a man dressed in a white tuxedo, very 1997.

"Well, I will give him this. He sure knows how to throw one hell of a party. Am I right?" Brian raised his glass of chardonnay in a toast motion toward Camille, while simultaneously removing his hand from her back. He only drank white wine, mainly chardonnay, saying it was the thinnest choice and kept his teeth from yellowing, so Hollywood of him. Camille wasn't sure either was true, but some things weren't worth the fight.

She smiled, turned to the bar where her fresh drink sat, raised it to meet Brian's wine, and said "To us. The reason why this station thrives. The reason these people get paid. And the reason I am falling apart at the seams." She clinked his glass while he looked at her, trying to look sad or confused, but the Botox not letting him look anything besides stone faced.

"Never mind," Camille quickly followed, turned, and took a drink from her glass. Even without her watchful eye, the boy had managed to make the perfect drink. Simple things rendered big thanks for her tonight as she fished a ten-dollar bill out of her dress to tip the boy and slapped it down on the counter. The boy jumped again, slightly irritating her as she left the bill on the counter and she and Brian headed out into the room, linked arm in arm.

Jazz music floated throughout the rich air filled with laughter and power. Camille took her arm out of Brian's, using it to grab his hand and lead him onto the dance floor. Never one to turn down a dance, Brian happily obliged, swinging her out in front of him, causing her drink to spill over the edge splash on the floor. This sort of thing would usually upset her, but tonight she didn't care. She wasn't that wound-up-tight mother of three and wife of soon to be no one. An entire chest-contracting hoot escaped her mouth, forcing her to laugh so hard she couldn't stop. She wasn't sure if she was laughing at the ridiculousness of her situation or just herself in general. Removing her hand from Brian's, she placed it on her knee as she stay doubled over, laughing hysterically. Brian kept right on dancing, to no one's surprise. He was nothing if not vain.

When she finally composed herself after a minute, she stood back up, started swaying her hips to the music, and put her straw back in her mouth, sipping and spinning. She could feel that she was being watched, not necessarily in a creepy way, just that eyes were on her. It could be anyone in the room, so as she spun, she looked. It took two twists for her eyes to finally lock with his. Connor Dixon flashed a half-smile at her, and for the first time it didn't feel off-putting; it felt genuine. Maybe it was the cocktail or the spinning, but for a split second she felt her heart race at the way he was looking at her. No one had looked at her like that in a long time. She maintained eye contact, noticing out of her periphery that Melia still stood next to him, her hand in his, but his eyes were all over her. She swayed her hips with a little more effort suddenly, moving like she was putting on a show. It wasn't until Brian grabbed her shoulders and spun her back to face him that she realized she was flirting with her boss, and the worst part was that she was likely misreading that entire situation.

He wasn't looking at her, she decided as she sipped her drink, her hand now back in Brian's as he spun her. She must have had it wrong. A man like that would never look twice at a woman like her. Hell, nowadays she couldn't even get the man who was forced to look at her every day to actually see her. A wave of nausea came over her when she began to realize how foolish she had been. She pulled her hand from Brian's one last time and shimmied off the dance floor.

CHAPTER 36

VERA

LIFE WAS SIMPLER IF YOU DIDN'T PLAY games, which was why Vera never ventured into sports. Competition ran through her veins, but games didn't. She employed this same philosophy in every aspect of life. She was a straight shooter at work, and she didn't beat around the bush in relationships. Life was too short to waste people's time with games; she knew this all too well. Her life had been a series of games once her father passed. A game of waiting for the other shoe to drop. A game of wondering where her mother was. A game of chance. When it came to games, Vera was never the lucky one. Always playing by the rules, desperate to win at all costs, but usually losing due to unforeseen circumstances. The wrong tiles in a game of Scrabble, a bad roll in Yahtzee. She flirted with quitting games as a child and officially gave it up as an adult. Which is why it was so incredibly out of character for her to be a few feet behind them hiding (albeit not well) behind a lemon tree that the Dixons obviously had brought into bring some color to the rooms, sipping champagne while she engaged in a game of cat and mouse.

The champagne flute was supposed to be ornamental. Destruction ensued with every sip, but the longer it sat in her hand, the more difficult it was to say no. Then there was Melia, the bracelet, the wink, and Vera's lips were on the glass. Slowly she tipped the glass back again, trying to convince herself that if she drank it slowly, then it wouldn't affect her as much. The glass was already

near empty as she had been trying to look casual behind
this tree for the last half hour as she watched Melia's every
movement. She was supposed to be here to watch Connor,
take him in, ask around about him, see if she wanted to
represent him, but she couldn't peel her eyes away from
the woman on his arm.

Melia, it seemed, hadn't noticed Vera watching her.
Truth be told, there wasn't much to watch. Melia stayed
fairly glued to Connor's arm, only releasing it when it
seemed he relaxed enough to allow her to free her hand to
greet guests. The entire exchange shouldn't have been
surprising to Vera, given her experiences with them in her
office. It was very clear that Connor ran the show. The
thing Vera couldn't wrap her head around was why? And
how? Being a strong, independent woman herself, she
always had a hard time understanding when women
succumbed to men. How, after everything women have
fought for, were there still women who didn't fight?

Trophy wife would have been Connor's more
obvious choice for a wife. Melia was pretty, of course, but
a simple pretty, nothing apparent. You had to look at her,
really study her to see it. Her porcelain skin that bled
seamlessly into her thin, blond hair that down hung just at
her bony shoulders. Roughly one hundred ten pounds
soaking wet, which laid thin on her five-foot-six frame.
Her eyes look tired, but her composure was flawless. To
the world she was put together and ready to be put
forward. But her eyes and skin told a different story—one
Vera saw the beginnings of in her office, but behind this
tree she saw more.

The gemstones of the bracelet caught in the
chandelier light when she removed her arm from
Connor's. Vera noticed for the first time that it was bigger
than hers—not that she was comparing, just an

observation. The first time she saw it, she was so in her own head about it that she didn't notice that it was quite a bit larger, in fact, and hung more like a thick bangle than a tennis bracelet. The red, white, and blue had her initially thinking it was some American piece that Connor likely bought her when he decided to run for mayor. A statement piece for the future first lady. But the way Melia had winked and the fact that Vera had been gifted a similar bracelet had her wondering if there was something else about the bracelet all together.

"Another glass miss?" a charming young girl who couldn't even be old enough to drink asked, scaring the shit out of Vera.

She jumped, shaking the tree a little, and immediately felt a pang of panic for spilling her drink, only to realize she hadn't. Her glass was empty. Her ornament had become necessity for the spy work she was involved in. Swallowing back her nervous fear of what too many glasses would lead to, she set the empty flute on the tray and grabbed another. The waitress smiled, turned, and was gone, leaving Vera to play Russian roulette now armed with a gun.

Just as she brought the barrel into her lips, she realized she wasn't the only one in danger. She watched as Melia's bracelet slipped up her arm when she extended her hand to meet yet another someone Connor was yapping about, and there under the spot where the thick band had covered was a bruise so dark Vera could see it from her hiding spot. She watched as Melia quickly reached for the bracelet and pulled it back down to cover the mark, still smiling, still maintaining eye contact with the new so and so. *She really is a pro,* Vera thought. Then without thinking, she put the barrel back in her mouth, and in one gulp, she pulled the trigger, leaving her tree in search of that young little waitress with the cure to her life's woes.

CHAPTER 37

ELIZA

NINA PARK WAS ONE OF THOSE women you only think exists on newspapers and TV screens. Not the celebrity kind that seems unattainable and ignorant, but the kind who was "every" woman, but brilliant and a ballbuster. Nina was once upon a time engaged to a man who ran for president. His name escaped Eliza now, but it didn't matter anyway. He wasn't the story; she was. Thai-American descent, Nina was stunning—one of those women whose appearances stop conversations in rooms among men, and start them among women. A Yale graduate with a law degree and thriving practice, she gave it up to be by what's-his-name's side during his campaign. Unfortunately for him, she realized she deserved better when he decided to lean conservative republican.

Some say her leaving him was the straw that broke the camel's back in his election campaign, and it was likely true. Over the course of his campaigning, it was she whom people seemed to gravitate toward. She was an even more modern-day Michelle Obama (if such a thing were possible), minus the chiseled arms. What she lacked in arm strength, she made up for in stunning platform comments and life-changing ideas. She was a woman on a mission, she was no one's patsy, she was simply Nina, and in the end, it turned out that was all she needed.

Nina walked away from Mr. Has-been and became a somebody. Her ideas that helped launch his campaign translated nicely into her run for office. She started small, local Pittsburgh government, then onto district attorney, and now in the Senate. Senator was hopefully a stepping stone to the White House, many guessed. The woman had something. That thing people can't look away from, and it wasn't just her beauty—it was her ideas, her brain, her passion, her desire for change. She was a breath of fresh air in a world breathing stagnant ventilation. And that breath of fresh air had somehow blown right into Eliza's midst.

Fan girl would have been putting it lightly. Eliza rarely turned the TV on, unless it had something to say about her future Mrs. President, Nina Park. For a woman so turned off by politics, at a time when the world felt torn by parties, Nina had made Eliza not only interested and listening, she had made her hopeful. Hope was something Eliza felt the world was lacking at large but she especially needed a little more of. Every time she looked into Piper and Kinsley's eyes and tried to answer their questions about all the horrible things happening in the world, it was Nina Park who made her feel okay to say she believed there would be a better future.

It took more cups of courage than Eliza would like to admit for her to make her way over to Nina. Miraculously, she was sitting alone at a table, watching people try their best to attempt dance moves, her phone face down on the table, but Eliza could hear it repeatedly buzz as she got closer. Instinctively, she gripped her clutch tighter between her arm and chest, her umpteenth glass of champagne in her other hand as she got close enough to not only hear her phone but also her humming to the music.

"You like jazz?" Eliza blurted out, feeling like a silly schoolgirl and immediately wishing she would have brought Nina a drink as well. How rude.

Nina turned, her asymmetrical bob moving in unison with her head. "Yes. Are you a fan, as well?"

Eliza wished in that moment that she was, that jazz was her favorite music, or that at the very least she could name one artist.

"It is growing on me . . ." She smiled. It was true — she did like what she was hearing, and she had an inner smile at her farm reference, which of course Nina would never understand.

Nina smiled, looked Eliza up and down in a way that almost made Eliza wonder if she was assessing her or admiring her, and patted the chair next to her.

"Have a seat." Nina nodded and angled her body toward the empty chair.

Hoping this wasn't just part of her political pretense, but truthfully not caring if it was, Eliza slid as gracefully as possibly while tipsy into the chair.

"Nina Park." Nina extended her hand to Eliza.

Eliza set down her drink on the table and reveled in the moment her fingers threaded Nina's.

"I know who you are," Eliza said with a sly grin.

Nina smiled in return, retracting her hand but maintaining eye contact.

"And you are?" Nina pursed her lips together, managing to make the question seem sweet instead of mocking the fact that Eliza had gotten so starstruck she forgot her own name.

"Oh. Oh my. Sorry. Of course . . ." Eliza stammered. "I am Willa Morgan." And as soon as she felt the name on her lips, she immediately wondered why she had said it.

Picking up her champagne glass and bringing it to her lips again, she heard Nina say, "It is nice to meet you, Willa. Tell me, what brings you to this party?"

And Eliza let the champagne flow into her veins as she leaned into her story.

"Well, I work for an overseas affiliate." Eliza felt the words flow out easier than they should have, veering toward humility by not mentioning she was the vice president of marketing.

And before Nina could ask any more, Eliza asked, "And what brings a lady of your amazing stature to this event?"

"Honestly . . ." Nina began, then looked over both shoulders to see who was around before leaning in closer to Eliza and whispering just loud enough to be heard over the music, "I have been hearing some rumblings about Connor Dixon, and I wanted to see this guy for myself. He has offered time and again to contribute to my campaign, and while I could always use the money, I am not about to take it from a supposed rapist." Nina lowered her voice slightly on the last word.

"A what?" Eliza choked on the last of her champagne she had tried to swallow while Nina was talking.

"There are stories . . ." Nina began and flagged down a waiter effortlessly with her slender fingers perfectly adorned with borrowed rings from Tiffany's, "but I have a hunch you may need another drink first."

Eliza felt the waiter set the two glasses down over her shoulder and onto the table. Nina smiled at the waiter and nodded, looking effortlessly graceful as only Nina Park could. Eliza picked up her glass, took a sip, and then she leaned forward, getting closer to Nina Park than she ever thought possible, and whispered, "Do tell."

CHAPTER 38

CAMILLE

CAMILLE HIKED UP THE BOTTOM of her dress as she sat on the cold toilet seat and set her drink on top of the sanitary napkin metal trash can attached to the bathroom stall wall. She giggled as she set it there, partly because the sober, uptight her would never allow germs that close to her glass, the other part laughing at the term, "sanitary napkins." *What in the hell does that even mean,* she thought as she sat.

Between the dress hiking and the sanitary napkin disposal bin, Camille was brought back to her wedding night. A night where her dress was so big she couldn't lift it alone to pee, so she had to find Eliza and Vera every time she needed to use the restroom or change her tampon. Every woman she knew used tampons or pads, not "sanitary napkins" She had tried to switch her birth control several times to line it up so that her period wouldn't land on her wedding date, but in the end, it was either let it flow on that day or all of her honeymoon, and she decided to sacrifice one day for a week of bliss. Not to mention that everyone had said no one has sex on their wedding night because they are too tired. Should have been a red flag, though, literally a bright red flag that things weren't going to last. Rain on a wedding day is good luck, but maybe a period on a wedding day was a big red mark on the marriage.

She sat longer than she needed on the toilet, waiting for the tears to come, but nothing happened. Instead of sadness, she felt anger. Who in the hell did Noel think he was? Did he think he could honestly do better? Had he taken a long look in the mirror lately? He wasn't a young pup, and that dad bod and old sweater wasn't doing him any favors. He was lucky to have her and dumb to lose her. Warm blood began to rush to her cheeks as she wiped, let her dress fall, and walked out of the stall. Heat from the anger made her start to perspire along her hairline. She grabbed a few paper towels and dabbed the beads of sweat before turning to the sink to wash her hands. Chills ran through her body as she saw what she thought was a ghost in the mirror staring back at her, the white complexion mixed with the booze in her eyes, forcing her to blink several times before realizing it wasn't a ghost. It was Melia Dixon.

"Camille?" Melia's soft voice questioned. "Are you okay?"

Camille wasn't a hundred percent sure how to answer that. She wasn't okay in the grand scheme of things, and though she wanted to believe she was okay in the form present in front of Melia, she knew that, too, was likely a lie. But since it seemed like everything in her life was a lie, Camille continued the charade.

"Oh, Melia," Camille began and dabbed her forehead lightly again, "I am fine. Just a little warm, I guess." She smiled and fanned herself with her free hand, realizing she still hadn't washed them and was likely wafting germs straight into her mouth.

"Do you need anything?" Melia asked, looking genuinely concerned.

"Oh no . . . just too much dancing, not enough water." Camille smiled and kept fanning against her better judgment.

"Speaking of which, I should probably head out and grab some," Camille began. "Water, that is. Grab some water," she continued, realizing for the first time she was feeling bad about her potential flirty exchange with Melia's husband.

"Okay. If you need anything . . ." Melia began, but Camille had already flung the women's restroom door open, hoping she had sanitizer in her purse still sitting on her seat at the head table. The table where Connor and Melia would be sitting, as well.

In the midst of her beeline out of the bathroom, she heard someone behind her call, "You move pretty well out there."

Camille froze. She knew who it was, and though every bone in her body told her to keep walking, she turned, and her eyes met Connor's, for the second time tonight.

Jolts of electricity zapped all over Camille. Someone had seen her. Though it was her boss, and against her better judgment, she walked toward him. He was standing over by the bar, in the back of the hallway to the restroom. No one else was around, making her wonder for a second if this was his own personal bar. She wouldn't put it past Connor to have a bar set up just for him. He was indulgent like that. He loved throwing his money around, even if no one else was there to see it. But here she was, seeing it with her own two eyes.

He smiled as she came closer, and for the second time tonight, it didn't unnerve her. He was more handsome than she had ever bothered to notice before, and the way his body laid under that suit was a bit of a crime. How was it that she hadn't noticed his aura before? He wasn't as old as his power would make him seem, and his casual confidence was more attractive after a few drinks. Camille had enough in her system to not only notice his physique, but to also forget about his wife.

As she sauntered over, leaning over the bar, allowing him to take a gander at her ass, one of the few features she reveled in about her body. Her waistline may come and go, but that ass was her saving grace. She had learned as teenage girl how to use it to get her way, too, and tonight she was going to use it to flirt with an attractive man and feel wanted, even if was just from afar.

He was her boss, and they were both married, and this wouldn't go anywhere, but she decided there was no harm in a little innocent flirting. So while he kept his back resting on the bar, she leaned back onto her heels, pushed her chest farther forward than she had all night, and held her head high as she casually threw back a sip of her martini and said, "Oh, you liked those moves, did you?"

CHAPTER 39

VERA

HALLMARK MOVIES WERE WRITTEN about moments like this. Girl meets boy and initially is turned off, but over time begins to fall. Then comes the culminating dramatic moment when they get in a fight or misunderstanding and everything goes to hell, only to then fall back together in one romantic gesture. Vera's life had never been the kind make-believe stories are made from. There was no girl meets boy, only girl meets girl, which already limited the audience. There had been no initial turnoff when it came to Spencer, only a flutter in her stomach she couldn't shake. There had, however, been the blowout, though there was no misunderstanding, just a huge obvious roadblock that they could no longer ignore. Now would be the time for a big romantic gesture, one that brought them back together and would likely leave them happily ever after. But this was no love story, and Vera wasn't that girl.

"Are you drinking?" the soft familiar voice came from behind Vera's back as she scanned the crowd for Melia, whom she had lost on her trip back to the bar.

Choking, Vera slowly turned, hoping she hadn't been found out, especially by her.

Spencer was a vision in multicolor organza halter dress that showed off her perfectly golden tan and flawless skin. She was flat chested, but instead of hiding that, she reveled in it, letting her outfits highlight all her other enviable features so you didn't even notice her lack of breasts. Her hair was down, straight, the ends beginning to curl ever so slightly from her natural wave she could never fully flat iron away. The winged tips of her eyeliner curved up a little higher as she scrunched her face to meet her sad and confused eyes.

Vera stood stoically still. She didn't know if she wanted to throw up or run, so instead she froze, staring for far too long at Spencer, leaving the space between them to grow stale and unpleasant.

Flippantly, she took a sip of her champagne to clear her throat, not realizing the consequences until she tilted her head back down and her eyes met Spencer's, her bleach blond hair falling off her left shoulder as she tipped her head farther to the side and a frown spread across her thin lips.

"Spencer?" Vera started, tilting her head down to break eye contact.

Knowing she should continue on, but not sure what to say, Vera pursed her lips together, continuing to stare at the shiny marble floor's tiles. She thought that if Spencer returned to her, she would wrap her arms around her, fall back into old times, and find the happiness she thought she had lost. But this woman standing before her had broken her heart, not to mention not responded to even one text or call. Ghosting was not a practice Vera found attractive. Just another game she had no interest in playing.

Realizing she wasn't happy to see her, but not yet sure of what she was feeling, Vera kept still and quiet, trying desperately to search through her feelings and identify what this woman standing before her now made her feel. She had hoped for this moment, waited for the elation she would feel, but instead she felt nothing. Then she realized that wasn't true. She did feel something. Anger.

It started in her lower ribs and worked its way up, beginning to make her heart race and her breath quicken. *Fuck you,* Vera thought by the time it hit her eyes, forcing her to raise her head back up and meet Spencer's eyes. This woman would not make her hang her head in shame; she had done nothing to feel that. There was no need to apologize for who you truly were. Vera was not going to be made to feel bad for being honest, not by Spencer, and not by anyone. Her choices were hers and hers alone, and she owed no one an explanation for anything.

By the time the anger hit her brain, it had also reached her fingertips, compelling her to grip the flute even tighter.

"Spencer," she started again, "what in the hell are you doing here?" She finished by lowering her voice and squinting her eyes to convey that this was not a happy coincidence. Then to really nail it home, Vera tipped back the champagne, finishing the glass, and placing it back on the bar. And while Spencer lowered her eye contact, Vera raised her hand and ordered another round.

CHAPTER 40

ELIZA

"THERE TRULY IS SOMETHING about you, Willa," Nina said as she took a sip of her drink. "I don't usually feel this comfortable with strangers." She set the glass down and looked Eliza in the eyes.

"You have an honest face and a protective quality to you." Nina placed her hand on Eliza's. "I bet you are a wonderful friend."

"Nina, you are too kind." Eliza smiled, hoping she would continue. They had spent the last several minutes with a mildly drunk Nina giving Eliza (or "Willa," as Nina thought) all the dish she had on Connor Dixon. Nina kept finishing every rumor by staying, "But that's just the rumor. No one has any proof." Eliza knew that meant that if she ever were to pass on the information, the unspoken rule was that it was nothing more than gossip, and it couldn't have come from a woman with possible presidential ambitions.

Eliza hung on every word Nina said. The woman had done her research, and for good reason. A huge part of her platform was women's rights, women's protection, and rape reform. Not to mention she was one of the champions of the #metoo movement, having survived a rape as a young adolescent. She never spoke about it until some of the more nameless women of the movement came forward, compelling her bare her truth, creating behind her a female army that would follow any orders she laid forth. She was a powerhouse, and while she had done most of her fundraising without corporate money, a presidential bid was going to need a lot more cash flow, something Dixon was willing to offer. Nina needed to know at what price though.

"Just between us girls, right?" Nina patted Eliza's hand.

"Of course," Eliza was quick to reply, wanting nothing more than for Nina Park to have the utmost faith in her.

"I should probably go mingle. My campaign manager would be utterly disappointed in me if I attended an event with this many potential connections and spent the entire evening gossiping with my new girlfriend." Nina pulled her hand off Eliza's and smiled, her eyes somehow catching the light and shimmering.

She definitely has that "something," Eliza thought as she maintained eye contact with Nina longer than she probably should have. That thing that endears people, that "strong yet kind" aura, a "best friend and yet stern mother" quality.

A leader shines, and Nina wasn't just shining, she was glittering.

Eliza felt her breath catch at Nina calling her "a girlfriend" and had to remind herself not to nerd out.

"Nina, it has been my pleasure." Eliza felt like it was the most cordial statement she could come up with at the time.

"No, Willa, the pleasure was all mine," Nina responded as she rose effortlessly from her chair. "I hope we can cross paths again." She smiled, leaving Eliza to think she really meant it.

"I would love that." Eliza rose to meet her, realizing for the first time they were almost eye-to-eye even in heels. Eliza usually towered over most women, but Nina only fell maybe an inch below her. This just added to her already powerful presence. A tall woman made men uncomfortable, just the sort of thing this world needed right now.

"I will have my people reach out, and maybe when you are back stateside, we can connect," Nina spoke as she began to shove her chair back in.

"Wonderful," Eliza answered and extended her hand to shake Nina's.

Nina, in turn, leaned forward and wrapped her arms around Eliza, stunning Eliza momentarily before she returned the embrace.

"I am more of a hugger," Nina said and then pulled away. "My father always said, 'A handshake can tell you someone's grip, but a hug reveals their heart.'" One last smile and she was gone, just one of the many bodies in a party full of others thinking they were "somebody." Nina didn't have to think she was, though. Everyone just knew it.

Still stunned by the entire exchange, it didn't immediately dawn on Eliza that Nina would never call. Not because she didn't want to, but because Willa Morgan didn't exist. In the flurry of excitement and gossip, Eliza had forgotten she was being someone else. She thought for a moment about chasing after Nina, telling her the truth, and hoping her apology would be enough for forgiveness and friendship. Before she dashed off, though, she thought about her honest face and realized Nina was likely not a woman who gave second chances. So instead Eliza headed toward the bathroom, for the first time in a long time wishing she had simply been herself. Just Eliza.

CHAPTER 41

CAMILLE

HAVE I EVER NOTICED BEFORE how blue his eyes are? Camille wondered as she sipped her drink through the tiny straw the beautiful blond bartender had added. Once Camille had taken a good look at the female bartender, it confirmed her suspicions that this bar was meant for Connor. Fully stocked and expertly staffed.

They had moved on from her dance moves and were now discussing the party at large, the players in attendance, and the plan for the night. Camille felt like a strong, sexy, confident woman for the first time in months. Noel had stopped looking at her so long ago that she forgot how to even get a man's attention. It turned out that if someone wanted to see her, it wasn't that hard. Connor had noticed her without her even trying; she had forgotten she still had that in her. The extra pounds mixed with the emotional baggage had added additional self-doubt and insecurity. It might have been the courage in the cocktails she had been drinking all night, but she was feeling like herself and enjoying every minute, even if it was fleeting.

"At some point I will have to make a speech, I suppose," Connor said casually, lifting his bourbon to his lips and taking a sip.

"You always give great speeches," Camille flattered. "You know you are a good speaker. It's in your blood." She smiled.

Connor met her smile and replied, "Maybe you should give the speech." His smile turned mischievous, his lips tightly pressing together while their ends curved up to meet the apples of his cheeks, under his narrowing eyes.

Camille almost spit out her drink before covering her mouth with her hand as Connor lightly snickered.

"Why in the hell would I give the speech?" Camille removed her hand from her mouth and questioned.

Connor's grin turned stern. "Why wouldn't you? You are the reason for the station's success."

"No. It is not just me. I am one of many people who make the station work." Camille slurred slightly but caught herself.

"Not true," Connor quickly added, not acknowledging Camille's drunken slip. "Have you seen the latest ratings and focus group results?"

"Not yet. Supposed to go over them on Monday." Camille leaned against the bar ledge for support but hoped it looked like a casual "I don't care about the ratings" lean.

"Well, maybe we can find time to go over them before that. There is something else I want to chat with you about, as well." He smiled at her.

Camille kept leaning, trying to sip her drink casually, assuming instead that she looked like a toddler learning to use a straw for the first time.

She lifted the outside edge of her upper lip to hint at a smile. Ratings and feedback were truly all that any anchor cared about. If the public didn't like you, then you were out. If they did, then you were Katie Couric. Camille had her eyes on being the next big thing and taking the station to new levels, ones not seen by a woman yet. There were many that came before her and tapped at that elusive glass ceiling, trying hard to beat the likes of Tom Brokaw and Matt Lauer. Though, it wasn't hard to raise above Lauer these days, following his scandals that got him kicked off NBC.

Camille wanted to be on everyone's lips, though. She wanted the world to know who she was. Her following had been consistent, but not changing. She had yet to reach the younger demographic or most men. She was huge with women thirty plus, but the gen-z-er's were not fully buying what she was selling. They really weren't buying anything these days, getting most of their news from Twitter and not the TV.

This was a valid concern for those in Camille's field. Either go viral or go extinct. PTSK had an online medium and received a lot of traffic from it, but there had been rumblings that they were going to spend more money and more time into growing their online presence. They wanted to start a twenty-four-hour news feed that solely existed online and ran live on all social media platforms. Similar to those annoying pop-up ads that show up in your Twitter feed that you can usually click out of, except this would suck you in.

No one had done it yet, or even came close for that matter. Every other station nationwide simply uploaded broadcasts to their website and tried to promote via social media. This would change the way people took in the news. And if there was one man who could do it, it was Connor Dixon. Connections at Twitter, Facebook, Instagram, Snapchat—you name it, he had it. No one else could get all the mediums to function together, but Connor could. When money talked, people listened.

If Connor was about to pull off the impossible and wanted Camille in on it, then she was going to play nice and lean into not only the bar, but his business chatter, as well.

"Well," Camille started, using the tiny amount of core strength she still had to pull herself off the bar. Setting her drink down to prop herself up with that hand, she reached out her other hand, the one with her wedding ring, and placed it on Connor's masculine bicep.

"I would love to chat about my future. You know I am interested in where the station is headed and what I can do to help us get to where we are going." She hiccupped, then swallowed, embarrassed, but started giggling.

"I have to go give that speech you were supposed to give," he smiled and winked, "but I will have my assistant go grab the ratings and proposals and drop them off. Then maybe after I get done stroking some egos, we can grab a minute to chat before the night is over. That work?" He pursed his lips together, and then he downed the rest of his bourbon before slamming it down on the bar top.

From the side she noticed his chiseled profile, high cheekbones, and perfectly angled nose. She felt her fingertips warm, reminding her that she was still gripping his arm. Squeezing his rock-hard bicep, she tried to relay a connection with her grasp. Nothing else in her life seemed to be heading in the right direction except this moment. Praise from the man holding the strings to your career. She wanted so badly to be the face of their new launch, and she was willing to stroke his ego a little to get there.

As she released his arm, they made eye contact. Camille turned and reached for her drink, bringing it to her lips and sipping slowly.

"Well?" He tilted his head as his fingers fiddled with the buttons on his suit coat, trying to close them.

"Oh, right." Camille smiled. "Sounds like a plan. I'll see you after. Good luck. Sorry I forgot my notecards."

Another sip as she raised mischievous eyebrows.

"I'll manage." He winked before looking down to finally fix his buttons shut. "And I'll see you later." He looked up, met her eyes, smiled, turned, and was gone.

CHAPTER 42

VERA

THE BAR WAS SHOULDER TO SHOULDER with people, and yet Vera couldn't shake the one standing next to her.

"Must you really be drinking like that? You know it's not good," Spencer began.

"Oh, now you are worried about my well-being?" Vera replied as the bartender set down another glass of champagne in front of her.

Vera took it and took a sip before turning to face Spencer fully. "It's funny to me how I have spent the last few days texting and calling and heard nothing from you. Then you show up out of nowhere and start telling me what's good for me? Shit, Spencer, you don't even know me. If you did, you never would've asked me to have a baby. You never would have guilted me into the conversation to begin with. You wouldn't have tried to change me. Did you ever stop to think that maybe the problem is you, not me? I mean, only one of us has a working uterus. The other's is hostile." Vera took another sip and continued. "Kind of like this entire exchange." Another sip.

The shock in Spencer's eyes cut bone deep. Vera knew she had gone too far, but in the moment, she was on a roll and let it fly. Now it was utterly apparent that she had crossed a line. And although she felt a pang in her stomach for the pain in Spencer's face, another part of her was strangely proud. Somewhere along the line in this relationship, she had stopped fighting for herself. Usually the one to wear the pants, time and love had her slowly removing them, baring herself more than she was comfortable with. She hadn't seen it when she was in the thick of it; one never does. The haze of love can make people blind to reality.

The last few days, lack of communication and abundance of alcohol had cleared the fog from her vision, and she was seeing Spencer in a new light. She was no longer that sun-kissed hippie in short shorts who danced her way through life; she was one of those women who thinks she can change people. They are everywhere, women who settle into a relationship with the hopes of forcing their partners' hands. Ask nice enough, shed enough tears, choose your fights, and over time, without realizing it, your partner begins to become putty in your hands.

Vera was no one's project—she was a damn masterpiece on her own, and she didn't need Spencer or kids to prove that.

Spencer's hair flew as she spun around and began to walk away as fast as she could. Never being a woman to wear heels made running away from problems a lot quicker. Vera stood, in her high-end high heels, and took another sip from her glass. Watching Spencer charge off, Vera tried to decide if she should go after her. That would require her setting down her drink, something she wasn't sure she could do, which was exactly why she did, the fluid sloshing up the edges of the flute, but it wasn't full enough to spill over the edge.

Running in heels was something Vera had strangely perfected, and so she caught up to the ballet-flatted Spencer as she passed through the large, antique metal door and into the concrete stairwell. Spencer, like

Vera, always took the stairs as part of her cardio, which was a hell of a lot easier when you weren't wearing heels.

Vera flung the door open, her heels clicking on the concrete as she entered the stairwell, and started up the stairs, yelling to Spencer to stop as she went. Spencer turned, halfway up the second flight, and waited for Vera to meet her. Vera clicked up the stairs toward her, stopping on the landing between the first and second flight, not willing to fully meet Spencer where she wanted.

"Spence, I am sorry. That was below the belt," Vera began, still trying to catch her breath.

Spencer stood still, one hand on the railing, the other on her hip. Vera always knew when she had crossed the line with Spencer because she would put one hand on her jutting hip bone. If both hands went on, then shit had really hit the fan, so Vera knew there was still a chance for forgiveness.

"I didn't mean to hurt you . . . or maybe I did . . . I don't know," Vera continued. "But the truth is you hurt me, too. You made me believe I wasn't enough. And over the last few days, I have missed you—I am not going to deny that—but I have realized that I am more than enough." She stopped to allow her heart rate to slow.

"I missed you, too," Spencer made a quiet concession.

Vera looked up as she, too, grabbed the railing to brace herself from the tipsy, winded feeling overcoming her. For the first time she could see that Spencer was crying. Usually this would have been enough for Vera to let her guard down, rush over, and take Spencer in her arms. They had performed this dance time and again, Vera holding a sobbing Spencer.

Vera never knew if she found the fact that Spencer cried so easily endearing and vulnerable or sad and weak.

And because she didn't want to judge, she let her mind go blank as her arms enveloped her.

This time, though, Vera stood her ground. There would be no embrace, only two women in juxtaposing positions hoping the other made the concession.

Spencer cleared her throat. "Vera, I was wrong. I needed space to realize that I don't need kids. I need you. I am sorry that I gave you the cold shoulder, but I needed enough time to get my thoughts in order. I thought it was you who needed to figure things out, but it turns out it was me. And by the time I realized it, I knew that a simple call or text wasn't going to do it, so I showed up at your office and Dash told me where to find you. I quickly ran home and changed, before hopping in a cab and sneaking past the security with a couple of model types". She lifted her hand off her hip and wiped the tears now on her narrow cheekbones.

Vera stood completely still, focusing on the rise and fall of her chest, which began to quicken again. Her vision became blurry, compelling her to panic at the thought that she was going to pass out. It wasn't until she felt her eyes squint tightly shut that she realized she wasn't going to faint. She was beginning to cry—a feeling so foreign to her that it made her feel nauseous. She released her hand from the railing and rested it on her stomach, leaning slightly forward, exhaling, hoping it would make it all stop.

The faint footsteps of Spencer's flats coming toward her coerced Vera to rise back up and use her free hand to spread all fingers into a stop sign in Spencer's direction. The footsteps halted.

"Don't" was all Vera could get it out before she looked away from her.

She swallowed hard, realizing this relationship had affected her more than she knew, but also knowing it had reached its conclusion.

Forcing her blurry eyes to look straight at Spencer, who had closed the distance between them to within a stair, she swallowed the pain and began her concession speech.

"Spencer, I love you. I will always love you. But I know for several reasons that this is not where either of us are meant to be." She swallowed again, hoping to force the tears in her eyes not to fall. "I want you to have everything you want. And I want to be who I am and not feel bad for the decisions I make. If we stay together, I will always know in the back of my mind that your heart wants a child. That is something you can't just turn off. You will find someone wonderful who wants to be a mother with you. I will just never be that woman, and I won't be anyone's disappointment."

Vera removed her hand from her stomach and reached it out toward Spencer, her final surrender to the life they almost had. Spencer slid her fingers into Vera's, not stopping the tears that were falling from her cheeks.

Vera took one last look at Spencer, took one last deep breath, and mouthed "goodbye" as she slid her hand out of Spencer's, fearing that if she said the words out loud, she wouldn't be able to stop the tears from falling.

Spencer nodded and gracefully turned, her bony shoulder blades protruding out of the open back of her halter dress as she headed up the stairs and out of Vera's life, almost as beautifully as she had entered.

Clicking sounds bounced off the concrete walls from Vera's heels as she descended the stairs, heading back to the party. It hurt, that couldn't be denied, but she didn't realize how good she was at letting go. Breaking up with Spencer had made her realize she had let go a long time ago, not of Spencer, but of herself.

CHAPTER 43

ELIZA

GOSSIP IN THE BATHROOM was usually in full force at events like this. Women in groups used the restroom as a respite from the male-dominated discussions floating around the party. Among other women, they could talk shop. Discussing dresses, affairs, bad hair, and jewelry envy.

So when Eliza flung the door open into the elegant, cream damask–wallpapered bathroom, she was surprised to find no one at the counter whispering about Suzie Q while her friend reapplied her lipstick. Instead she noticed only one other set of feet under the stalls. The quiet unnerved her a bit, but then she settled into enjoying a break from the hustle and bustle.

As she opened the last stall door, the other occupied stall opened, and a woman dressed in an all-white, silk, fitted gown with a small train that dragged on the floor behind her emerged. Eliza was a little grossed out by her couture gown wiping its way across the bathroom floor. The woman didn't seem to notice or care as she headed toward the mirror, using her middle fingers to lightly pull back the skin around her eyes she thought looked wrinkly. *What does this young beauty know of wrinkles?* Eliza thought. The woman smiled at Eliza through her reflection in the mirror and nodded. Eliza smiled in return and unwittingly nodded, though she wasn't sure why that had been part of their exchange.

Shutting the door of her stall, Eliza realized the woman looked familiar but she couldn't place her, so through the crack of the door, she took one last peek at her. Her red hair was fastened in an up-do that was fancier than Eliza's at her wedding. Curls were pinned perfectly on top of her head, allowing you to focus only on her form under that stunning tight dress. She watched as the woman patted her stray baby hairs flat onto her head, turned, picked up the front of her dress slightly with her hands, and exited the bathroom.

Eliza turned, hiked her dress, and took a seat, thinking for a moment about the woman's red hair, a trait that only a few possessed, and fewer could pull off. Then it dawned on her. Aria Tilbury. She was an actress on that long-standing show on PTSK, the medical drama one, the one Eliza had tuned in from time to time but wasn't fully vested in. But she did know enough about Aria to know that she was one of the actresses of *MD*, which Eliza always thought to be such a clever name, both standing for *doctor of medicine*, as well as *medical drama*.

Aria Tilbury was one of the women Nina had mentioned in her exposé to Eliza. *MD* was one of the first programs that Connor had put on the air when he took over at PTSK, and Aria hadn't initially been one of the break-out actresses, but she seemed to work her way up the ranks as other cast members fell off. Nina said the rumor was that Connor had approached her and propositioned her with job security, as well as a chance to become the star, and all she had to do in return is sleep with him when he wanted. Aria declined; he pushed. She said no; he didn't listen. And when things were done, he promised to make her a big star if she kept her mouth shut. And if she didn't, he would make sure she never worked in Hollywood again. He had that kind of power. She knew it, and most importantly, he did too.

Interrupting her thoughts, she heard Connor's voice booming over the party, though muffled in the bathroom stall.

"Good evening. I just want to take a minute to say thank you . . ." was about all that Eliza could make out through the muffle and her newfound general disdain of him. Tuning out his obnoxious voice was a lot easier than she imagined. Maybe all those years ignoring her daughters' arguments were coming in handy.

Eliza started to think of all the stories Nina had told her. Brisk but disgusting accounts of Connor's obvious abuse of power and reckless disrespect for women as a whole. There were at least five women whom Nina had heard about, Aria being one of them. Women who needed Connor to make a name for them, and so he used them in whatever way he wanted. And in exchange for not opening their mouths, he didn't shut down their careers. To her knowledge, none of the women had agreed to this exchange. All of the encounters had been nonconsensual if not unconscious.

Connor's voice broke back in, even louder, as the door to the bathroom opened. Eliza shivered a little at a break in her thoughts, but smiled knowing that someone else had decided that whatever Connor Dixon had to say wasn't that important. Eliza had finished but remained sitting, somehow feeling as though if she exited the stall, the woman likely fixing her makeup in the mirror would be on to her. As if she would somehow be able to see everything that Eliza knew and had been thinking.

Luckily the woman didn't stay long. Through the crack, Eliza only saw the flash of a black gown as the woman turned from the sink and headed toward the door.

"And of course we couldn't have done any of this without . . ." Connor's voice loudly flooded into the bathroom as the door opened again. Eliza closed her eyes, willing it to close and no longer have his voice enrage her.

Once the sound was muffled enough for her to unclench her fists, she opened the door to the stall, heading to wash her hands. She realized in that moment that Aria Tilbury had not. Not only was that disgusting, but rather ironic for a woman who scrubs in several times an episode.

Waiting for the water to heat up, Eliza noticed a Kraft envelope on the counter, resting up against the mirror. On it were two simple words . . . *Willa Morgan.*

CHAPTER 44

CAMILLE

CONNOR'S ICE WAS MELTING in the lowball glass as he hoisted it in the air. "Last, but definitely not least, I want to give a huge shout-out to Camille Givens." Connor scanned the crowd and found Camille leaning against a pillar. He extended his glass toward her and winked. Camille returned the gesture with a smile. It was all a little ridiculous, she couldn't help but think. She was no derby champion; she was more a show pony. The woman they strutted out to show that they were so progressive in their view of women. Which was all rather peculiar, she snickered to herself, since it was wildly known that Connor was not only a flirt but a misogynist. He looked at women as sport. *His poor wife,* Camille thought as she tipped her drink to her lips and scanned the crowd for Melia. She wasn't a woman who stood out in a crowd, so it wasn't surprising to Camille that she didn't notice her.

"Without her, our connection with the audience drops dramatically. She is a great anchor, friend, mother, and wife!"

The last word felt like a bullet. Camille, in her search for Connor's better half, hadn't even noticed he was still talking her up, until he fired the last shot. She choked a little on her drink, forcing her to cough. But not wanting to cause a scene, she turned and headed back toward the quiet bar in the corner where she and Connor had met earlier.

The coughing fit led to tears, though she wasn't sure they were actually from the coughing. The blond bartender brought her over a glass of water without being asked, setting it down on a coaster next to her. Camille nodded and took several gulps, hoping it would calm the cough and stop the tears.

"Are you okay?" She felt Connor's hand on her shoulder before she turned.

Setting down her water, she turned to face him, wiping her eyes as she did.

"Oh my. Are you crying?" he asked, looking more concerned.

She coughed, lightly this time, bringing her hand from her eyes to cover her mouth.

"Oh. No. I . . ." She coughed again. "Champagne went down the wrong pipe and threw me into a hacking fit, which made my eyes tear up." She lied.

"And here I was thinking my kind words moved you to tears." Connor smiled.

Camille smiled in return, bowing her head to hide her blush. It felt better than she would ever admit to receive praise, especially now. Looking back up at Connor, she couldn't help but wonder how complimentary he would truly be once he found out his perfect narrative of Camille being "every woman with the great family life" was about to come crashing down. She wanted to avoid what that meant to her career as long as possible and hopefully become irreplaceable before that.

With her future in flux, Camille knew her best bet was to entertain Connor's ego.

"Great speech," she began, to which he smiled and raised his drink toward her again.

"Someone had to give it after you bailed," he coyly responded and took a drink.

"Right." She grinned. "Thank you again for stepping up. Quite a guy you are."

"Anything for my star anchor," he responded, placing his hand on top of an envelope he had set on the bar.

"What do you have there?" Camille motioned with her head toward the envelope.

"Oh . . . these are the reports we talked about," he replied.

"What?" Camille said a little louder and leaned in closer. Now that he had finished his speech, the band had fired back up and was louder than before.

"I said these are the numbers. Do you want to go somewhere quieter and look them over and talk about what's next?"

Camille knew it might not be the best of ideas, but she needed a win right now, and it seemed the only place it could come from was her career.

"Yeah. We are staying in the turret penthouse," she said loudly, but not so loud as to draw attention to the fact that she was inviting her boss to her hotel room. It wasn't like that, but she knew people would think otherwise.

"Of course. I forgot that you are friends with Vera." He smiled.

"You know Vera?" Camille asked, feeling slightly confused. Sure, she and Vera hadn't been close recently, but how did she not know about Connor's connection to Vera?

"Yeah. I am consulting her on a project. Trying to get her to help me with a career move." His upper lip lifted slightly, leading Camille to wonder what he had in store.

"Oh really? Care to share?" she asked as she motioned to the bartender for another glass.

"All in good time, Camille. All in good time."

"Right. Well. Since we aren't talking about your career, let's talk about mine." She smiled as she reached for the drink that seemed to almost magically appear.

"Let's," Connor said and motioned for Camille to lead the way. "After you." He nodded in the direction of the exit.

Camille turned, drink still in hand, and headed toward the exit, wondering if she should first tell Eliza where she was going. Then she shook it off because they wouldn't be gone long. No one would even notice they were absent. He would fluff her ego with the numbers, hopefully offer her the online gig, and then they would be back to cheers with drinks from the blond bartender.

She had an eerie feeling of eyes settling on her, watching her, as she pressed the button for the elevator. She turned, scanning the crowd, but it seemed everyone was so caught up in themselves that they didn't notice her, a feeling she knew all too well. She had become so good at being invisible that she took it for granted, especially in moments like this where one prefers invisibility.

As the elevator doors opened, she realized Connor was nowhere to be seen. She placed her hand on the door, keeping them from closing, and again scanned the room. She caught his eye, about twenty feet behind her, visiting with one of the stars of one of his sitcoms. He mouthed "Sorry" and spread all five fingers wide, telling her he would be up in five minutes, and motioned for her to leave, ending the exchange with a smile.

Camille backed into the elevator and pressed the button to reach the hotel lobby, where she exited and walked out in the rain that was beginning to fall on this warm summer night. The smell of the petrichor mixed with the stale leftovers from a passerby's cigarettes was a heavenly aroma for Camille. And she took in deep breaths, enjoying every second as she walked in a drunken haze to the private entrance of their suite. She knew the only thing that felt right about this was the way the air smelled and the feeling of the rain landing on her cheeks and breasts. But she was too drunk to care and too sad for another disappointment, so she threw caution to the wind and opened the hotel room door, filled her glass, and waited for her boss to arrive.

CHAPTER 45

VERA

AS SHE SWUNG THE DOOR OPEN, walking back into the party, Vera once again wiped any residual tears from her cheeks, took a deep breath, and swallowed every remaining feeling she might not have left in the stairwell. And just when she thought she had composed herself, she nearly jumped out of her skin when she heard someone behind her.

"Girl trouble?" A small voice sent shivers throughout her body.

She didn't need to turn around to know who it was. She would know that voice anywhere. And if the voice weren't obvious enough, her body's reaction to it would have been.

Melia was a sight for sore eyes. Something Vera couldn't remember experiencing in a long time. Eyes so weary that only a few things could rouse them, and Melia was one of them.

Vera swallowed again, though she knew in this instance that all residual feelings for Spencer were gone.

"Girlfriend," she responded, watching Melia's face drop ever so slightly. "Ex-girlfriend, I meant," a quick correction on Vera's part that seemed to save face for Melia, as well. The exchange confused Vera even further since Melia was a married woman. A woman married to a man. Why was Vera getting the vibe that she was into her? Vera shook a little, partly from the thought, but also to shake the idea off. This woman was spoken for, and even if she wasn't, she didn't speak Vera's language. So whatever

Vera thought she was feeling was nothing more than wishful thinking. But she couldn't help but wonder why she felt the need to keep reminding herself of that.

They stood there, longer than they should have, both women bewildered by the other, not identifying what either was thinking. Their eyes locked on each other, not breaking contact, in a staring contest that neither agreed to but couldn't help but participate in. Vera found herself so lost in Melia's eyes that she didn't see Melia's hand reach out to her until she felt it.

Vera lost the contest, shifting her eyes to their interlocked hands. It couldn't have been more than a few seconds before Melia pulled herself closer to Vera, compelling Vera to look back up at her.

"You like it?" Melia asked, not breaking eye contact.

Vera felt every muscle in her body go limp, not understanding how she was maintaining her upright posture on her expensive heels. She wasn't sure how long she stood there either, staring back at Melia, trying to figure out the answer to a question she didn't fully understand.

Melia lifted Vera's hand up to her face. Vera held her breath as she waited for Melia to kiss it. Then continue up her arm, pull her into a back hallway, and kiss her up her neck, until their lips were joined together.

Melia broke eye contact, looking to Vera's hand, forcing Vera to assume this was the moment, the moment when all her underlying feelings about a straight woman who rendered her naïve would come true.

"The bracelet," Melia said, turning Vera's hand back and forth, letting the jewels catch the light, "do you like it?" She looked back up at Vera, who had lost all color in her face.

Vera pursed her lips together, blinked her eyes a few times to break the spell their eye contact had on her, and forced any lusty thoughts about Melia out of her mind. She cleared her throat and regained the composure of a woman who ran DC with her wit and wherewithal and looked down at the bracelet then up at Melia with colder eyes this time.

"Oh yes. What a generous gift from you and Connor." Vera lingered on Connor's name a little longer, reiterating to Melia that not only was she aware that she was straight, she was also acutely aware that she was married to a powerful man. Vera felt the muscles around her jaw tighten as she held her chin up a little higher, reminding herself that she had the upper hand here. That powerful man wanted her to help him, not the other way around. She puffed out her chest slightly as she remembered that she was so good at her job that this man's, Melia's man's, future political career success was likely determined by whether or not she decided to run his campaign. And just to cap it off, Vera told herself that not only was all of this true, but she had bigger balls than most of the men in this room. And if Melia couldn't help but notice, Vera wouldn't mind that, as well.

"Oh," Melia's voice broke into Vera's mental power-pose moment, "it wasn't from both of us." Melia smiled. "Just me."

And just like that, Vera felt her shoulders drop slightly, but she did her best to be the woman in her head, not the one with the heart.

CHAPTER 46

ELIZA

HER SHAKING HANDS CLUTCHED the thick envelope as she tried to rack her brain. There had only been two other women in the bathroom, Aria Tilbury, and the other woman she didn't get a look at. Neither woman knew who Willa Morgan was. In fact, as Eliza stood there, she knew there was only one person who knew Willa; Nina. The only rational idea she could come up with was that she had snuck into the bathroom as one of the women exited and placed the envelope on the counter.

Feeling suddenly like a covert spy, Eliza quickly ducked back into the stall, locking the door behind her, setting her clutch back on the top of the toilet paper holder, and stared once again at the envelope with her fake name scrawled in black ink. Hoping it was an invitation to some event that only Nina invited her closest kin to, but knowing it was something much less intriguing, Eliza slid her finger under the envelope seal.

Crisply folded white paper met her fingers as she reached into the envelope. Pulling it out, she set the still weighted envelope on top of her clutch and unfolded the letter. The same handwriting that had graced the front of the enveloped lined the paper. It took a second for Eliza to realize what she was looking at. The spacing of the words threw her initially since she expected a letter of sorts; instead it appeared as more of a list. Once she recognized the intent of the letter, she began to glance over each item listed.

Olivia Lindquist
Avery Bellows
Grace Noah
Allison Pratt
Sarah Gilman
Stella Hill

For a moment, Eliza wondered if Nina sent her the wrong invite. She didn't recognize a single name on this paper. Confused but convinced there must be a reason, Eliza kept on reading the names.

Taylor Russell
Lauren Anderson
Aria Tilbury

Eliza felt her breath catch in her throat for a moment. And just as she reread the name "Aria Tilbury," the bathroom door opened and she jumped a little, suddenly feeling like her cover had been blown. She peered out the crack in the stall door to see a women she didn't recognize visiting with one she did. Another actress she couldn't place but recognized.

As the two women went about their mindless chatter, Eliza turned back to the list, now more vested in what it meant.

Quinn Norel
Bailey King
Everly Wood

The list after Aria's name was a who's who of young women in Hollywood who had recently been on popular TV shows. Again, Eliza had heard of them but couldn't initially place them. In this moment she wished that Willa was a woman who knew more about popular culture than Eliza did.

As she scrolled farther down the list of all women, some she had heard of, some she hadn't, Eliza was still confused. The list was long, roughly some thirty or so women, but she didn't see her name on it.

As the visiting women exited the restroom, Eliza scanned the paper again, trying to figure out its meaning. That is when she saw it: nestled in among the many other names, one she had overlooked in the initial read through.

Rose Ryan

Young, stunning, actress on the rise who had recently fallen out of sight. She was the it girl from that show Rhett watched from time to time, some crime drama that seemed to be sweeping popular culture. Rose, a virtual unknown before the show, had become the breakout star, only to leave midway through season two, and she hadn't been heard from since.

It wasn't the entertainment headlines about her departure that rattled Eliza, it was what Nina had said at the table.

"My source said Connor is the reason for Rose Ryan leaving the business, and it wasn't on her terms. I hear he is having her blackballed because she blue balled him." Nina had smiled at her quip.

Rose, Aria . . . it couldn't be. Eliza felt her stomach lurch. She realized she was looking at a list of all the women Connor had attempted to assault. Eliza had to swallow the bile that burned its way up in her throat. This list made her sick. If what she was looking at was true, that likely meant there were many more where these came from. Eliza felt her hands tighten around the paper as the feeling in her stomach turned from sickness to rage.

This was the exact behavior that had been upsetting her for months now, creeping into her daily life and awakening the beast in her. The woman who wanted justice for the plight of women. The girl who wanted men to know they are not in control. The lady who wanted an America reboot, but this time with women in charge. She had wanted so badly to affect change. To be a part of the solution to a masculine epidemic. Now here she stood with a bullet in her hands, and all she needed was a gun.

As if it were beyond her control, her eyes darted back to the envelope resting on her clutch. It had still felt heavy when she set it down, so she picked up and peered in.

She wasn't sure if what she saw at the bottom of the envelope excited her or scared her, but she knew that she had her gun. Now all she had to do was follow through with the plan Nina set out for her. She would be the unsung hero for so many women, and maybe even free a small part of the scared girl in her mind.

Throwing the envelope and its contents into her purse, she took a deep breath, smoothed the front of her dress with her slightly clammy and shaky hands, turned the lock on the stall, and walked out into the bathroom.

There in the mirror, for the first time, she saw a different woman. She saw Willa Morgan, a powerful woman who took no shit and made no apologies. Eliza raised her chin and smiled slyly at this woman in the mirror.

And as she nodded to the woman she wanted to be staring back at her, she had one more sickening realization. There was one person who needed this information even more than Eliza. And though Nina had angled, she kept it secret. Eliza knew that someone needed to know. She rushed out of the bathroom and into the party, scanning the crowd quickly for Millie. Eliza didn't want to admit to herself that the sickening feeling in her stomach was telling her she may already be too late.

CHAPTER 47

CAMILLE

KNOCKING ON THE HARD METAL DOOR echoed off the walls, causing Camille to jump a little. Goosebumps pricked her skin as she made her way over to the door, drink still in hand. She had been waiting for Connor for only a couple minutes, so it shouldn't have alarmed her when the door finally sounded. As she turned the knob, she was surprised by the way the metal felt cool on her palm, making her keenly aware for the first time that she was nervous, her hands growing clammy and cold

Connor's smile lit up the dark evening sky as she flung open the door. Dry under the umbrella he had brought, or grabbed from the hotel lobby, he was obviously less drunk than she was to be forward thinking enough. He collapsed and opened the umbrella a few times, shaking the raindrops in all different directions before he entered the room.

Handsome but not kind of man who turned heads, and it wasn't even that Camille was all that attracted to him. It was in this moment that she needed to feel a little better about herself, and as much as she hated to admit it, having a man, especially a man with such power, take a shining to her was helping rub her ego that was hanging on by a thread.

"What do you think of the place?" Connor extended his hand high, waving it around the penthouse.

"Oh," Camille said, "it is lovely. So, kind of you guys to put Vera up in it."

"I am glad that you get to use it by proxy." He smiled. "We had some fancy designer come in, and his vision for this space was one of the most unique I had ever heard, and so we let him run with it."

He turned his back, though Camille could still feel him smiling, admiring his money and good sense in taste on display.

She took a drink as he wiped his shoes on the rug and headed into the living room as though he owned the place, which Camille supposed he did.

She followed, stopping momentarily at the drink cart, almost forgetting her good manners through her drunken haze.

"Did you want a drink?" She nodded toward the bar. "You are paying, though." She smiled.

"No." He smiled back. "I'll save myself a few bucks."

"Okay." Camille looked down at her drink, suddenly feeling a little sheepish about drinking the alcohol he paid for. Not bad enough to set it down, just taking a moment to recognize the joke in it. Here she was in a penthouse he paid for, drinking the booze he provided, for a party he was hosting. *Maybe I do owe him something, she thought,* but then she quickly shook her head of the degrading assumption that just because a man does something nice, you then owe him something in return.

She watched as he made his way over to the couch and took a seat in the middle, only leaving room for her to sit next to him on either side. Setting the envelope down on the coffee table, he turned toward her and patted the area next to him.

"Come and sit. Let's go over these numbers."

Nothing about the situation seemed amiss. There was no misunderstood brushes against her as had made his way over to the couch. He hadn't offered her more to drink or insisted they try any other paraphernalia. For all intents and purposes, it seemed as though he truly was there to talk about where she was headed in the company.

Camille felt her shoulders ease up as she checked off the mental boxes of potential red flags as to why she shouldn't sit down. Once she felt everything seemed up to par, she was ready to take a seat and have her ego stroked a little.

Connor pulled the papers out of the envelope. Camille felt their thighs touch as the slit of her dress hiked a little higher from taking a seat. The goose bumps that had momentarily vanished found their way back to the top of her skin as she brought the glass to her lips, hoping the drink would make them dissolve again before Connor saw them and had other thoughts.

"So," he began, turning to face her, "as I have told you time and again, you are a hit with the fans. People really seem to flock to you. I mean, I can see why." He smiled, though for the first time all night it alarmed Camille instead of flattered.

She took another drink, trying to set her mind back at ease, but the smile had made the red flag begin to blow in the nether of her mind.

Connor turned back to the coffee table, pointing at something on the paper that Camille couldn't make out and said, "Your popularity among women in the thirty-to-fifty-five range who are married, stay-at-home mothers is on the rise. It seems they really relate to the fact that you are a wife and mother and make no qualms about hiding the difficulties associated with that."

And before Camille could even stop it, she blurted out, "Well, that's about to change when I get a divorce." And as soon as the words escaped her obviously over-served lips, she regretted them. There were a million reasons not to tell Connor about that part of her life yet, but the biggest of all was that it seemed he was about to offer her a promotion based on that fact that she was someone's wife and mother, and she had just blown the lid right off that whole facade.

"Camille." Connor's face dropped.

Camille instantly knew that this was worse than ruining her chance of a promotion, the pity in his eyes. She suddenly felt like she wanted to hurl, knowing she had no choice but to stay here and wear it like a strong woman should. Connor may have been the first person (outside of Eliza, who didn't count because she was part of Camille) whom Camille had told, but he would be far from the last, and she needed to get her shit straight for how the people were going to respond and look at her.

So instead of throwing up, she tilted a little on the couch, allowing the slit of her skirt to rise a little higher, hoping it yelled confident and carefree as she took another sip from her drink, looked Connor straight in the eyes, and with her best publicity voice said, "It's fine. I am fine."

Then she took another sip, willing the tears to fall back with the vodka, and watched as Connor's face went from pity to roguish.

He placed his hand in the slit on her dress, pressing his palm into her thigh, grabbing it slightly. It took longer than normal for her to react as he leaned toward her and whispered in her ear, "Don't worry, babe. I'll make everything better."

CHAPTER 48

VERA

IT SURPRISED VERA HOW THIN and boney Melia's fingers felt in between hers. Although if she were being honest, she wasn't sure what surprised her more: the feeling of Melia's fingers or that feeling she felt throughout her body as Melia had grabbed her hand.

"I want to show you something," she said as she led Vera out of the party area and into the same staircase she had been in moments earlier with Spencer, a memory that seemed like forever ago now that she was with Melia.

With her hand still entwined in Melia's as she led her up the stairs, Vera again saw the bruise that Melia's bracelet had been unsuccessfully trying to cover. It was fresh, still red, bordering on brown. Vera knew how to tell an old bruise from a new one; her mother bruised easily toward the end. The new ones were obvious from their light tan outer edges that would eventually purple up, begin to gray and fade. When they were new, even the gentlest touch could send jolts throughout your entire body.

Vera tugged harder than she meant to as she stopped in her tracks and pulled Melia's arm back toward her. Melia stumbled a little before turning and facing Vera.

"What the—?" She locked eyes with Vera, thrown by the change in direction.

"What is this?" Vera lifted her wrist and shook it.

"It's the bracelet I had made. Similar to yours—"

"Not the bracelet. What is this?" she demanded again, this time lifting the bracelet farther up Melia's wrist, grazing the bruise and causing Melia to jump.

"It's not what you think. He's really not that bad. It was my fault," Melia started.

Vera locked eyes with Melia and saw them begin to glaze over. The same eyes she had seen in her office with Connor. Melia was retreating into the role she was supposed to play.

"No!" Vera shouted louder than she intended, causing Melia to jump and pull her hand out of Vera's.

Right before Melia's eyes had gone completely dead, Vera walked up and met her on the same step, eye to eye, and she reached for Melia's hand, this time holding it between both of hers.

"Don't do this. Don't lie to me. Don't play a part. Don't be who you are supposed to be. Be you. Be honest. Be Melia," Vera begged as she kept her eyes locked on Melia's, watching the darkness lightly peel back toward the edges.

Melia looked down at her wrist, then back up to Vera, and she watched the darkness fade out as the tears flowed in. Vera stood stoic, silent, waiting for Melia to say something, but instead she just quietly wept.

After a few minutes, Vera took one of her hands off Melia's and crouched down, using her hand to brace herself on the cement step as she took a seat. Melia followed suit, taking a seat on the same stair, their knees touching, hands still interlocked, Melia's tears letting up as her body sat down.

"It wasn't always like this. He was a good man for a very long time," Melia started.

From there she went on to tell Vera about the truth hidden in the lies of a marriage the outside world thought was wedded bliss. As it turned out, Connor started hitting her only a couple years ago. Melia said she wasn't sure what prompted it, but it was around the time he took over the company for his father. The first time it happened, he had come home drunk and disheveled, overwhelmed, and had promised he would never do it again. He even began to talk about adoption with her for the first time in years.

The vows and dialogues lasted only a month or so until he hurt her again. This time, instead of promises, he made threats. If she told, he would ruin her. If she left, he would make her life a living hell, and the worst part of all, she said . . . he could do it. So she had stayed, prayed that things would get better, and hoped he would find other outlets. But the mark on her wrist told Vera that the prayers hadn't worked, and Melia's eyes told her she had become hopeless.

The strong woman Vera had seen in the eyes of a meek girl was still there, honestly even stronger than before. Most would think a strong woman would walk away, but those were the ones who didn't understand domestic abuse, especially abuse from a man of endless means. The fact that she stayed, braved the storm day after day, and put on a brave face made Vera not pity her, but respect her. What choice did she have? If she left him, he would likely ruin her life or kill her, and he could do either with the snap of his fingers. But if she stayed, though she was miserable, she had secretly kept the upper hand. Melia had a secret that could ruin a man who seemed untouchable; she simply needed the right person to help her do it. She needed Vera.

"We are going to fix this," Vera said. "I am going to fix this."

"I knew you would." Melia met her gaze, the tears mostly dry. "That's why I sent him to you in the first place."

Most had dismissed Melia, but Vera smiled, realizing that she was wilier than the world thought, and was about to be the woman they would all know.

CHAPTER 49

ELIZA

ELIZA COULD FEEL HER CHEEKS FLUSH as she tried to catch her breath by holding on the back of a dining room chair. Trying not to draw attention to herself (though she wasn't sure many noticed her anyway), she scanned the crowd back and forth, over and again, trying to spot Millie's black hair and likely loud cackle if she was still on pace with the drinking she started earlier that evening.

The band's top volume made it impossible to hear in there and was making it hard for even a mildly sober Eliza to focus. Squinting her eyes, she tried to see as far across the room as she could, hating to admit to herself in that moment that she wished she had her readers she had gotten the year before. They helped, especially at the end of the day, but the age shame that came with them left her leaving them home more often than her eyes would like.

Her search for Millie had come up fruitless when she spotted Brian out dancing in the middle of the floor, making a scene with his arms in the air, and trying to accrue as much attention as humanly possible, a trait that only seemed to become emphasized with each drink he downed.

Eliza took one more breath, heading through the crowd of horrible, mainly white folks attempting to dance, and wriggled her way up to Brian's side, managing to avoid getting hit by his obnoxiously large dance moves.

"Brian!" Eliza hollered in his direction, trying to sway with the music to not draw attention again. He kept swinging in circles to the band's rendition of "Dancing

Queen" by ABBA, which was apparently his "jam," or at least that was what she thought he was yelling over the music as he flung himself around.

"Brian!" she hollered again, cupping her hands over her mouth, trying to raise her decibels.

He turned until he realized that Eliza was the one yelling.

"What can I do for you, little lady?" he yelled back, still violently swinging his arms and hips.

"Have you seen Millie?"

"Who?"

"Oh . . . um . . . Camille? Have you seen Camille?" she shouted back.

"That girl is not my responsibility off the clock," he yelled, turned, and started thrusting his hips in the direction of some big-boobed blonde who had shimmied her was over toward him.

Annoyed, and yet slightly jealous, of Brian's ability to have that kind of carefree fun, Eliza made her way off the dance floor and was heading toward the lobby area when she felt a hand on her shoulder.

Instinctively, she placed her hand on the hand before turning around, assuming it was Millie, or at the very least Vera.

"I have been looking everywhere for you . . ." she started, but when she turned it wasn't Camille or Vera—she was face to face with one of the players on her husband's team, Aiden Cole.

His mother clearly having given birth to him in the height of *Sex and the City* fame, Aiden was named after Aidan Shaw, Carrie Bradshaw's one time fiancé, a fun fact that they had put up on the jumbotron at one of the rare games Eliza had actually attended. Fresh out of high school, he was barely twenty and was already being touted as the second coming of somebody who Eliza wouldn't know anyways. A cute, young kid, built beyond his age, but with a baby face. He was supposed to be the best shortstop the organization had ever seen, that much Eliza had gathered from hearing Rhett on the phone.

"Mrs. Kingfield?" He looked at her quizzically, then looked at her hand, which was still holding his hand.

"Oh dear," Eliza started then quickly released her hand from his. "I am sorry. I thought you were my friend I have been looking for." She smiled, trying to smooth the waters and make the entire exchange appear less sexual.

"No worries." He spoke with a southern accent that just added to his overall charming appearance.

"Rhett here?" He began to look around the room.

"No. I am here with some girlfriends. One works for the station," Eliza responded, trying to scan the crowd discreetly over his shoulder.

"Oh fun. Y'all having a good time?" He took a sip from his beer.

Eliza realized that this poor young man was out of his league at this party and was desperate for someone to talk to, and while her bones were telling her to go find Millie, she decided it was best for Rhett if she stood for a minute and made his "next big star" feel a little more comfortable in the crowds he was going to have to get used to running with.

"We are. Just seemed to have gotten separated. But anyhow . . . are you enjoying yourself?" Eliza asked as she looked the sweet country boy in the eyes, ignoring the fact that he was drinking underage and likely under contract.

"Yes, ma'am, I believe I am. I do wish I felt a little less out of place. I don't know many people outside of baseball, so I am afraid I am in a little over my head in this kind of party." He took another gulp, using the back of his hand to wipe his lips after the drink.

"Well it is your lucky day then." Eliza smiled at him, realizing she could kill two birds with one stone.

"Is that right?" Aiden tilted his head to one side, waiting for her to continue. "And why is that?"

"Well, I don't know many people here, not unlike you. However, I did notice one of the PAs from my friend's show when I first walked in. A tallish blond woman not too much older than you. She also looked a little out of place, and I am sure she would appreciate the company of someone like you." Eliza winked at Aiden, trying to seal the deal and boost his confidence at the same time.

"Well, ma'am," Aiden said as he began to blush and looked down toward his wing-tipped cowboy boots hidden under the hem of his perfectly tailored suit, "while that does sound nice, I have to admit that I don't believe she is my type."

"You haven't even met her yet," Eliza said. "Do you not like blondes?" Now she tilted her head back at him.

When he didn't respond right away, Eliza began to get slightly irritated. She needed to find Millie, not play matchmaker for a playboy cowboy who already had a petulance for being picky.

But when his silence lasted longer than she thought possible, his head still looking down at his boots, she noticed that his boots were fidgeting back and forth, the beer in his hand trembling slightly. And when she looked back up at his face, he finally met her eyes, and she saw it. The truth he could never tell if he wanted to be who everyone thought he was meant to be.

"It's not that she's blonde," Eliza started. "It's that she's a—"

"Mrs. Kingfield, please don't tell anyone." And just like that, she realized she wasn't the only person at the party pretending to be someone else.

CHAPTER 50

CAMILLE

THE BUZZING IN HER EARS was so high-pitched it felt more like a siren in her head. "Are you fucking kidding me?" Camille shrieked as she tried to push Connor away from her. She quickly realized that between his muscular build and her lack of sobriety, there was no moving him, no stopping him from where he wanted to go.

"Connor! Stop!" Camille yelled again as he slid his hand up higher through the slit of her skirt and in between her thighs, using his other hand to shove her shoulders back onto the armrest of the couch.

"You wanted this to happen," he said barely over a whisper, almost as though he didn't believe it for himself. "You have been flirting with me all night, wanting to come up here with me, damn near asking me to."

She felt his hot breath on her neck as he began to kiss her collarbone between sentences.

"Dammit, Connor. Please stop. This is not what I wanted," she said, lowering her voice, hoping that a mellower approach would defuse the situation.

"Don't back out now, Cami. You want that internet job, right?" He began to kiss her neck and up around her ear.

"Connor. I don't—" she started before he put his lips on hers and forced his tongue in her mouth. Camille tried to turn her head the other way, but he freed his hand from her shoulder and grabbed her face, jerking it back toward him and looking her in the eyes.

"This is how things are done, Cami," he began, stopping for a moment to move his hand under her panties and beginning to rub her crotch. "You want this job, and there are things that I want, too." He lifted his eyebrows as he shoved his finger inside her.

All she had wanted was to feel like a woman for a night. The kind that men still found attractive, the kind that could still make a man smile in her direction. She couldn't remember the last time Noel smiled at her. This night was supposed to go so differently. She was going to set all the bullshit in her life aside, enjoy her success, and leave with a promise of better things to come, a promise she hadn't felt in a long time.

The slit in her dress was not an invitation, but merely a rejection of the idea that she was no longer sexy. An attempt to outwardly convince herself that she was still a confident, sexy woman who deserved love and respect. Her cleavage showing was her way of putting her best foot forward. She was proud of her ample bosom. These breasts had provided nourishment for her three healthy children, and the ribcage they sat on was keeping her alive, even in the midst of the walls closing in around her. While she didn't mind if others admired her cleavage, it was not a solicitation.

She had dressed up tonight to try to feel good about the woman who, under all of it, was crumbling. Lying to herself that it didn't matter if others noticed—of course it helped when people nodded approval in your direction. But this was not what she wanted, not what she had thought about when she squeezed her slightly-larger-than-before figure into this dress earlier tonight. And as Connor forced his fingers in and out of her, his other hand moving her head side to side as he kissed her, she had the frightening thought that maybe she had asked for it.

One less cocktail, one less body part peeking out of her dress, one less flirty line in hopes of a promotion. Would that have changed the outcome of tonight? Camille wondered. Had she sent all the wrong signals? Was this her fault?

For a brief moment, she wondered if she should lay there and take it. Her life, it seemed, was falling apart. This was merely par for the course. Could she simply let Connor do what he needed so she could get where she wanted in her career? Was that truly how this worked?

"Cami," he said in a near whisper as he jerked her head to look at him again, breaking her stream of unpleasant thoughts, "this is just between us. You know that, right? You tell anyone and I will destroy you. Understood?"

In that brief second with his evil eyes peering into hers, and his hand still inside her, she decided this was not her fault, and it was not the way her story would go. She might be the woman in the middle of a midlife breakdown, but she was no one's lackey.

So, before she could think otherwise, she summoned every muscle in her body, and knowing it would hurt later, jerked her head forward as hard as she could, colliding with Connor's.

Bone crashing into bone created a sound unlike any Camille had ever heard. A cracking sound that reverberated throughout her entire head and into her neck made her so caught off guard that Connor couldn't even scream before Camille felt his weight fall on top of her. The final push she needed for her body to black out completely.

CHAPTER 51

VERA

THE STAIRCASE WAS BEGINNING TO FEEL a little too stuffy for Vera to be able to catch her breath. "You need to go back out to the party and socialize. Continue to act as though nothing is amiss," Vera said to Melia, their knees still touching in the stale stairwell.

"Nothing is going to get resolved tonight, and if it is at all possible, you need to hang in there a little longer. You can't let on to Connor that anything is off. With men like him, there are two outcomes: one, he is too busy to notice you or that anything is off, or two, he becomes keenly in tune and obsessed with your every move. We need to try to avoid the latter," Vera said, looking over her shoulder several times to make sure they were still alone.

"I am not worried about Connor," Melia said and looked Vera in the eyes. No hints of the scared woman Vera thought she would see, the one who had been abused, mistreated, and hurt. Instead mixed in with the bravery of before, she saw something new. She couldn't quite place her finger on it, but it almost looked like deliverance.

Vera let the weight of the situation hold them both in the staircase a few moments longer. The corners of Melia's lips began to turn up in sync with the corners of her eyes. Warmth from her half-smile melted any unresolve Vera was feeling in that moment.

"We should get back in there," Vera said, breaking the moment, and she began to rise off the cold step. Only a few inches off the ground, Melia reached for her hand and pulled her back down, placing their faces inches from each other now.

Melia leaned in, closing the gap between them. Vera felt her heart lurch into her throat. The last time she got mixed up with a straight woman had been back in college when dipping your toe into the other pool was part of the experience. But Vera had learned the hard way that you can't turn someone just by falling for them and swore off any straight woman with a need to test the waters from that day forward. And though Melia was married, there was something about her that Vera couldn't quite place.

When Melia's face was centimeters from her own, Vera could smell jasmine, citrus, and vanilla, instantly bringing her back to her mother's bathroom on Christmas Eve while she watched her line her lips for church. Before they left the room, she would spritz Chanel No. 5 on her neck and inside her wrists, followed a quick spritz in Vera's direction. Chanel was only worn for the best of occasions, when nothing else would do.

Vera closed her eyes, awaiting Melia's lips' soft touch on hers, breathing in the reassuring smell of luxurious childhood moments.

But instead of on her lips, she felt Melia's lips touch the edge of her ear as she whispered, "You are exactly who I thought you would be." And just as Vera was about to pull away from a woman and a statement that confused her, Melia continued, "And I am so glad I found you." But as she drew her lips away from Vera's ear, she stopped and pressed them to her cheek. Vera felt herself lean into the kiss her eyes still closed.

Then Melia was up, standing, smoothing her hair, and gathering herself to head back out into the world as the stoic, simple woman whom everyone looked at as Connor's arm jewelry. It looked good for the business that he had a stable home life with a doting wife, and what was good for business was good for Connor. And Melia would play along if she knew what was good for her.

But not now, not since she brought Vera into their life. Melia had all but secured Vera's help running Connor's campaign if for no other reason than to be close to Melia and formulate a plan to get her out. Though, that hadn't been the plan when Melia began dropping hints to Connor about the genius Vera was, she was happy to have her in her court. It was going to make everything a lot easier to navigate.

"So," Melia began, looking up from smoothing out her dress and making eye contact with the now-standing Vera, "you will help Connor run then?" Melia nodded at the end of the question, making it seem more like a statement.

Vera felt her eyebrows scrunch together as she stared back at Melia, confused.

"Melia, why would I help Connor?" Vera asked, adjusting the sides of her dress as well.

"Helping Connor would help me," Melia retorted. "You would be around more, so you can keep an eye on things. Not to mention if you keep him busy campaigning, he will be too busy to even notice me. He is destined for infamy. You will see." Melia instantly grabbed onto the bracelet covering her bruised wrist, twisting it slowly.

Vera's eyes darted toward the bruise and then quickly away. She didn't love this idea. It felt wrong for her to help a man like this gain even more power. But if it meant helping a woman escape, then maybe it was worth it. And she didn't have to help him win—just help him try. That thought made Vera smile.

"Does that smile mean you will?" Melia cut into Vera's thoughts.

"Yes. Yes, I am on board." Vera smiled.

"Oh, wonderful. I have a friend who works for the *Circadian* who is here tonight, and I know he would love to break the story." Melia smiled and turned to head back to the party.

Melia turned to face Vera one more time with her hand on the door handle. "We are going to make a wonderful team, Vera. Just you wait and see." Then she smiled, turned, and was gone, leaving Vera standing alone in a cold stairwell, weirdly feeling played and yet awestricken, much like she had been in college.

CHAPTER 52

ELIZA

ARMED WITH FAR TOO MANY SECRETS than she could fit into her small clutch or her tight dress, Eliza scanned the room one more time for Vera or Millie. When she realized that neither was there, she decided to head back to the suite, hoping that maybe her two over-served friends had somehow managed to get back there and pass out. Not to mention that running into Aiden had reminded her that she left her cell phone back in the suite, and had likely scared the shit out of Rhett as this point in the night by being alone in the city and not returning any calls or texts for hours.

Eliza hadn't realized how stuffy the basement ballroom had been, filled with too much ego and power to take in a decent breath, until she stepped outside into the light rain. Normally, she would have returned back to the lobby for an umbrella in weather like this, but tonight it felt oddly perfect to have a little of the lies and ego drip off of her with each raindrop. The warm night air lent itself perfectly to a cleansing mist. One Eliza wasn't sure could fully clean her of some of the nefarious thoughts she had swirling in her mind after the note, the names, and the needle.

At the bottom of the package lay a syringe filled with a dark brown, translucent liquid. A dropper filled with a tanish brown soda colored looking just like the liquid she used to suck up in the clear straws of their large fountain drinks on those hot summer days with Millie sitting outside the Tom Thumb gas station. There was no childlike innocence here though, no note, no instructions, no prescription sticker listed on the side of the plastic, and oddly enough, no Millie. Just a needle and a list of names in an envelope left for the woman she had become. Needles had never frightened her, not even as a child. She took shots like champ and took bullets for her friend. Times hadn't changed.

As she walked in the rain, she couldn't stop thinking about the syringe in her purse. She wondered what the brown liquid was, who it was for, and what the hell she was supposed to do with it. Who leaves someone a needle full of medicine? Drugs? Whatever it was—who leaves it with no instructions?

Strands of wet hair had begun sticking to her cheeks and neck as she opened the door to the suite. The walk wasn't a long one, but it was long enough for the warm air to mix with the damp rain and start to prick her arms with goose bumps.

She opened the door to the suite.

"Millie?"

"Vera?"

"Is anyone here?" Eliza called as she slid her pumps off and felt her wet bare feet stick to the cold tile floor as she rounded the corner into the living room.

An audible gasp escaped her throat as she saw Millie completely lifeless under Connor in the exact same state. Eliza dropped her clutch and rushed over to them, trying to figure out what the hell happened, hoping they were still alive, or that at least Millie was. She was surprised at how easy it was to pull Connor off Millie, watching his body roll over the edge of the couch, bumping the coffee table before hitting the floor with a loud thump. Ignoring his well-being completely, she used that same surprising heroic strength to push the velvet couch that still held an unconscious Millie back so she could get a better angle to assess her.

Dropping to her knees, her cold, wet feet touching the edge of Connor's arm, Eliza put her fingers to Millie's neck, while also resting her head on her chest, listening with all her will for a heartbeat. Instead, her head rose quickly and forcefully as Camille tried to catch her breath in a loud, catching inhale. Her eyes shot widely open, and her body stiffened as if already in fight mode. Camille's eyes darted back and forth as her mind tried to catch up, her breath doing the same.

"Oh my God! Millie!" Eliza leaned down, wrapping her arms around her lucid friend, thankful she was no longer checking for vitals.

Camille's darting eyes settled on Eliza's strawberry blonde hair resting on her chest, and she exhaled for the first time since coming to. Closing her eyes again, feeling the weight of her friend calm her nerves, Camille lay motionless on the couch. Eliza relished the feeling of her head rising and falling on her friend's chest, thankful she was alive.

After a few moments, without moving, she called to Millie, the back of her head the only part facing her, "Mill, what happened?" knowing that if she turned to face her, the truth would likely be harder to say out loud.

CHAPTER 53

CAMILLE

ELIZA'S ARMS WRAPPED AROUND HER. Holding on for dear life was a feeling Camille was all too familiar with, one in this moment she both hated and relished. She was thankful that Eliza came, knowing deep down that she always would, but hating that she had to keep finding her like this. She couldn't help but feel ashamed, watching the back of her friend's head rise and fall with her still-labored breathing.

She took one more deep breath before trying to form words in her dry throat and explain to Eliza what had transpired over the evening with Connor and how she had found herself in this predicament. Her head pounded at the spot where she connected with Connor's skull, every word of the evening making it throb even harder.

"So, I guess in a way I asked for it," Camille finished the story, not able to make eye contact with an erect, and now facing her, Eliza.

For the first time, she realized that Eliza's cheeks were wet, glistening in the moonlight that was streaming in from the rainy evening. She wasn't sure if they were pity tears or leftover bits of rain from her walk over; she assumed the first but prayed for the latter.

"Mill," Eliza started, looking down to wipe the now-confirmed pity tears with her fingertips before continuing, "I am so sorry." She looked at Camille.

"Eliza, you have nothing to be sorry for," Camille said as she tried to sit up on the sofa.

"Don't," Eliza started. "I am sorry. Truly sorry. Sorry I wasn't here earlier. Sorry I didn't know where you were most of the night. Sorry this happened to you. But most of all . . . I am so sorry you feel like this is somehow your fault."

Camille watched as something shifted in Eliza's posture. Before seemingly mothering, kind, and warm, now her shoulders pushed back, her posture more rigid with fists beginning to ball. Though she was still on her knees on the floor, she suddenly felt ten feet tall.

After scanning her body, Camille's eyes met hers; the once-glistening, borderline blubbering, sad doe eyes had hardened. The muscles in her face tightened around darkened eyes with a fire lit in them that could only be seen by the one person who knew her best.

"This is in no way, shape, or form your fault. You are not asking to be sexually assaulted just by enjoying the attention of a man. You are a woman going through a shitty time, and just because you flirt and accept a compliment does not mean you are inviting him to come inside you."

Camille was struck by her sweet friend's last sentence. Eliza was a woman of many facets, but anger was one Camille hadn't seen on her. Keeping her emotions and life in check was something Eliza had perfected, but the woman kneeling before Camille now, while maybe out of line, was also on point.

Just as Camille was relishing in the new, strong Eliza, she felt her jerk, jolting the edge of the couch back, a break in the resilient stance Eliza had just struck. And before Camille could question her, she heard Connor let out a voluble groan. Shifting on the floor, still face down, but starting to come to.

Camille felt her entire body stiffen again, freezing her back into the place under his body weight. She tried to reach for Eliza's hand, but Eliza was already on her feet, her wet dress sticking to her thighs as she stepped over Connor and headed toward the door.

"Eliza!" Camille whined out in a hiss, hoping not to breathe any more life into Connor.

But Eliza didn't respond. She didn't even turn to her as she rounded the corner and disappeared, leaving Camille soaking wet, frozen, back in that tub after nearing death, except this time she was trying to reconcile the fact that she hadn't done this to herself. If only shame were that easy to erase.

CHAPTER 54

VERA

APPARENTLY, VERA HAD BECOME a sucker for a damsel in distress. Still sitting on the cold cement steps of the back stairwell, Vera realized the gravity of what she had done. Not only did she find herself falling for a woman who may or may not be available to her, she had agreed to help said woman's abusive and arrogant husband run for office.

If she wasn't so good at her job, she wouldn't have worried, but she was excellent, and that meant that Connor, an abuser, was likely about to become the next mayor of New York. Another white man getting what he wanted, and taking what he needed along the way. Power was a drug that Vera knew all too well, but the abuse of power was something she wasn't sure she wanted to be a part of.

As she got to her feet, she felt slightly uneasy on her high heels, and she wasn't immediately sure if it was from the alcohol, the dizzying effect of Melia, or the severity of the situation. Vera clutched the railing as she slowly descended the stairs, her mind spinning, again unsure what the culprit was or if it was the combination of factors. Her gut instinct was to open the door, find Melia, retract her offer, and ask for forgiveness but vouch to help her get out. But as her hand wrapped around the cold metal door handle, she knew Melia would never let her back out, so she took a deep breath and decided her better course of action was to find Connor and get to know the man she was about to make mayor.

Warm air blew past her shoulders as she entered back into the party room, and the crowd hadn't missed a beat in her or Melia's absence. Jazz music echoed off the walls, forcing the guests to talk even louder, though the booze was likely raising their voices on its own. Vera felt her eyes squint shut, forcing her to reset and get back in the atmosphere that surrounded her. She needed a drink, and knew she shouldn't, but the current situation called for it.

Making her way over the bar, Vera was approached by a sandy blond–haired man with his curly, chin-length locks tucked behind his ears and round, Harry Potter–style frames that Vera couldn't decide whether they made him appear hipster or passé.

He reached into his pinstriped navy suit pocket as he ponied up next to her at the counter.

Vera tried to ignore him, though he seemed intent on speaking to her.

"Jameson Gold. Neat," Vera called to the bartender, avoiding eye contact with the stranger.

"I'll have what she's having," he called out to the bartender after her as he produced a notepad from his jacket and set it on the counter.

Vera turned, glancing at the illegible markings scribbled on the pages before him and turning back as the bartender slid her drink in front of her. She took a sip of the warm, amber liquid, a larger gulp than was appropriate, but she wanted to enjoy a longer burn on the way down.

Once the burn made its way into her stomach, she set the drink back down, keeping her hands on the deep south glass, and turned to her new bar mate.

"A reporter are you?" Vera looked at him, already knowing his answer.

"What gave ya that idear," he said, his Boston accent appearing stronger now. He brought the drink to his lips. Vera gave him a quick once-over. He was likely in his early thirties, fit, and wore a suit well over his sun-kissed summer skin. If she weren't gay, she would definitely be interested. Her eyes followed his pinstripes down to his shoes. The Prada shoes with flower appliques made her wonder if he wouldn't be into her either—though if she had learned anything working in DC, it was that the shoes do not make the man, and they definitely don't make the man gay.

The clink of his glass brought her eyes back to his hazel, almond-shaped ones hidden under his thick lenses.

He cleared his throat, Vera assumed to try to hide the New England in his accent.

"Vera, right?" He grabbed a pen out of his jacket pocket, awaiting her verification.

"Yeah, that's correct." Vera smirked and took another, much smaller sip.

"I am Deacon Hunter. I work for the *Central Circadian*." He paused. Vera racked her brain, trying to remember if she had ever read anything by him.

"I am working on a piece on Connor Dixon. Was that his wife, Melia, I saw you emerge from the stairwell with?"

Vera knew instantly where this was going, and she was not about to participate. Deacon was looking to paint Melia as the distant, cold wife who batted for the other team, leaving Connor no choice but to find a warm embrace elsewhere. Or worst yet, he knew the truth and was about to blow the whole thing wide open and make everything much harder for Melia. Either way, Vera wasn't having it.

So Vera turned away from Deacon, slammed the rest of her whiskey down her throat, allowing herself a moment to enjoy the burn before turning back to him and saying, "You know what, Deacon? I just realized I haven't seen my friends in a while. And I think I need to find something lighter. Maybe champagne." She looked at him, realizing he was wanting to say something, so she turned and moved slowly away from him.

Before she was out of earshot, she heard him call to her, "You don't strike me as the kind of woman who prefers champagne over whiskey."

Vera turned, her hair bouncing over her shoulder, and called back to him, "Welcome to New York, Deacon. Things aren't always as they seem."

CHAPTER 55

ELIZA

NOT THE TYPE TO DRINK into a stupor since her younger years, Eliza had still managed to skirt the phenomenon of "blacking out." She had heard people explain it, use it as a defense in TV court case, and even use it as an excuse for their bad behavior, but she, for one, had always known when to draw the line. However, when she would look back on this moment, this life-or-death instant, she would have no recollection of what came next.

She would remember being on the couch, her arms draped too tightly around Millie, willing her to breathe but holding her so constricted she might have been preventing it. She would remember the elation in feeling Millie's chest rise and fall, hearing her breath catch in her throat as she tried to speak. She wouldn't forget the anger that coursed through her blood as Millie retold the events of the evening. And she wouldn't forget the flame that leaped from her angry fists into her legs as she rose from the couch after hearing Connor fight consciousness. The last thing she would recall was the sodden fabric of her now darker green dress bonded to her thighs, wet from the rain and yet damp from the sweat pouring out of her body, an unconscious reaction to the anger fueling the fire inside her as she headed out of the room on a mission.

Eliza's eyes had turned black, no longer seeing anything around her, no longer caring about the consequences of her next actions. She was fed up, beyond the point of no return. Starting long before she even knew it was there was an anger against the patriarchal society, she hadn't even realized she had fallen victim to. A world where the wants of men were put before the needs of women, one she had been hidden from her whole life. A life in the suburbs, one with no ups or downs, one in the middle, in Middle America, in a white, still-married family, in a white neighborhood, in a white city. Always told she could do anything, be anyone, with an undertone of "as long as it is not too much" or "anything too highbrow."

Women are teachers and homemakers. And there, of course, is nothing wrong with that, but if you want more, then why the hell can't you have it, she began to wonder when she went off to college. But then she had met Rhett, fallen in love, given up her dreams for his, and fell back into her white, simple woman existence.

For too long, though, she lived this white existence. Enjoying the privilege it brought, finding comfort in complacency. It wasn't until she had opened her eyes, looked outside her house, her city, her world and noticed all the shit that had been going on around her. She didn't need to be a working woman who was paid less than a man, or even raped, to be outraged. She wanted a world for her daughters where stories like the ones Millie reported on, and Nina had told her about Connor, did not exist. For so long she hadn't known how to do her part, how to make a change, be a part of the solution. After all, to the outside world she was nothing more than a wife and mother—what change could a woman like her really erect? But as her white world turned dark, she suddenly knew what to do. It wasn't going to be a big part, but it was a start.

Her hands moved with swift precision, no sign of doubt or nerves, as she reached into her purse, pulling the thick envelope out and reaching to the bottom. Initially, the syringe at the bottom of the package had confused her, but as her fingers slid past the list of all the other women Connor had assaulted, Eliza realized what Nina had intended the needle for.

The chandelier lights in the bar area lit the brown liquid with a warm glow as Eliza pulled the syringe out of the envelope and into the light. The genial glimmering thawed the edges of her eyes with a supporting cheer, as though the needle were giving her an approving smile. Turning on her heel in the puddle that had formed from her still lightly dripping dress, she headed back to the living room, holding the needle up in the air like a pistol.

Millie's eyes narrowed as Eliza entered the room. She was still not able to speak, paralyzed with each breath Connor was fighting to take, his eyes now fluttering imperceptibly. Eliza made momentary eye contact with Millie as she knelt down next to her, placing her hand on the side of her cheek, allowing her darkened eyes to smile at her. Millie's eyes returned the favor, the last acknowledgment that Eliza needed before removing her hand from Millie's face and turning toward Connor.

As Eliza placed one hand over his mouth as he fought to become lucid, his eyes locked with hers. As they widened, the whites growing larger, Eliza's darkened, looking past the white world he was living in, feeling her body warm with the pleasure of his fear. And with the bravery of all the women he had hurt, she jabbed the needle into his neck, pushing the brown solution into his body. Her smile finally spread over her teeth as she watched his eyelids began to close and his limbs went lifeless.

CHAPTER 56

CAMILLE

CAMILLE FELT THE BREATH flood back into her body the moment Eliza stabbed the needle into Connor's neck. A flush of warmth brought her back to life as his slipped away. Her mind was still a little fuzzy on the events, not fully comprehending the gravity of what just happened. She wasn't initially sure if Eliza had just knocked him back out or if she had killed him. She knew she should hope the first, but she truly prayed for the latter.

Eliza turned, put the cap back over the sharp end of the syringe, and set it on the coffee table, the vial rolling a little before coming to a stop in the middle of the table, resting against the edge of Connor's drink glass. Camille watched as Eliza turned back to her, seeing for the first time a different woman than the one she knew. Eliza had always been self-confident on the surface, but now there was an air of power around her, almost a purpose radiating off her. Eliza cupped Camille's face in her hands, the ones that had just taken care of her perpetrator, and brought her forehead to her soft lips, kissing it with intense purpose, the bruise pulsing under her lips.

Eliza drew back, looking Camille in the eyes, then back to Connor, placing her index and middle finger along the side of his jugular. "He will never hurt you again, sweet girl. He will never hurt anyone again." Then she kissed Camille's forehead once more and walked away to grab ice from the bar for Camille's head.

Camille swallowed hard, not sure if she was fighting back tears of relief or the bile surfacing as she came to grips with the fact there was likely a dead man on the floor. She didn't feel bad about it, just ill at the thought of death in her presence. Dying was something she had contemplated time and again, but now in the company of it, it felt both ironic and poetic, a combination that was strangely leaving her ill.

Eliza, on the other hand, seemed not the least bit fazed over the entire exchange. As Camille stared back into her now-darkened eyes, she could've sworn she almost saw enjoyment. The look sent chills up her spine. An Eliza she didn't recognize might have been the thing that was actually making her more nauseous than a dead body. Something in Eliza's posture, eyes, and sly smile had unhinged Camille slightly. She would be forever grateful to her friend for her heroic actions, but she worried she may be forever changed by them, as well.

While Camille's mind was still trying to register the stature of the new woman before her, she realized that Eliza was still speaking. Squinting to clear the eye contact that had rattled her, Camille turned off her brain and opened her ears, realizing she could only focus on one thing at time.

"This wasn't the first time he did this, Millie," Eliza was saying.

"I ran into Nina Park, who told me he has done this to countless women, using his power and threatening their career if they didn't participate in his sexual needs."

Before Eliza could continue, Camille found her voice, clearing her throat lightly.

"Nina Park?" she asked, raising her eyebrows, astonished that her friend had not only been in a conversation with one of their icons, but had also managed to get an unknown scoop on Connor from her.

"Right. I know," Eliza chimed in proudly. "I approached her and began talking. She was kind and forthcoming. I liked her even more than I anticipated, if that is possible."

Eliza stopped, her posture suddenly shifting, her shoulders losing their power and drooping slightly forward. Camille waited quietly, just like her therapist had taught. People will break the silence with truth if you let them.

Swallowing hard, Eliza looked back up from her sullen posture. "Well . . . I wasn't exactly truthful with Nina." She swallowed again.

Camille waited.

"The thing is that . . . well . . . it gets complicated. Um . . ."

And just as Eliza was about to continue, the two women heard the fidgeting at the suite door, stopping both their hearts and forcing them to hold their breath. There was a dead man at their feet and someone at the door.

CHAPTER 57

VERA

ALMOST AS IF ON CUE, a waiter appeared next to Vera, nearly shoving the drink tray into her arm as he asked, "Drink, ma'am?" So, now with a champagne flute comfortably back in her hand, she searched the room for either Melia or Connor. Taking a sip, she moved farther into the ballroom, watching people drunk dance, the vodka telling them they looked good. In another world, she would have been one of them, back in her lighter college days with Eliza and Camille egging her on, dragging her uptight ass out on the dance floor. She would never admit to it then that those were some of her fondest memories, the three of them looking a fool on a random dance floor.

As the bubbles tickled her throat while she swallowed her champagne gulp, Vera realized that she hadn't seen Eliza or Camille for a while. It dawned on her suddenly how strange that was. The three were rarely out of eye shot from each other for more than fifteen minutes, a trick they had tried to maintain at frat parties so as to never find themselves in a compromising situation.

She felt her heart skip a beat, then speed up, banging harder against her ribcage. Her eyes began to dart around the room now, no longer casually scanning for a man she didn't really care about—now searching for the women who were her everything. Every strawberry-blond and dark-haired woman on the dance floor or sitting at a table made her heart leap with hope, only to be let down when they turned their head, or Vera further assessed their dress, realizing that it was not Eliza or Camille.

Setting her drink down on a table, Vera turned her back to the ballroom, assuring herself they were not in there. The clicking of her heels on the marble tiles sounded their alarm as she walked faster and faster, her eyes scanning the hallways and bars stationed throughout the larger room for any sight of her friends. She could feel the champagne in her stomach beginning to rise, mixing with the nervous bile that was beginning to flow, forcing her to try to swallow down not only her fear but heartburn.

Swinging open the bathroom door, Vera called out, "Camille? Eliza?" praying they had snuck off and were holed up in a stall drinking alone on the cool, tile floor. When no one answered, she bent over, checking underneath the stalls for any sign of life. She banged each stall door open, hoping that they were empty, but aimlessly hoping they weren't.

As she rushed out of the bathroom, feeling the color now draining from her face, she felt a flush of anger in the realization that maybe Eliza and Camille weren't in danger. Maybe they had forgotten her and left. Shaking her head, trying to rid the thought, she caught Melia out of the corner of her eye. She was visiting with someone Vera did not recognize, smiling as though she weren't a woman living a lie. Melia saw Vera, and her toothy smile melted into a closed-lip grin as she winked in Vera's direction and bashfully lowered her head. Vera felt her face contort into a confused grimace, unsure of what the exchange meant. And while her face was unsure, she felt a pang in her gut. The kind that women are told never to ignore. Eliza and Camille were in trouble; she knew it. She rushed to the elevator, pressing the up button over and over, knowing it wouldn't speed the arrival, the unease in her bones praying that it would. Seconds suddenly felt like hours as the doors finally opened, and Vera stepped in, pushing the inside button repeatedly, as well.

Once the doors opened into the lobby, Vera rushed out, trying not to run as she made her way through the hotel guests milling around the plush entrance. Once outside, she began to run, ignoring the pain her feet were in from her heels, and not even feeling the rain now pelting her face. She ran as fast as her tipsy mind and screwed-up body would allow. Fumbling with the key card, strands of her hair stuck to her face, she tried to open the suite door, hoping she wasn't too late.

CHAPTER 58

ELIZA

MURDER WAS A SIN, not to mention a crime. Eliza had not premeditated it, never thought about how or when to do it, not directly anyhow. The calculation had occurred in every angry thought, every feeling of female injustice, every pang she felt in her stomach as Nina listed off the women one by one. She hadn't been aware that it would lead to this, but she wasn't sorry it had.

Something in Eliza had shifted. A new sense of power and pride that she didn't know could exist. And as she began to explain how the course of the night had unfolded to Millie, though she had lied about who she was, she had followed through with who she wanted to become.

The relief and power pumping through her blood was immediately replaced by fear the moment she heard shuffling at the door. Though she had become a badass in the moment she stuck the needle in Connor's neck, she was still a mother and a wife to a public figure. She couldn't go to jail; she couldn't be held responsible for her actions. They were beyond warranted. Connor was a bad man who did bad things, and it was only a matter of time until someone did the right thing. And while part of her felt resolute in her actions, the other was about the vomit as the door jiggled open.

Eliza felt her breath stop, freezing her in place and wiping her mind clear. She hadn't even realized that she was holding Millie's hand until she felt her fingers tighten around her palm. Silently, they both stayed listening to the rain fall on the window panes, getting louder now that the door was open.

"Camille?" They heard a voice shout.

"Eliza?" The voice came again.

Eliza was so lost in a mind fog of fear that the voice didn't register when calling for Camille, but the second time when she heard her own name, she knew she recognized it.

Then, just as Eliza was trying to fight the fog and place the voice, Vera appeared in the living room, her wet hair sticking to her face, her damp dress also clinging to her legs.

"Oh my God!" Vera gasped, covering her mouth with her wet hand. Her dress leaving puddles on the floor, just as Eliza's had.

Eliza watched as for a minute Vera's eyes darted around the scene—now a murder scene—trying to assess what had transpired.

Vera removed her hand from her mouth, swallowing hard. "I knew something was wrong. I just knew it!" Tears formed in the corners of Vera's eyes, and Eliza could feel Millie's hand begin to lightly jerk in hers, Eliza knowing Millie, too, was crying.

"Is he?" Vera started but couldn't get the words out.

Eliza looked her straight in the eyes, tightening her grip on Millie's hand, and without an ounce of regret responded, "Yes," stronger than she had ever uttered a word in her life.

Vera wiped the tears from her eyes, shaking her head lightly. "Good," she responded.

Eliza felt her head jerk back a little, taken aback by Vera's abrupt and fervent response.

"Good?" Eliza asked. Though she did feel good about it, she wanted to know why Vera also felt it was a good idea.

"Yeah. Good." Vera stood taller on her heels, pushing her shoulders back.

Eliza's eyes searched Vera's, trying to figure out what she knew. Both women were in a standoff of sorts until Eliza felt Millie squeeze her hand and she squeaked out, "E, tell me what the hell happened with Nina."

"Nina?" Vera tilted her head quizzically.

Eliza turned from Millie back to Vera. "Nina Park. This all happened because of her."

"What exactly *did* happen?"

CHAPTER 59

CAMILLE

CAMILLE'S HAND BECAME CLAMMY in Eliza's as she listened to Eliza explain the transgressions Connor made and the scene she walked in on. She tried to keep deep breathing to force herself not to go rigid again as she heard the words spill out of Eliza's mouth.

"Well," Eliza began, "I introduced myself to Nina Park, who proceeded to tell me she was at the party tonight to vet Connor after a reporter friend told her he was a serial rapist of sorts. She listed several women whose careers he had made or broken based on their willingness to participate in his sexual advances."

Eliza stopped, looked back at Millie, who was still laying on the couch, silently breathing.

Camille nodded at Eliza and she continued, "But, see, the thing is that I was lying to Nina. I told her my name was Willa Morgan and fed her a whole story about my career and purpose at the party."

"What? Why would you do that?" Vera interrupted.

Eliza looked down at the rug, avoiding her glance from a now paling Connor.

"I don't know. I wanted to be someone else for the night. I wanted to feel important and powerful. And my alter ego helped get me there. It was dumb, I realize, but it is what it is," Eliza finished.

Camille understood. It was hard to constantly be put into boxes based on what people thought they knew about you. She had spent her whole life trying to break out of boxes and sometimes wished she could just be someone different all together. Admitting this would make her even weaker than she was, so instead she gave Eliza a tight-lipped smile and slight nod as she continued.

"See, the thing is that I was going to tell her. After I walked away, I wanted to go back and clear the air, but I felt it would only ruin things, so I left it. I figured no harm no foul."

Eliza took a deep breath and continued. "But then something strange happened. After Nina told me all about Connor, I was enraged. I thought I was doing a good job of hiding it, but it must have been written on my face because when I went to the bathroom later and came out of the stall, there was an envelope sitting by the sink with the name Willa Morgan written on it."

Camille watched Vera's eyebrows scrunch together and eyes narrow at Eliza.

"I opened it and inside was a list. A list of women's names."

Eliza looked back at Camille and then to Vera.

"Initially I didn't know what I was looking at until I saw the name Aria Tilbury and Rose Ryan. Nina had mentioned them as a couple of the women Connor supposedly raped. And then I realized I was holding a rape list."

The word "rape" triggered Camille's breath to catch again in her throat and a warm sensation ascend up her neck, flushing her cheeks.

"Then I peeked at the bottom of the envelope and saw a syringe. Again, I didn't understand, but I placed the list back into the envelope and put the envelope back into my purse as it dawned on me that I hadn't seen Millie in a while. So, I hurried out of the bathroom, trying to forget about the list, and the needle, and focus on the pit in my stomach that was telling me that Millie was in trouble."

The rigidity Camille was trying to fight was seemingly climbing into every one of Vera's limbs as Camille watched her face twist in anger and fall in sadness.

Vera called across the room through catching breaths, "Camille!"

Camille looked her way, trying to make eye contact through her blurry, wet vision. Fighting the rigidity had turned into tears.

"I am so sorry. I should have known. I should have been here. I am so sorry."

Vera kept repeating it over and again, "I am so sorry."

She didn't need her friends to say it. The look on their faces told her they felt every ounce of sorrow. She wouldn't want them to. They were here now—Eliza having rescued her and Vera, she knew, would help from here. She may not have a husband, but she had amazing women in her life who loved her like no man could.

"It's okay," was all Camille could muster, but it was enough for Vera to stop repeating her repentance.

Camille turned her gaze back to Eliza, waiting for her to finish the story, but she sat silent, her shoulders still high, knees on the ground, but neck tall and strong, now staring at Connor's body.

When she didn't speak and Camille could no longer stand the weight of Vera's expecting glance, Camille finally cleared her throat, tightened her grip on Eliza's hand, and spoke.

"He blacked out on top of me. I passed out, too." She swallowed, trying to force some fluid into her dry mouth. "And when I woke, he was on the floor and Eliza was clutching me." Camille squeezed Eliza's hand again.

"While I told her what happened, Connor started to shift on the floor." Camille felt her stomach turn, remember him fighting consciousness. "Eliza got up with a passion, heading toward her purse and returning with the needle." Camille swallowed as Eliza finally released her stare from Connor, her eyes now connecting with Camille's.

"And she jabbed it in his neck." Camille took a deep breath. "Then he just stopped moving."

Camille watched Eliza's eyes narrow and grow black again before she turned to Vera.

"And I would fucking do it a million times again. Bastard got what was coming to him," she said.

Camille's jaw dropped as Vera's smiled back at Eliza.

CHAPTER 60

VERA

VERA HADN'T REALIZED SHE WAS still standing in her heels until Eliza had ceased talking and Camille began, when the anger pulsing in her body forced her to finally recognize that her feet were throbbing. Reaching down, she slipped the damp stilettos off her red feet and walked over toward Eliza and Camille, taking a seat in a worn cognac leather armchair adjacent to the fireplace, feeling herself immediately stick to the soft fabric.

Bile was now rising in Vera's throat, mixing with the anger she was already harboring for Connor and his abusive ways with his wife. Vera felt like she would like to have been the one to kill Connor herself.

She felt her shoulders rise up toward her ears and her fists begin to tighten around the heels of her pumps, still in each hand. If she was angry before, now she was full-out enraged.

She decided that instead of trying to quell the anger, she would lean into it. This man was a monster. Using women as objects, not humans, and clearly not caring who he hurt, as long as he got what he wanted. In the fairy tales she heard as a child, the monster always died, the bad guy always was reprimanded, and the moral of the story was one that supported the good guy's intentions.

This wasn't a story, though. This was real life, and though the bad guys may get what was coming to them, they also usually got away with it, leaving the good guy in the lurch. Vera wasn't about to let her friends be blamed for their good deeds that society would deem as bad. No good deed goes unpunished, but Camille and these other women had been punished enough. This was where the story would end. Right here in this room. This was, after all, what Vera was best at. She was a fixer. She was the very best.

And though she knew she shouldn't because it was not her secret to tell, she opened her mouth.

"He was beating Melia too," Vera said, her jaw muscles tightening as she gritted her teeth together, remembering the bracelet-covered bruise.

"What?" Camille's eyes widened as she tried to sit up on the sofa, the cushions giving way under her and the velvet creasing in new directions.

"Yep. For a while now, it seems. That's why she wanted him to hire me, so I could help her get out," Vera responded.

"Of course he did," Eliza called, glancing back and forth between the women as if they were in a tennis match. "That shouldn't surprise anyone!"

Vera felt a pang in her stomach at the sharing of Melia's private secret. But she didn't do it to gossip—she did it to cement in Camille's mind that they had done the right thing. And as she looked back at Camille, Vera realized maybe she, too, needed to say it out loud, make it real, as the final nail in the coffin of their last shreds of guilt.

And as that guilt washed away into the puddle still forming at her feet from her dripping dress, she stood up, now barefoot, felt her jaw lock into a strong position, glanced at both of the women looking up at her, and declared, "Okay, let's clean this mess up."

The way she said "mess", as though they had simply spilled milk allowed Vera to detach from the actual task at hand of getting rid of a dead body and look at it more as another day at the office. She was used to cleaning up messes at work, but never had she gotten her own hands dirty on the job. Running through how to get herself and her friend out of this mess if they got caught had shaken her usually unwavering veneer.

Walking over to the women, she felt her moist, bare feet sticking slightly to the floor as she approached Eliza and extended her hand to her.

For the first time, Vera saw herself reflected in the dark of Eliza's eyes, a malevolence she didn't remember seeing before now. Vera realized her eyes bore the same gaze, a look of triumph and twist she couldn't quite place. She felt her tight smile spread into a toothy grin as Eliza placed her hand in Vera's and rose to meet her, still towering several inches over her.

Then each woman grabbed onto each of Camille's hands and pulled her off the velvet couch, a slightly damp imprint left behind. The three women embraced, being careful not to step on Connor, though it wouldn't have mattered anyway. They held each other for what felt like an eternity, Camille letting out a few wallowing cries before her breath seized one last time.

Vera released her arms from around the women, her eyes finding Camille's, still tear-ridden and baggy, but now edged with the same wrath that had crept its way into her and Eliza's.

CHAPTER 61

ELIZA

ALL THREE WOMEN NOW STOOD, staring down at the body. Killing him had awoken the beautiful monster in Eliza. A beast that had lain dormant for far too long was now creeping into her soul. She was now wife and mother with a thirst for justice at any costs, as long as the punishment fit the crime.

But right then there was the task as hand, or rather at their feet. They needed to get rid of the body and cover their tracks. Though she didn't regret her actions, she didn't want to face the legality of it all, either.

Eliza suddenly sprang into action, along with Vera, whose brain she knew was already planning their alibis and cover-ups. They had certainly never murdered before, yet they were acting as though they knew the drill.

Eliza headed toward the staircase, taking the steps one by one, a mixed feeling of excitement and dread forcing her mind to dizzy. Once at the top of the stairs, she grabbed the sheet out of her suitcase that as luck would have it she had brought along to keep her from all the filth and smut that littered hotel beds, balling it up in her arms a warmth of humor at the situation growing in her chest, she turned to head back down the stairs.

Out of the corner of her eye, she noticed the basket on the dresser. Next to it sat two empty bottles of wine or champagne—she couldn't tell from across the room—and a note lay next to them. She was tempted to go over and read it, wondering what was going on between Vera and the Dixons, but she decided better of it, realizing the urgency of the task below.

Grasping her soft linen still balled in her arms, she descended the stairs to see Vera sweeping the room for any traces of Connor having been there. Luckily, his time there had been short, leaving him little chance to leave his mark.

Millie was in the kitchen area, scrubbing her drink glass fervently, while Vera was wiping the coffee table and side tables off with a towel soaked in vodka from the bar.

"Vodka?" Eliza called as she landed at the base of the stairs and made her way over toward Vera, the smell making the entire suite smell like a college party gone bad.

"It was the closest thing I could find to a cleaning product." Vera smiled and continued wiping. "I figure alcohol kills everything, right?"

The irony of the comment sent both women into hard belly laughs. Eliza doubled over the lump of sheets in her arms, trying to catch her breath and enjoying the levity of the moment.

Millie rushed back into the room to find out what all the commotion was about, and without even uttering a word, she, too, broke into laughter. Eliza felt her face grow warm and flush as her stomach began to ache from the laughter pains. They needed to laugh; they needed a moment of careless, pure joy, because after they finished their task tonight, they would never be the same. They all knew it.

When she felt the last bit of laughter escape her lungs, Eliza went over and set the sheet on the ground next to Connor's feet. Then with Vera's help, they shifted the coffee table away to make room on the floor for them to spread the sheet.

Eliza caught herself smoothing the edges of the sheet against the rug, as she would when she made the girls' beds sometimes. Quickly, she straightened up, not allowing herself to think of her girls at a time like this. She had no time to go mushy.

Looking back at Vera, and then to Millie, she remembered these were *her* people, they were in this together, and everything was going to be okay. They had yet again survived what they thought would kill them, instead they were the ones still alive.

CHAPTER 62

CAMILLE

MILLIE COULD FEEL ELIZA'S MIND slipping into the gravity of the situation. She had killed a man. Without any hesitation or second-guessing, she had ended a man's life before he could threaten Camille's again. She had done this before, not the killing part, but the leaping without thinking all to save Camille's life. And now, as Camille watched the gears behind Eliza's dark eyes begin turn, she knew it was her turn to help her friend. She owed everything to Eliza; she had saved her life twice.

So, without hesitation, and without thinking twice, Camille took Eliza's hand, calmed her nerves, and was about to take the reins.

With strength she didn't know she had, Camille turned and pushed the velvet couch, the scene of her attack, back, making room for her to crouch behind Connor's body.

He was ashen, and his flaccid body had become heavier without the muscle control to hold it together. Regardless of all that, Camille shoved her hands under his shoulder and hip bone, pushing up and forward with all her strength until she was able to roll him onto the sheet spread across the floor.

Once the other women had gotten over their amazement in Camille's strength and motivation, they got up, flanking each side of her, and together they began to roll Connor's body up in the sheet.

Out of breath, Camille panted for a moment next to the now-covered body of the man who had not that long ago had forced himself on her. While she knelt beside him, her body trembling from fatigue and anger, Eliza rose to her feet, heading again back to her purse, the needle in her hand.

Camille watched as Eliza stuffed the syringe back into her bag and fished around for a moment before lifting her car keys out.

"I am going to get the car and pull it up to the door. You guys pack up our stuff," Eliza chimed as she slipped on her tennis shoes she was wearing earlier in the evening and headed toward the door.

The light from the streetlamp outside flooded in as Eliza opened the front door and stepped out into the still-rainy night. It was only shortly after ten, but the street that faced their room was a quiet back alley. And the lack of New York sidewalk congestion made it seem as though it were the very middle of the night.

Camille scurried back into the suite, rushing into the bathroom, shoving their lotions, potions, hair products, and makeup into whatever container she could find. They would sort it all out later; this would do for now. She could heard Vera's bare feet pad up the stairs to where she had left all her belongings, having arrived before Camille and Eliza.

Opening every door, checking every crevice before leaving the bathroom, it dawned on Camille that now every space in the suite was a crime scene. Obviously, everyone knew they had stayed in the suite, and if something were left behind, that wouldn't be anything that would hint at what actually happened in this room tonight. Camille felt herself exhale at that thought—only they knew what happened; only they knew what would look suspicious. To everyone else, this was nothing more than a few longtime friends meeting up for a party and heading back to their fancy suite, tipsy and content. If a straightening iron was left behind, it meant they were forgetful, not felons.

CHAPTER 63

VERA

TINY PUDDLES OF WATER STILL LAY in the bottom of the tub where Vera had soaked earlier in the evening. Back when her biggest concern at hand was the bracelet she had been gifted and the cocktails she couldn't help draining. Now, she found herself hustling around the bedroom, throwing clothes and shoes into her bag, stuffing her basket full of the goodies Melia had given her, and scanning the room for anything she overlooked.

The room was darker now, the once-bright sunlight that had been streaming in the skylights was now a black frame being pelted by the rain. Had this been any other night, it would have made incredible sounds to fall asleep to. Vera loved the sound of the rain, a reminder that everything could be washed clean again, even the dirtiest of things.

Padding back down the stairs, she spotted Camille throwing Eliza's belongings into a bag, and she couldn't help but notice that Camille didn't seem stressed. She was packing as though she were heading out on a trip, not someone about to hop into a getaway car.

"Cam, you okay?" Vera called, setting her things by the door before walking over to help.

"Oh, I am good. All good." Camille looked up but kept on folding. Cramming would have seemed a better option in this case, but delayed shock or stress had left Camille creasing instead of stuffing.

"Well, better anyways." She looked down again and continued on her way.

Vera was perplexed, but left well enough alone. She felt bad enough about not being there earlier when things got out of control, coupled with the months of guilt for not being strong enough to admit her faults. So she was feeling as though she needed to respect Camille's boundaries and let her process how she needed to process.

Against her better judgment, and somewhat against her will, Vera walked up behind Camille and wrapped her arms around the soft of her belly, resting her head into her hair. Camille stopped, freezing in place and easing at the tenderness of the gesture from a friend for whom compassion was not in her conduct.

Vera didn't say anything, letting her body language say it all. They had been through so much, too much, and yet they were still here, still together. Without a word, she told Camille that she was here, always here.

And while Vera was silent, Camille quietly, as though telling a secret, whispered, "I am getting a divorce."

Vera knew the vulnerability it took for Camille to say those words out loud. Knew the courage it took to admit that to your hard-ass friend whom you weren't sure you could trust anymore. Again, Vera found herself lacking the words, so instead she kissed the back of Camille's head and held her tighter, feeling her body begin to writhe with silent cries.

Neither woman was sure how long they stood there, probably only seconds, minutes at max, until Camille finally straightened her posture, a clear sign to Vera that it was time to move forward. They had left nothing unsaid in those silent moments.

Vera headed back into the entryway, sliding on her flats before grabbing a few of the bags from a still slowly, methodically packing Camille.

After dropping the bags by the door, Vera walked back into the living room, where Connor lay wrapped in a bed sheet. Her dress now felt heavy from the dampness, which matched the feeling in her head. Things had moved so quickly and erratically that she had all but forgotten she was drunk upon entering the suite. The magnitude of the situation mixed with the need for immediate action had sobered her into the headache state, somewhere between tipsy and needing another.

Trying to fend off the urge, she began to move the sofa back into its original spot, followed by the coffee and end tables. And just as she stood there, a welling of pride for her strength and forethought, Eliza burst in the door, the rain pouring down behind her drenched hair.

"I have an idea. Let's go."

CHAPTER 64

ELIZA

THERE WAS NO EASY WAY for three women to carry a deceased male body out and into the back of a car. This might have been the only time in her life that Eliza wished she had a sedan with a trunk that was a separate entity from the seating area, rather than the SUV she drove.

Connor was a muscular man, in great shape, likely at or below the average weight for a man of his stature, but that didn't make him any less heavy. Muscle when not in flexion weighed more than fat, making Connor a heavy and awkward load.

After trying and failing at many different positions—Vera and Camille holding his head, Eliza at his feet, then Eliza and Camille at his feet and Vera at the head, and so on—they eventually settled for Eliza hoisting his top half over her shoulders (though she was the thinnest, she was also in the best shape); Vera was in the middle, both her arms under his lower back; and Camille had her arms wrapped around his calves.

They made it to the car in two segments, stopping halfway for everyone to catch their breath. Once they set him on the bumper, the three women, using all their arm strength, rolled him in until he hit the back of the back seat.

Relieved to find the alley was empty and strangely camera-less, there they stood there, breathless and panting, the moment sinking in as the rain did the same. They were sopping wet at this point, looking like drowned rats in ball gowns with sensible shoes. A different day, they would have laughed about their looks; a different day, they would've laughed about many things.

Walking back into the suite, the women grabbed bag after bag, throwing them into the SUV, Camille taking time to make sure they covered Connor with their bags, though no one would ever be able to tell there was body in the back of high-end SUV. In the same fashion she had folded, she was still packing. At first it was clothes, now luggage, but deep down it was likely her emotions.

Once the car was loaded, the three women headed back into the suite, each venturing off to perform a once-over and make sure nothing was amiss, each of them leaving behind a trail of rain water as they walked.

"All good?" Eliza called out to the other women as she stood in the living room she had looked over one last time.

"Yep," Millie hollered from the bathroom.

"Uh-huh," Vera said as she came back down the stairs once again.

"Then let's get a move on," Eliza called and turned to head out of the suite.

All three women climbed into their spots in the vehicle, never even asking about Eliza's plan, just blindly trusting their friend and her uncanny ability to figure out how to get rid of a body.

Eliza reached over her left shoulder, pulling the seatbelt across her chest and clicking the buckle in. The irony of her now following the law with a body in her trunk was not lost on her as she turned the car on, the rain glistening in the headlights that lit the back alley.

The rain made pulling out into the dark, traffic-riddled streets more difficult than it already was. The car remained silent, except for the quiet, crooning voice of Leon Bridges spilling out of the speakers. Eliza was grateful that her friends knew enough to not elevate and already stressful drive by mucking up the quiet.

Finally, after a Lyft car sped by, Eliza was able to sneak out easily into the busy roads of the city that never sleeps, something she was beginning to wonder if she would ever do again, move swiftly without feeling watched. The rain mixing with the headlights, streetlights, fog, and humidity in the New York summer air made everything around them a blur of colors and shapes.

Weaving over to the far right, willing herself to be more sober than she was, she tried to squeeze her way in among the honking blobs to merge onto the New Jersey Turnpike South, heading back to Darlington. This drive was one she could almost do blindfolded, and tonight it seemed she might have to unless the rain ceased. It felt like days ago that she had made the trek from home to NYC. So much had happened since then, things she could never forget, even if she wanted to. A smile spread across Eliza's face as she squinted her eyes, trying to see through the rain as she realized she didn't want to forget, she wanted to relish.

CHAPTER 65

CAMILLE

CAMILLE STARED OUT THE PASSENGER seat window, watching the rain fall in streams down the glass, forcing her to keep her eyes focused on what was close up, not far off. She had climbed into shotgun without even calling it, a position she was used to being in when it came to Eliza. Eliza was good at calling the shots when things got shitty, and things right now couldn't get a whole lot worse.

Cars splashed water up onto the side of the SUV as they sped past Eliza. Camille glanced over at the speedometer, wondering why people were blowing past them.

"Are you seriously going fifty in a sixty-five?" Camille remarked.

Eliza kept white-knuckling the steering wheel, slightly hunched forward, her forehead scrunched in all the spots she hadn't gotten Botox yet. She didn't turn to Camille, just calmly stated, "I am trying not to get pulled over. I don't know about you, but I really don't think a meeting with the cops is something I am up for right now. You and Vera are still drunk, I had a syringe full of God knows what in my purse, and not to mention that we have a dead man in the back of car."

Camille sat quietly, staring at Eliza, waiting for her to continue, but she didn't. She was too focused on following all the laws and trying to drive in a mild tsunami, making her wipers work overtime, and still not maintaining any sort of actual visibility.

"And buckle your damn seat belt," Eliza said.

The beeping from the passenger seat belt had been drowned by the rain, or Camille's lack of focus on the situation in general. A shell of a woman was not something she was used to being. She was better known as the strong one, the woman most women wanted to emulate. But things around her seemed to be in a constant fall now. Crumbling to pieces quickly, not allowing her any time to process her new normal. Divorce, job drama, and now murder.

She flipped down the sun visor and slid open the mirror, the light illuminating throughout the car. The woman looking back at her was one she didn't recognize. She looked puffy, tired, with tear-stained eyes and red marks on her cheeks. *Is it possible I got fatter in the last couple hours?* she wondered. Just as she was about to full out shame spiral, Vera called from the back seat, "Shut the visor. I am sure it hard enough for E to drive as it is."

Camille was grateful to be stopped in her tracks, almost as if her friend knew what was going through her mind. Slamming the visor shut, she tried to slam the door on the negative thoughts, knowing full well it wasn't that easy. She turned, giving Vera a tight-lipped, but genuine, smile as the rain pelted the car from all directions. Vera's face was lightly lit by the glow of her cell, reflecting the smiling whites of her eyes as she stared for a moment at Camille before going back to typing on her phone.

Even in the midst of a crisis, she was still working away, keeping up, and touching base. The glow reminded Camille that she should check in with Noel, who was no longer worried about her whereabouts except when it came to the children. A pit formed in her stomach as she pulled his name up on her screen.

Ignoring the slew of texts from colleagues wondering where she was and asking if she had heard anything about the social media position, Camille touched Noel's name, hoping that he, too, had reached out, maybe said he was sorry and he was wrong. Though, she wasn't sure that was what she truly wanted. Love was a complicated thing and being married was a mess unto itself.

Allowing just a moment of reflection as she watched the headlights stream in and out of the blurry windshield, Camille came to the startling realization that maybe she didn't really love him anymore either. She had tried to keep them together, tried to fight the vapidity that had riddled the last few years of their existence, but if she were really being honest with herself when she thought about him, she knew she loved him, but was not *in love* with him. Over time he had become her roommate, a complacent companion who would someday repeat the details of her life when she was gone as proof of witness. Anyone could fill that role. And as she sat in the soft leather seats of her best friend's luxury SUV, she realized that Connor's body wasn't the only one that was dead. She had been emotionally unresponsive for years. It was high time she woke the hell up.

CHAPTER 66

VERA

VERA SAT CROSS-LEGGED under her almost dry evening gown in the back of Eliza's car. She glanced over her shoulder every now and again, knowing the suitcase and bags were still covering Connor's body, but checking just to calm her mind. Driving in weather like this would've normally brought her to the brink of a panic attack. Vera hadn't driven a vehicle in over four years, having returned her Mercedes when the lease was up, figuring with the plethora of car services apps, there was no need for her to get behind the wheel. Not to mention it allowed her more time to multitask on her phone from the back seat.

And here she was again, in the back seat, trying to take on several things at once. There was the mental anguish she was fighting, having taken on the campaign of a man who was not only no longer running but was no longer breathing, and the back and forth battle of the what-to-do-with-Melia component. Vera couldn't help but wonder for a split second if she was strong enough to hide something like this from her. But as she returned random emails and texts, most about work, some personal, she remembered that she was a badass woman who could do anything she set her mind to. Melia would be better off with Connor gone, and the rest was just details, and she was good at the details.

Being on her phone was part therapeutic, part practical, and part scheme. People wanted to constantly tell her that she was dependent to her phone, but she didn't care. The glow of the blue light and constant "need" for her was addicting in a way she saw nothing wrong with. There was a calm that resonated throughout her body when her phone was in her hand, and right now it was helping her to forget what they were doing and where they were going—two things she didn't know the answer to and was afraid to ask. Not to mention she decided it would look a lot less suspicious if she didn't go radio silent. She had always been the type to immediately get back to people, no matter the time or day, so this shouldn't be any different.

In the midst of returning an email to a client, a text popped through from Melia. Vera felt her heart stop; her fingers froze. Clicking on it would cause her phone to let Melia's know she had read it, and she wasn't sure she was ready for what it said or what she would say. She blinked slowly several times, trying to focus on the pitter patter of the rain and the two women in the front seats, neither of whom were speaking. Eliza was leaning forward, grappling to see through the rain, and Camille's head was faintly swaying to the discreet music.

Taking a final deep breath, Vera pressed on the screen, bringing Melia's text to life.

"Where did you go?"

Simple enough, Vera thought. *She was just looking for me. Probably wanted me to meet her reporter friend, since she likely announced that I would be helping Connor run for office.*

Vera lifted her gaze to the sunroof of the SUV, the rain streaming toward the back of the vehicle. She watched the water work its way as she tried to find the words to write back. *Where am I?* Vera thought.

"Guys," Vera called as she lowered her gaze back to the front windshield, "we need to figure out our story.

Melia is asking where I am, and I am not sure what to say."

Vera saw Eliza's eyes leave the road and meet hers in the rearview mirror. Strangely though, Eliza's eyes didn't look scared or even concerned by this question. Vera found the exchange both comforting and frightening at the same time.

Eliza's eyes returned back to the road, and she started talking. Both Vera and Camille's eyes locked on her every word. In that moment, Vera realized that damaged women were the most dangerous kind because they already know how to survive.

CHAPTER 67

ELIZA

THE RANG SANG AS IT HIT the windshield and trickled down the glass. "I ran into Camille at the side bar after she had gone over some numbers with Connor. They had discussed her as the new social media news presence they were working toward." Eliza paused and quickly glanced at Millie, her smile verifying that would be nice.

"Millie had been celebrating since Connor rejoined the party, and I decided to get her back to the suite before she made a fool out of herself and jeopardized her promotion." This time Eliza smiled at her forward thinking.

Camille turned back to Vera, nodding. "I had had quite a bit to drink." Verifying that part of the story was true.

Once Millie spun back forward, Eliza continued as though these following events were not fabricated and she was simply recalling the events of her evening.

"You did whatever you were doing, and after a short while, you couldn't find us and headed back to the suite to make sure everything was okay," Eliza glanced up into the rearview mirror again, making eye contact with Vera. "And just so we know, what exactly *were* you doing?"

Vera looked sheepishly down at her phone, the glow lighting her face as she bit the inside of her cheek. Then she exhaled. "I was with Melia—"

"What do you mean *with* Melia?" Millie using her fingers to make air quotes around the word "with."

"Not like that," Vera started again, then paused. "Well, kind of like that, I guess. I don't know. I am strangely attracted to her, and there is this whole bracelet thing and—"

Millie cut her off again. "Bracelet thing?" She turned back around and cocked her head.

Vera went on to tell them about the bracelet in the basket, the flirtation between her and Melia, and lastly about the bruises on Melia's wrists.

"That bastard." Eliza gritted under her teeth again, almost as if she didn't want the dead Connor in the back to hear her.

"And that's not all," Vera continued. "She asked me to champion his run for mayor of NYC. And somehow between the look in her eyes, the bruise on her wrist, and her hand on my knee, I agreed."

"Well, he's not going to win," Millie snickered a little while turning back around.

"That's not the point," Vera responded. "What do I tell her now? I have to keep this a secret from her and yet still do my job."

"Okay," Eliza chimed back in, taking charge of a situation that Vera was losing ground on which was odd since damage control was Vera's forte.

"So, you came to check on us after you left the stairwell with Melia. When you got to the suite, I had put Millie to bed and was reading in the living room. Though you wanted to rejoin the party, you didn't want to head back out into the rain, and so you poured yourself one more cocktail." Eliza stopped and again glanced at Vera in the rearview adding, "against my wishes."

And with her eyes back on the road, she kept on with the story.

"After your drink and my reading, we called it a night." Eliza stopped again, allowing it all to settle into the spaces of each woman's mind.

Breaking the moment of silence, Vera spoke up, "And then what? What are we doing now? Where are we going? What do we say happened after?"

The rain had somehow found a way to fall harder in the last minute, and there was now lightning illuminating up the sky around them as thunder broke the humid summer air outside the car, the low bass sound vibrating the glass on the windows. Eliza had become hyper focused on the road, her storytelling going silent.

CHAPTER 68

CAMILLE

NYLON FROM THE SEATBELT rubbed against Camille's still slightly damp, soft neck skin as she turned back to Vera. "Text Melia that you went back to the suite to find us," Camille said, turning back to Vera.

"Okay," Vera said and began poking around on her screen.

"And as far as the rest of it," Camille began, "I woke up super early the next morning, before dawn had even broke. And the hangover was so intense that I couldn't go back to sleep, and so I made coffee and headed into the living room, accidently awaking the two of you, who were asleep on the couch and armchair"

Vera was staring at her, waiting to see how this would all play out. Eliza, for her part, was doing everything in her power to keep them on the road, the vehicle moving even slower, but still heading south.

"Between the coffee and commotion, you two awoke, and as part of my self-wallow shitty morning, I told you all about the divorce and my miserable existence that had forced me to drink myself silly the night before." Camille felt the truth of the confession make her stomach churn a little.

"Then Eliza," Camille said, smiling at Eliza, though her eyes never left the road, "she suggested that we head out to her house for the night as a getaway from the gravity of my reality."

Then Camille turned to face Vera. "Just us girls out in her guest house, drinking, bitching, and healing."

"Eliza's house?" Vera questioned.

"Yes," Camille furrowed her brow as she responded, a little caught off guard by Vera's, question. "That is where we are headed."

"What?" Vera raised her voice a little, realizing how odd it was that she hadn't asked until now. "We are going to Eliza's? What on earth are we going to do there?"

Camille turned back to Eliza, waiting for her to answer the question they both had, but Eliza was far too stressed with the task of driving to give them any more information than a simple, "I have a plan," with her eyes never leaving the blacktop.

Camille didn't need more than that but knowing that Vera would likely not be satisfied with simplicity, she tried to head her off by continuing with their "story."

"And so, whatever happens next we can explain away by saying we spent the next day or two enjoying a light buzz and deep conversation. Beyond that, Rhett will be our alibi, not to mention each other," Camille finished, clearing her throat of the ineptitude that had been stuck since Noel and her had decided to separate and Connor had forced himself on her and allowing for the first time her pride to rise up and her lungs to take an actual deep breath.

They were going to be okay. She trusted these women, and together they were going to get through whatever came next. The only thing standing in their way was Eliza's silence and this damn rain.

CHAPTER 69

VERA

WHILE VERA DIDN'T LOVE THE NARRATIVE, the story seemed simple and solid enough to stick. She wasn't sure why the hell they were headed to Eliza's, but she was willing to let it play out. She didn't have a better idea— and there was a body in the back that needed disposing of.

Her phone screen lit back up. Melia responded to her text.

"Did you find them?" her text read.

Vera applauded her use of punctuation. All the younger people in her office no longer used it, and it made deciphering texts even harder than it already was.

"Yes," Vera started to type back, and then followed the script she had been told by the two women steering this ship.

"Camille got over-served, so we put her to bed." Vera finished the text.

Then she waited as the three dots blinked lightly on the screen. Melia was typing and Vera was testing her patience and strength.

They had been in the car for a couple hours now, and Vera was beginning to wonder what exactly would happen once they got to Eliza's. The usual brazen side of her would normally ask, but as the buzz wore off and the exhaustion of the night settled in, she became too tired to do much more than text.

"Oh, poor thing. Hope she feels better in the a.m. I wanted you to meet my friend Deacon from the *Circadian*.

He is going to announce that you are running Connor's campaign online tonight!"

Vera felt her stomach lurch as she read those words. Little did Melia know that there would be no actual campaign to run, and Vera had already met Deacon and wasn't sure yet if he registered as friend or foe for Team Dixon.

"Oh, sorry," Vera started, "I think I am just going to stay in for the night. Don't want to go back out in the rain. Maybe I can meet him in the morning before I head back to DC?"

Vera figured adding that in would make the optics look even better because she was organizing plans for herself for the morning. That way when they "headed" out to Eliza's super early, it wouldn't seem like she was planning that all along.

More blinking dots. More patience.

The two women in the front were silent now, too, the music and rain the only sounds in the vehicle. Vera didn't have to see their faces to know they, too, were dog tired. It was after midnight, which in and of itself would make anyone of their age sleepy, but couple that with the measures of the evening, and every woman in that car was worn out all the way to her bones.

"Sounds good. I will try to find Connor and see if we can meet you guys for brunch somewhere."

Again, the words lurched Vera's stomach. Melia, simple, sweet, broken, but brave Melia, was about to go looking for a man she would never see again. He was an abuser and a rapist, but that didn't mean she didn't love him once upon a time, or at least care for him. He had been her partner for a long time, and she was about to find out that time had come to a close. Vera looked away from her phone for a moment, watching the rain droplets trickle down the car window, and wondered if Melia would be sad or relieved when she found out he was gone. Vera hoped she would be relieved but was afraid the submissive side of her would be sad.

Staring out the window, Vera remembered Eliza calling her a black widow spider, a term at the time that Vera wasn't sure was endearing or offensive. Now, in the dark of night, with a body in the back of the car, and the woman who killed him driving them to the middle of nowhere, Vera couldn't help but think it was actually Eliza who was the black widow, the word finally forming into pride. But this spider had lived up to its name, killing a male counterpart, making Melia a widow herself. The question now was whether she was black like the rest of them.

CHAPTER 70

ELIZA

ELIZA USUALLY ENTERED HER PROPERTY through the large steel gate out front, the clicker rendering her admittance, but tonight she did not want to risk waking the dog, much less the family, so she took the winding gravel side road to the very back of the property and entered from there. With a hesitant exhale, she turned off her headlights, again to hide their entry, and slowed the car to avoid any excess noise that may come from the tires pressing on the gravel.

It was pitch black except for the reflection of the moon in the puddles on the ground. It had been raining here, as well, Eliza realized. She didn't need the light. She knew her way around the property by heart and feel. She smiled, knowing the rain would make the process a lot easier.

No one spoke as the women were bumped around in the car, veering through the trees and up toward the guest house and animal pens. Vera's face was no longer lit from the glow of her phone, and Millie leaned forward, squinting, trying to decipher where they were headed. Both women had been to the property many times before, but never in the middle of the night, and definitely not with a mission at hand.

The stress in the car was palpable as Eliza put the car in park alongside the large brick barn that housed their horses, hiding the car from sight of the house. It was important that Rhett know they were here, but not yet. She would move the car once they were done.

Eliza shut the ignition off, finally giving the wiper blades a much-needed break. Then she turned to face Millie and Vera, angling herself to look back and forth between the two of them easily. Their gazes were already on her, waiting expectantly to hear the plan unfold. Eliza took a deep breath, feeling quite confident in all her actions tonight.

"Okay. Let's throw all the bags into the back seat, and then we need to unwrap him from the sheet and take off his clothes."

She finished, leaving the two women puzzled as she turned back around, opened the front door, and quietly shut it. A few moments later as she was heading to the back of the vehicle, she realized the others were sitting still, frozen, likely not fully understanding since she had only given them part of the plan. She figured it was better that way. Too much information gave them too much to argue with.

"Move!" she called, only as loud as she allowed herself, so she didn't accidentally awaken anyone, human or animal.

Camille and Vera came to attention, finally hopping out of the SUV. All three women were still dressed in their evening gowns, but now with more sensible shoes and weather-strewn hair. Grabbing a hair ties from the center console she pulled her hair back into a pony at the nape of her neck, Eliza popped open the back gate, then bent down in the trunk and began tossing bags over the headrests, landing them on the seat Vera had just sat on.

Quickly, Connor's body came to view in the sheet, still damp from the rain, even after the three-hour drive. The moisture allowed a transparency so the women could see through to the paling skin of a man once in power.

Eliza relished the grotesque nature of it all. She had single-handedly stripped him of that power, and now it was she who harnessed it.

Grabbing one end of the sheet still wrapped tight enough to make carrying him easier, Eliza commanded the other women to also grab their respected ends. They had done this not that long ago; they knew where to go to make the task as simple as possible.

Hoisting him out of the car, Eliza put the twisted sheet end over her shoulder and began to walk toward the back of the horse barn. The rain made her footing more difficult as her sneakers slid in the mud, but she marched on, the droplets falling down her lashes. She wasn't crying—nothing about this would bring tears. It was simply Mother Earth's way of rinsing clean their sins, or maybe cleaning the dirt off their hands from dealing with a filthy man.

Eliza could hear Millie and Vera behind her, complaining that they needed a break, it was too heavy, can we stop for a minute, but she kept right on. There was no time to waste, and they needed to suck it up.

Once finally around the bend in the barn, they came upon another fenced-in area. It was a mud-covered bog that held animals that were hard to make out in the dark and rain. Eliza didn't need to squint, though. She knew exactly where they were.

"Okay," she said as she turned to the women and set Connor in the mud at her feet, "let's unwrap him, strip him, and toss him in." Then she knelt down, the mud now higher on her gown.

"And then what?" Millie said through her panting breaths.

Eliza looked over her shoulder toward the fence, the other two women's eyes following, trying to figure out what was in there.

"Then we feed him to the pigs."

CHAPTER 71

CAMILLE

CAMILLE HAD BEEN CALLED A PIG many times in her life. Every day she received several emails and letters at the station from fans and foes. Some letters were words of encouragement or praise, others criticizing everything from her hair, to her weight, to the way she said "roof." The ones that hurt the most were the ones about her figure. She had spent her life yo-yo-ing in the weight department, never finding a permanent home for longer than a few months.

The camera added ten pounds, she would tell herself every time she read yet another email calling her a fat ass, chubby, or a pig. Though she was aware that pigs had the reputation of eating anything and everything in sight, she wasn't sure that Eliza had her head on straight when she suggested that they feed Connor's body to her hogs.

"Eliza," Camille pleaded, still catching her breath while she watched her two friends begin to unwrap and undress a dead man, "this isn't a mafia movie. You can't feed a human body to pigs in real life!" Pressing her palm to her forehead, she forgot for a moment that there was a bruise there until the pain buzzed through her skull.

Eliza heard her but didn't respond initially, too busy trying to lift a lifeless leg out of a tailored, thousand-dollar suit.

"E!" Camille raised her voice again, though not at a respectable level for the middle of the night when you were in the business of hiding a body.

Eliza paused, the pants halfway down Connor's legs, before saying, "Millie, I know what I am doing. You have to trust me." She made eye contact with Camille before continuing, "You know I am good for it." Camille watched Eliza's eyebrows raise, signaling to her friend that they had been in the shit together before, and it was indeed Eliza who got them out of it.

Camille took a deep breath, realizing that she truly had no better plan of her own, kneeled down in the mud between the other women, and began to unbutton Connor's soaking wet dress shirt.

She closed her eyes for a second while she did it, trying to stop the perverse feeling that was creeping in from the edges. It was only a few, short hours ago that Connor had forced his way into her dress, and now here she was removing his clothing. She swallowed the bile that had begun to rise up from her empty stomach, forcing the feelings down with it.

Trying to undress a dead body while being pelted by rain, and knee deep in mud, was no easy undertaking, the mud making everything slippery and the rain causing everything to feel heavier. The fabric on Camille's dress was so heavy that she immediately thought of how much weight it would add to the scale. Her mind went there more than she liked to admit.

The darkness of the night mixing with the mud made it hard to even see their hands in front of them as they worked feverishly to undress him. Out in the middle of nowhere, the only light was that flickering off the almost full moon in the sky, one that was hard to see with the rain clouds filtering past it.

A pile of wet clothes and sheets lay next to the three women as they once again lifted a heavy, only boxer brief–wearing Connor and stumbled and slipped over to the edge of the pig fence. The hogs had rustled awake at their sound and were now noisily grunting at the fence edge. They we huge hogs, the kind you see at state fairs that win prizes for their overall size. *What a luxury,* Camille thought, *to be rewarded the larger you get.*

The sound of the pigs clambering over each other, their hooves slipping and readjusting in the mud to gain better access at the grub that was about to come their way, startled Camille a little, though she knew better than to show any more fear in a moment like this already littered with terror.

Eliza had her thin, but muscular, porcelain-skinned arms bent up under Connor's armpits, holding his head in her bosom. Vera was at his legs, her arms wrapped around them as if she were holding a football. That left Camille in the middle, under Connor's spine, his white belly with a chestnut treasure trail below his belly button staring up at her, making the bile rise again.

"Okay," Eliza whispered, loud enough for them to hear, "on three we throw him over. One . . . two . . . three . . ."

CHAPTER 72

VERA

TO VERA'S SURPRISE, THE HOGS backed up as Connor's body tumbled over the top of the fence. With a thud muffled by the rain softened earth he landed on the ground, the mud and pooled rain water splashing up around him, the pigs descended on him as though they hadn't eaten in months.

Vera rested her hand on the top of the fence, leaning her body against it while trying to catch her breath. Looking down at her once-nude dress that was now almost black from the mud, her eyes shifted over to Camille, who was standing, also glistening in the mixture of the moon and rain hitting her. Was it possible that amid all this chaos and blood she looked at peace? That was something Vera couldn't remember seeing on her in a long time. Vera owed this to her. She had made so many mistakes when it came to their friendship, but this wasn't one of them.

Looking past Camille, she could only make out Eliza's outline in the dark, her green dress also black from the mud and rain, her wet hair pulled back, and her fists resting in her hip bones. A flash of lightning lit the sky, and for a moment Vera could almost swear that Eliza looked like Superman in her stance, her chin held high.

Once her panting ceased and she began to allow her wits to creep back in, she became keenly aware of the sounds coming from the other side of the fence. If she hadn't known better, she would've thought it was the sound of a seam ripping out of a pair of pants, but it wasn't, and the sound made her gag and throw up at her feet.

Both Camille and Eliza turned toward her, their eyes leaving the hogs for the first time since Connor went in.

"Oh my God, Vera." Eliza made her way over to her. "Are you okay?" Her damp hand now rested on Vera's back. But as the sounds of teeth grinding through flesh, much like a dog ripping apart a shoe continued, so did Vera's heaving. There was barely anything in her stomach, she had hardly eaten since she left DC, so it looked as though it was simply raining out her mouth, as well.

Once everything was out and she was left to dry heave, Camille and Eliza took her each by the arm and carried her back into the car, both following and returning to their seats in the front.

"You okay, Vera?" Camille turned around.

Vera took three deep breaths, finally calming her stomach and mind from the sounds and responded, "Yeah. It was just the sound and . . ." She felt her chest start to heave forward again and so she stopped.

"Yeah. It was a lot," was all Eliza said, turning on the ignition.

Camille turned back to face Eliza. "Where are we going now? We can't just leave him there. What if he is still there in the morning?" Vera couldn't see Camille's face, but she was sure it was paling at the thought.

"We aren't leaving. We are heading to the guest house. Rhett needs to see our car in the a.m. and be able to verify that we were at the house. And then we can check on the pigs before dawn and see if they did what I was told they could do."

"What if they don't?" Camille's faced twisted into a panic-stricken scowl.

"They will." Eliza retorted calmly, yet boldly.

Camille looked on, waiting for more, but when Eliza remained silent, Vera suddenly chimed, "If they don't, then we will have ourselves one hell of a bonfire tomorrow." They phantom smell of burning flesh turning her stomach again, leaving her praying the pigs would do as Eliza said.

Eliza put the car in drive as Vera chimed in from the back. "What you were told they could do?" she asked rather quizzically. "Did you buy homicidal pigs?"

"No," Eliza responded calmly. "When Rhett bought them, he said the guy made some funny passing comment saying that if you ever needed to hide a body, fourteen lactating sows could devour an entire male body in an hour or so."

Eliza moved the car forward in the direction of the pig pen, and Vera and Camille waited for her to go on.

"And there are eight of them, so I figure that he will be gone in the next three hours. We will just have to check for his teeth likely. I don't know if they will eat those. I think they can't digest them or something."

"Or something," Camille echoed Eliza's last sentiment. "How in the hell do you know that?"

"I saw it on Animal Planet or CSI or something. I don't know. That part I am not sure of. I guess we will see," Eliza said as she put the car back in park and hopped out into the rain again.

"We will see," Camille echoed again as she and Vera watched Eliza pick up the heavy pile of sheets and clothes, sliding in the mud, and throwing them on the hood of the car with a thud, making both Camille and Vera jump.

Climbing back into the car, she shivered a little as she put the car in drive and they slowly made their way to the guest house, a couple yards away, Vera swallowed any remaining tinged saliva in her mouth and asked, "Why didn't you throw the sheets and clothes in?"

As Eliza put the car in park, she turned back to Vera. "I don't know if they can digest those as well. And I don't want the pigs to get sick," she said matter-of-factly, like they hadn't just fed a human body to those very same pigs.

Then Eliza reached back, grabbed her bag, opened the door, and headed into the guest house. Camille turned, fetched her bag, gave Vera a shrug, and also hopped out of the car.

Watching her two friends move with such confidence ignited that same conviction in Vera, something she usually possessed without effort, as she finally took one last deep breath, grabbed her bag, and ran through the rain into the shelter and warmth of the cozy guest house.

CHAPTER 73

ELIZA

THE GUEST HOUSE WAS RARELY USED at the Kingfield property. Most of the guests chose to stay in the large house with Eliza's family than out on their own toward the back of the property. That didn't stop Eliza from fully decorating the space with rustic cottage charm meets industrial chic.

She had thought of everything down to the dishes and towels, all themed with farm animals that hinted more toward charming than childish. All three women had instantly removed their muddy shoes before entering the house, a gesture that thrilled Eliza more than she wanted to admit. She was a clean freak who liked to fake ambivalence when it came to the topic. People always thought clean freaks had OCD, and she wasn't about to be labeled.

Eliza stood in the ship lapped entryway, both women flanking her, as she shimmied out of her heavy, soaking, and now incredibly dirty dress, the green and brown material pooling at her feet on the floor.

She turned to the other women, her hands over her breasts, only in her underwear, and declared, "I have a bunch of extra comfy clothes in the rooms. Take off your dresses and let's each grab a shower."

Eliza turned and headed toward one of the two bathrooms in the house, her damp feet padding on the rustic wood floors. Behind her she could hear Millie and Vera struggling to get out of their wet dresses that were sticking in all the wrong places and were muddy all over.

Their laughter floated through the air, finding a resting place in Eliza's heart and warming her soul.

•• •• ••

All three women were now in the living room, strewn across the large sectional and side chairs. Each dressed in sweats, their hair still wet, but now warm from the shower. No trace of mud or mayhem existed on them as they sipped on the coffee Eliza had brewed and tried to eat some of the cookies and crackers they left in the guest house for guests' late-night needs.

Wine would have been a more appropriate choice given everything that had happened that night, but the optics of them "showing up in the early a.m." that they had planned to tell Rhett wouldn't explain wine on the counter, so coffee it was. Not to mention they were trying to stay awake to check on Connor before Rhett awoke for the morning.

It was after four in the morning now. The alcohol and adrenaline having worn off and the exhausting truth settling in had the women trying everything in their power to fight the fatigue.

Eliza had thrown their dresses, along with Connor's clothes and the bed sheet in the dryer, an action the other two women had questioned at first. But Eliza explained that if they dried them, they would be a lot easier to burn when they had a bonfire the next night. They needed to get rid of everything that had come from that night.

As the dryer hummed in the background, and the women sat under the dull candlelight so as not to draw any attention to the guest house, they actually followed Eliza's given narrative, talking mainly about Camille and

Noel's marriage falling apart and what that meant for them and the kids going forward.

Eliza was surprised by Vera's empathy for the situation, until she spilled the beans about her and Spencer, and uterus-gate. Only then did her overexertion of kindness and understanding make more sense breaking through her tough exterior.

But just as the night was giving way to the dawn, the women each had closed their eyes, allowing their bodies to finally give into the enormity of the night, and the fatigue that rattled in their bones.

CHAPTER 74

CAMILLE

"COCK-A-DOODLE-DOO" ECHOED through the walls, vibrating the inner part of Camille's eardrums, forcing her eyes to fly open.

"Shit," she called out from her end of the sofa, "this place is like a regular animal house." She smiled at her clever joke, only to see Eliza jump to her feet and hustle out the door, barefoot running through the still-mucky grass toward the pigs.

Camille's smile turned into a tight-lipped grimace as she made eye contact with a now-awake Vera, suddenly remembering what happened a few hours before. They were supposed to stay awake, supposed to beat Rhett out to the pigs, supposed to make sure they were in the clear. If clear heads would of prevailed, someone would of remembered to set an alarm, but with the rush of emotion and scattered thoughts of pulling of a murder, time wasn't at the forefront of their mind.

She rushed to her feet, Vera doing the same, and together they ran to the window to watch Eliza, figuring it would look strange if they all came running out at once.

Camille felt her breathing stop when she caught sight of Eliza near the pigs—but she wasn't alone. Standing next to her was a morning-haired Rhett holding something in his hands that Camille couldn't make out from where she was. She tried to squint as she watched their conversation, trying to figure out if it was a friendly or accusing one.

She felt Vera move away from behind her toward the door, opening it quietly and stepping out under the awning, still out of sight but now in earshot. Camille followed suit, realizing she was still holding her breath.

"Yeah, it was kind of last minute. She needed to get away. I didn't want to wake you or the girls, so we just made coffee and hung in the guest house," they heard Eliza say.

"Oh, that's terrible," Rhett started, leaning in to hug Eliza. "I am so sorry for Camille. I can't believe it though. They always seemed so happy."

"I know. I was shocked, too, but I guess you never really know the things people are hiding."

Camille heard Vera gasp lightly and cover her mouth, the stabbing of those words hitting a little too close to home for all of them this morning.

"Well," Rhett said as he pulled away from Eliza, "the girls and I will try to respect your girls' weekend on the farm. We'll try to stay out of your hair." He smiled and kissed her forehead, causing another stab in Camille's stomach, leaving her longing for a man to treat her the way Rhett treated Eliza.

"Thanks." Eliza leaned up on her tiptoes to kiss him, her hands resting on his shoulders.

"You head back to the cottage. I'll feed the animals this morning," Rhett said, turning toward the pig pen.

Camille and Vera watched, trying not to be seen from their spot under the awning, as Eliza reached for Rhett's hand, casually following him over to the hogs.

"I will in a minute. I think they may have fallen back asleep so I can help you for little while." Eliza smiled up at him.

Camille felt her lungs finally release as she watched Eliza and Rhett throw slop into the pig pen, nothing looking amiss, no one pausing or cocking their head.

Quietly she and Vera slipped back into the guest house, both finding their spots on the couch. Camille closed her eyes again, realizing for the first time that it was okay to do so. It was over.

CHAPTER 75

VERA

VERA WATCHED CAMILLE FINALLY RELAX under the soft flannel blanket on the other end of the couch, knowing that her friend was finally at peace. One of the tragedies in her life had come to an end. Another was on the horizon, a battle that Vera was sure would get ugly before it ended—but she had them, and the three of them could do anything together. Divorce seemed straightforward compared to murder.

Vera, for her part though, wasn't able to go back to sleep. She wasn't the type to relax into a moment, and she also wasn't the type to be away from the online world for long. Keeping up appearances meant everything right now, and so she dug into the bottom of her purse, fishing out her phone and a charger. She found an outlet over by the chair that Eliza had posted in before and slipped under a blanket, plugging her phone in, ready to take back her power.

As soon as the screen came back to life, though it was only after six a.m., she already had a slew of texts and emails to return. This was why a woman like her could never sleep.

She clicked on the texts first, seeing immediately that she had missed several from Melia as the night had progressed. Her stomach lurched.

"Have you seen Connor?" 12:21a.m.

"I am starting to get worried. No one has seen Connor in a few hours." 1:43 a.m.

"Vera, where are you? The cops are here." 2:22 a.m.

"I am freaking out. Connor is missing. I need you here." 4:12 a.m.

"Vera?" 5:17 a.m.

Vera felt all the color rush out of her face. She didn't know what to say to Melia. She wondered if she shouldn't say anything at all yet, maybe wait until Eliza was back and they could talk it though. But then it dawned on her that Melia's phone would now show that Vera had indeed read the texts. She had no choice but to respond.

So, with her fingers lightly shaking, she began banging on the glass screen of her phone.

"Oh my God, Melia. My phone died last night. What is going on? Can you talk?" Vera hit Send.

The typing dots blinked on the screen. Vera had wished they wouldn't.

"I am at home now. Police came right away. They are trying to figure it out. I don't know what's going on. I was going to go to your suite last night but the cops wanted everyone questioned and me to go home in case he came there. Where are you?"

Vera typed the story as Eliza had stated: "We woke up super early. Camille needed coffee and she spilled some troubling personal information to us. Eliza suggested we get out of the city for the weekend and spend some time relaxing at her farm in Maryland. We just arrived a little bit ago." Vera reread the text, making sure it fit the narrative, then sent.

Blinking dots again, but they quickly turned into three words. "I need you" was all Melia wrote.

If one could ever physically feel their heart break, Vera was feeling it right now. She didn't know what to do. They hadn't devised this part of their plan. She worried it would seem odd if she wasn't there to be alongside the woman whose husband she was going to try to get elected but was now missing. But she also didn't want to abandon Eliza and Camille at a time like this.

Vera froze, staring at the screen, not sure of what to do. In her heart, she was torn between the woman she had strange, hidden feelings for and the women she loved beyond measure but who would be okay without her now.

"Let me talk to Eliza. She drove us here. I will see what I can do to get back to DC. Can you come there?" Vera hit Send just as Eliza opened the front door.

CHAPTER 76

ELIZA

SOMEHOW IT HADN'T DAWNED on Eliza until she was on the front rug that she had not only run out of the house without shoes but had performed several chores alongside Rhett barefoot. Her toes were now covered in mud and blades of grass, a farmer's norm.

She tried to rub some of the mud off her feet, swishing them back and forth on the rug before Vera appeared before her, towel in hand.

"Well?" Vera asked.

"They did it," Eliza started as she leaned down, wiping her feet off with the towel. "They really did it."

Eliza felt her mouth break into a smile and then a giggle. She couldn't control it; it just happened. She had hoped that what the man told Rhett was the truth, and now it had worked. The pigs had finished Connor off, bones and all.

Eliza's giggle was infectious, forcing Vera to start to laugh, as well. *It's ironic, really, when you think about it, a pig being eaten by pigs,* Eliza thought, making her laugh even more.

Vera finally shushed her, gesturing toward the living room where Camille was soundly sleeping.

"She is finally resting," Vera said.

Eliza peeked around the corner at her beautiful friend, finally safe and sound in slumber. Then she headed to the kitchen, motioning Vera to follow, tossing the towel in the laundry room on the way.

Pulling another mug from the cabinet and filling it with steaming coffee, Eliza took a seat on at the kitchen table, Vera doing the same next to her. Eliza brought the mug to her mouth as Vera slid her phone over in front of Eliza.

"Read this," Vera demanded.

Eliza set her cup down and picked up the phone, skimming the conversation as in the background Vera asked, "What do I do?"

Handing the phone back to Vera, Eliza took another sip of coffee and said, "Go. You should be there. It will look odd if you don't. Especially if the press already knows you are working with the Dixons, which it sounds like they do."

With another sip of coffee, Eliza was relishing her role as the one in charge for once. She watched as Vera looked over the phone again, contemplating her words.

"You are right. Of course I should go. I just don't want to leave—" Vera started but Eliza cut her off, wafting her hand in the air as if shooing a bug away.

"Don't even think about Millie and me for a second. Things here are good. Done. I will find the teeth eventually, but for now they are somewhere in the mud and may never even be seen again. Tonight she and I will burn everything and toast to redemption." Eliza grinned, her teeth shining in the sunlight streaming in from the sliding glass door.

"Redemption," Vera repeated as she looked down again at her phone, typing something out and then showing it to Eliza.

"Okay. I am on my way. Hang tight. You okay?" The text read.

Eliza watched as the blinking dots appeared on the screen.

"Yes, but I am thankful you are coming. I don't know what to do," the text from Melia said.

Eliza looked up at Vera. "You go this. Stick to the narrative. You will be fine." She took another sip of coffee as Vera got to her feet.

"Take my car. The keys are in it. I will have Rhett bring Millie back to the city and I can get my car later," Eliza said.

"Are you sure?"

"Yes. Of course. It is no big deal. He will be eager to go once he hears that I ran into Aiden Cole at the party." Eliza smiled, remembering the secret she now kept on the boy who had been deemed "the next big thing."

"Okay. But if you need me . . ." Vera started again, but Eliza whooshed her hand in the air again, waving her thoughts and presence away.

"Go," Eliza assured her.

Eliza watched Vera head to the door and slip on her shoes, now dry from their time in the dryer.

"Oh," Eliza called out from the kitchen, trying not to wake Millie, "try to connect with Nina if you can. We need to know what she knows."

"Right." Vera called back before turning and shutting the door quietly behind her.

Hearing the car engine come alive outside, Eliza realized that Nina was their wild card. She was part of the whole scheme. She may not know her real name or if Willa had pulled it off, but she knew enough to cause a problem, a pit that sat in a small ball in the bottom of Eliza's new nerves of steel.

CHAPTER 77

CAMILLE

ONE MIGHT ASSUME THAT AFTER everything Camille had been through in the last twenty-four hours, her dreams wouldn't be dreams but more likely nightmares. Instead, however, with a large part of this mess behind her, she didn't experience either, just pure black calm, and a deeper sleep than she had had in months.

She finally awakened early afternoon to the sound of birds chirping outside the sun-streaked window, the glare of which was now warming the side of her cheek. Camille's eyes fluttered open, trying to register where she was, but not being immediately sure. As her blurry vision smoothed, she saw Eliza sitting at a chair in the corner, sipping coffee and paging through an old *People* magazine.

"You know a lot has happened since that twenty-year-old Cartrashian got pregnant, right?" Camille smiled as Eliza looked up at her from her rag mag.

"Well, some of us aren't as caught up on pop culture as others." Eliza returned the smile. "How are you feeling?" she asked, reaching for her coffee and taking a sip, the steam still wafting about the rim.

"Actually, I feel great," Camille began. "Best sleep I have had in God knows how long."

"Good." Eliza smiled over the rim of her cup.

"What time is it?" Camille asked, stretching her arms over her head.

"Just after one," Eliza responded. "You hungry?"

"Starved," Camille responded, realizing for the first time that she hadn't eaten or thought much about food in over a day.

"I will head to the house and grab some goodies and come back," Eliza said, slipping on her shoes.

"Where is Vera?" Camille asked, looking around but not seeing her.

"Oh. She headed back to DC," Eliza began. Then she went on to explain what happened with Melia and how it would look better if Vera were there with her, being the families "fixer" and all.

"Don't fret though," Eliza finished after seeing the panic settle back into Camille's eyes. "Everything will be totally fine." Eliza walked over to the couch, took Camille's cheeks in her hand, and forced her to look her in the eyes.

"I promise. Everything is going to be okay." Then she kissed the top of her head and turned to go.

"I'll be back with supplies," she called as she shut the door behind her, the warm air rushing in and mixing with the air-conditioned chill in the air.

Camille enjoyed the warmth that flooded over her, bringing a sense of calm along with it. She hadn't realized she was cold until the warmth hit her skin. Truth be told, she likely wasn't cold, more nervous.

Reaching onto the live edged walnut table that Eliza had adorned perfectly with the books and magazines, Camille grabbed her phone, which her wonderful friend had remembered to charge for her amidst of all the chaos. Glancing at the magazines, Camille wondered if Eliza knew they would end here, but she knew in her heart that her friend was simply the type of person who kept everything ready and up to date for a "just in case" situation.

Her phone lit with texts and emails from several people at the network—some from a drunken Brian wondering where she was, most from others asking if she heard about Connor, and the latest text was from Noel, which made her heart jump and quickly drop, remembering where they were.

"Are you okay? What is going on with Connor?" the text read.

Obviously, word had gotten out on social media that Connor was MIA, leaving Camille feeling foolish that she thought it wouldn't hit so fast. She knew she needed to respond to Noel and let him know where she was and what was going on, but first she needed to see what was being said.

Popping open her Twitter icon, it didn't take much scrolling for her to come across headline after headline about the missing head of the network. She clicked on a report from *Now! Online* and read the facts that were out there so far.

- Connor was last seen giving a toast to the crowd.
- He seemed fine, maybe tipsy, but the bartenders say he was drinking a lot and was seen with many different people.
- His assistant had fetched him the recent stats on the network.
- His wife reported him missing shortly after midnight.
- There was speculation that he was participating in some unsavory acts, an exposé that one of the larger newspapers had been working on.

No mention of her, which allowed the muscles in Camille's chest to loosen enough for her to finally breathe again. She exited out of Twitter and was about to text Noel when she noticed she had a few missed calls and voice mails.

She clicked on the voice mail icon, bringing the phone shakily to her ear. The first one was from another high up at the network wanting to talk to her. The second was a frantic drunk one from Brian. The third was from one of the PAs on her show checking in on her. The last one forced her to stop breathing yet again.

"Hello, Camille Givens. This is Detective Mark Gilmer. I need to speak with you regarding Connor Dixon. Please call me back at—" But Camille didn't hear the number. The phone fell out of her hand and onto the floor.

CHAPTER 78

VERA

VERA DROVE FASTER THAN the speed limit, no longer caring if the authorities stopped her. She had gotten away with much worse before seven a.m. A trip that should have taken closer to an hour and forty-five minutes, she had done in just over 85 minutes. Pulling into the parking garage at her office was an unfamiliar feeling since she had always walked to work, leaving her feeling off.

Looking in the rearview mirror, Vera realized that she was more than off—she was a fucking mess. She searched in Eliza's center console, looking for and finding wipes. Thank God for moms. She wiped last night's makeup, sweat, and murder off her face. Then she finger brushed her hair back and threw it up in a tight bun with a hair binder she also found in the console. She bit her lips and pinched each of her cheeks, trying to bring them to life. Then she grabbed her purse and headed into the office.

Taking the stairs to try to reset her morning, Vera arrived in her office to a waiting Dash, already at work typing away. Vera had the good sense to call Dash on her way into the city, asking her to come in on the weekend, something Dash was familiar with.

"Coffee?" Dash looked up from her screen, reaching out a black cup toward Vera.

"Oh my God! You are an angel!" Vera grabbed the cup, tipped it back, and drank half the cup in one gulp.

"And keep them coming," she said, Dash responding with a nod.

"Mrs. Dixon will be here soon. She is coming in on her husband's jet. The cops will be here after lunch. They want to speak with you and Mrs. Dixon," Dash said as Vera headed toward her office.

"Oh," Dash called after her, "and I tried to reach out to Nina Park, but her office hasn't returned my calls. I will keep trying."

"Thank you, Dash," Vera said before downing the rest of the coffee and wiggling the cup in her assistant's direction.

•• •• ••

Vera was onto her second cup of coffee and halfway through her email responses and Twitter feed regarding Connor when Dash opened her door, leading the way for a sunglass-covered Melia to enter.

She was dressed in a long, black trench coat, though it was the middle of the summer, her hair pulled back and through the back of a baseball cap with a New England Patriots logo on it. She clearly was no more put together than Vera, and was in much worse shape.

Slinking into one of the chairs in front of Vera's desk, Melia took off her sunglasses, setting them back into her large Louis Vuitton purse and setting the purse on the other chair.

There was no sign of tears in her eyes, though Vera understood that part of her was likely glad he was missing. If Vera didn't know the truth about what happened to Connor, she might have suspected that Melia did something to him.

"Vera," Melia began, her voice soft and mellow, "thank you so much for coming back to help me. I don't know what to do."

She sounded mildly believable, which Vera knew would play well in the press.

"Of course," Vera responded.

They made eye contact for a moment, sending charges throughout Vera's body, forcing her to readjust in her chair to forget them.

"So, tell me where we are at? What do you know? What do the cops know?"

Melia spent the next ten minutes explaining to Vera that the cops were trying to talk to everyone who was there last night, which is why they wanted to speak to her. She told her that her friend Deacon had published a small blurb last night after she had spoken with him, confirming that Connor was running for mayor and Vera was heading the campaign, so people would definitely be looking to her to be the face of information on the Dixons' behalf.

Vera felt her stomach flip. Lying was part of her job, she knew, but lying when you were involved in that lie was a whole other thing.

"Oh, and the network is freaking out. They want to spin this into good press somehow. Apparently, there is talk that the *Circadian* is about to run an exposé on Connor that won't put him in the best light."

"The *Circadian*?" Vera looked at Melia quizzically. "Isn't that the newspaper your friend Deacon works for?"

CHAPTER 79

ELIZA

ELIZA FIDDLED WITH THE DOOR HANDLE of the guest cottage, her arms full of canvas grocery bags and goodies from the main house, making it hard to use her hand freely. She finally got the door ajar, shoving it open with her hip bone. Slipping off her shoes, she noticed that Millie was still on the couch, staring off at the window across from her.

"Mill?" Eliza called, heading toward her, not bothering to shut the door.

"Mill?" she said again as she stepped in between her and the window, setting the bags on the floor.

"Mill?" Eliza waved her hand in front of Millie's eyes. "Hello?"

Millie finally shook her head lightly, blinking her eyes quickly several times, coming back to reality.

"What the hell?" Eliza said, still standing, her arms now crossed over her chest.

"Ummm . . . I . . . Umm . . ." Millie began.

Eliza widened her eyes and shook her head back and forth, silently asking Millie what was going on.

Millie swallowed. "The, um, cops called."

"Okay?" Eliza asked as though she expected this (she did).

"They, um, want to talk to me," Millie finished.

"Then you will talk to them. You have nothing to worry about. You did nothing wrong. This is on me, remember?" Eliza's hands now shifted to her hips, back into a power pose.

Millie's eyes met hers. "Did they call you?"

"No, but I am sure they will," Eliza responded, reaching down and grabbing the bags again.

"Let me get you something to eat. Then we will touch base with Vera, see if the cops called her, and then we will call them together, okay?"

"Okay," Millie responded blankly.

"Did you check in with Noel?" Eliza called as she walked into the kitchen.

Eliza went to work unloading the bags and heating the pan. The one thing she knew about her best friend was that her favorite comfort food was bad-for-you white bread and the most processed cheese around melted together into the all-American grilled cheese. Mix in some tomato soup for dipping, and you had one happy Millie.

Eliza's girls had embraced her with huge hugs when she entered the house, as though she had been gone for weeks and not a day. She held them, their warm cheeks snuggling into her stomach and chest. Rubbing their backs, she couldn't help but tell them that everything was all right now.

Piper had looked up at her, her arms still wrapped around her moms' waist' and asked, "What did you do in the city, Mom?"

"I did the right thing. I changed the world for the better," Eliza said, smiling down at her daughter.

"You did? How?" Piper tilted her head.

"She helped Auntie Millie with a tough time," Kinsley chimed in before Eliza could respond, her arms also still holding her mother. Eliza thought Rhett must have talked with them about Millie.

"That's right," Eliza cooed down at her girls. "Women help women. That's the only way we will get through this man-driven world, if we stick together. We catch each other when we fall. We are the net."

"Just like the spider mom." Piper smiled, proud of herself. "The black widow spins a web, catching things too. And the girls are the most powerful, remember?"

"I do remember, Piper." Eliza stroked her youngest's head. "I guess that makes me a black widow, huh?"

"Yeah. You are," Piper chimed again.

Eliza smiled at this, her inner pride swelling that she made the world a safer place for her girls by killing off one more disgusting male spider, a species the world definitely needed less of.

Now back in the cottage, Eliza buttered her bread, unwrapped several pieces of cheese, and put the bread on the pan, the sizzle echoing in the small kitchen. She enjoyed the warmth from the pan and the moment, because she knew that once she brought the grilled cheese into Millie, the lies would continue. First to the cops, then the network, and likely elsewhere. A smile spread across her lips, Eliza warming not only from the stove heat but from the idea that she enjoyed this lie. Nothing about this situation rattled her. Dare she say it settled her?

CHAPTER 80

CAMILLE

CAMILLE TRIED TO CALM HER shaking fingers, taking a deep breath before opening up Noel's text thread again. His text hadn't seemed overly nervous. Why would it? He knew nothing and was simply doing her a courtesy by checking in since her boss was MIA and it was making the news.

"Hey. Thanks for checking in. I am okay. I actually headed with Eliza back to her place for an impromptu girls' weekend. I will be back on Sunday night," Camille typed.

The blinking dots appeared quicker than she expected.

"Glad you are okay. Sounds good. Kids are good."

Simple, no fuss, no genuine care. *Things really have shifted for us,* Camille thought. In the blink of an eye, Noel was moving on, half expecting her to do the same, she supposed.

"Okay. Good to hear. They can text me if they'd like," she wrote back, wanting to write something more about the failure of their marriage, the end of an era, and how could he already be fine and finite, but she hit Send.

Blinking dots again.

"What is going on with Connor?"

Camille's breath caught, but this time she steadied herself, taking a quick, deep breath, reminding herself that she could do this; it started here and would get easier the more she said it.

"I don't know. I just saw it on Twitter not that long ago. I guess he is missing. I only saw him a few times last night. Not sure what is going on." And as she pressed Send, she began to believe it.

Eliza walked into the room, holding a plate that Camille couldn't see the top of but could smell instantly, the aroma releasing her shoulders and bringing a much-needed smile to her face.

The cheese melted over the edges of the perfectly golden bread, leaving a bronzed crust, the perfect grilled cheese. Eliza had been making them for Camille since middle school. They were the one go-to they both knew would never fail to bring Camille back up.

Eliza took a seat on the couch next to Camille, their thighs touching, and she leaned her head onto Camille's shoulder, allowing Camille to feel for a moment like the protector, the strong one of the two. The feeling was fleeting, she knew, but she appreciated Eliza' gesture almost as much as the grilled cheese.

Sinking her teeth into the melty goodness, Camille's stomach barked, unable to wait any longer for her to put something in it and calm herself from the outside in.

Swallowing, Eliza lifted her head from her shoulder, turning to her friend. "I know you are scared, but I am here. I texted Vera, and she is on her way to speak with the cops right now at her office. Seems they are talking to everyone who was on the guest list, which might be why I haven't heard from them. I was a plus one, so my name isn't on there. But I am sure they will figure out I was there, too, and I will make the same brave call you are going to. But for now, I am here, and you can do this."

Camille continuously munched on the grilled cheese as Eliza gave her the pep talk. And when all that was left was the buttery residue on her fingers, Eliza handed her the phone.

CHAPTER 81

VERA

DETECTIVE GOODWIN AND SERGEANT VINCELLI were quite the pair sitting in Vera's conference room waiting for her and Melia to join them. Vera had asked Melia to come to DC, feeling more comfortable handling things in "her" town than in the business that is NYC. Not to mention she didn't feel like returning to the scene of the crime.

Goodwin, a young woman likely in her early thirties, had an athletic build and hair cut high and tight, leaving Vera wondering if she had served. The wrinkles on her face from the stress of the job did nothing to help her already plain look, but Vera was sure she was the type of woman who didn't have time to be beauty conscious anyhow.

Vincelli, on the other hand, was a short, plump man, with rosy cheeks with a buzz cut. He looked to be older than Goodwin, but not by much. The stress didn't wear on his face as hard. He sat, leaning back on the back legs of the chair, tempting faith, Vera thought.

Vera found out that Melia had already spoken with a different cop in NYC, Detective Gilmer, and had told him everything she knew about Connor and what could have happened to him. She looked like Vera felt, exhausted and put out. But it was Vera's turn to get questioned, so the two women headed into the conference room.

Vincelli leaned his chair forward again, the front legs hitting the marble with a crack, Goodwin shooting him a look. Both then stood to greet Vera and Melia.

"Hello, Mrs. Dixon and Miss Sutton. I am detective Goodwin, and this is Sergeant Vincelli." Goodwin gestured over toward the chubby man, whose belly was brushing up against the edge of Vera's glass table, before extending her hand out to the two women.

"I believe you spoke with my partner, Detective Gilmer, in NYC, Mrs. Dixon?" Goodwin questioned as she took a seat, Vincelli following suit.

"Yes, I did. Late last night ... or early this morning ... I guess I don't know what to call it," Melia said, sounding frazzled. Vera put her hand on top of Melia's shoulder, trying to calm her.

"Don't worry, Mrs. Dixon. We know this has been a tough day. We are here to help. I will have a few follow-up questions for you and some general questions for Miss Sutton, as well." Goodwin opened a folder sitting on the table in front of her.

"Of course. Whatever you need," Vera said, patting Melia's shoulder one last time before removing her hand and clutching them together in front of her on the table.

The foursome would spend the better part of the next two hours revisiting all the events of the night before to their recollection—Goodwin doing most of the questioning, while her sidekick loudly smacked on gum and took the occasional note.

Vera had told the story just as Eliza had detailed, and it seemed as though the cops bought it hook, line, and sinker. They didn't seem too worried about the hours in which Connor was missing, but more in the hours leading up to then.

"So, you two were together around the time that Connor went missing. Is that correct?" Vincelli asked, slyly smiling at Goodwin as though proud he asked a helpful question.

"Yes," Vera said, looking at Melia. "Yes, we were together."

"Yes," Melia chimed in, as well, "I was doing my best to get Vera to agree to head Connor's mayoral run. I had heard she was the very best, and I wanted Connor to have the best." Melia finished by looking down, almost as though she were going to cry.

Vera couldn't help but think the whole thing as a little overacted, but then again maybe the woman was truly sad. Who was she to say?

"So, after you left the stairwell?" Goodwin asked, leaving the question open ended.

"I went to break the news to my reporter friend, Deacon, knowing he would tweet the news out immediately and we would have one more thing to celebrate at the party. I thought it would be a fun surprise for Connor," Melia said, looking down again, "but I never found him."

Vincelli and Goodwin's eyes shifted over toward Vera, waiting to hear what she did next.

"I went to look for my friends, and when I didn't find them at the party, I went back to our suite, where I located them." Vera looked Goodwin straight in the eye, leaving her no reason not to believe the story.

"Mrs. Dixon, do you have any reason to believe someone would want to hurt your husband or that he would run away from someone?" Vincelli piped up, speaking a little louder than he needed to.

"I don't know. Honestly, my husband is a powerful man, and powerful people have enemies. But he hid a lot of that from me. He tried to keep things simple for us. As simple as they could be." Vera watched as Melia rubbed her bruised wrist, making her face begin to tighten.

"Miss Sutton?" Goodwin asked.

"Honestly, I have no idea. I literally agreed to this job a few hours ago, mainly because Melia is so convincing. I figured if she was this amazing, he must be too." Vera looked over at Melia, who gave her a soft smile.

"Well . . ." Goodwin looked a little frazzled as Vincelli reached into the back of the folder, pulling forward a set of printer paper stapled together in the top corner. He threw it across the table, the packet sliding and landing in front of Vera and Melia.

"Then what do you have to say about this?" He stood, leaning over the table, suddenly acting like one of those cops in a TV drama.

There in bold letters, across the top of the paper, it read:

"Dirty Dixon: Sex, Drugs, Shock & Payroll" by Deacon Hunter.

CHAPTER 82

ELIZA

ELIZA AIMLESSLY SCROLLED THROUGH her Facebook feed as Millie punched in the numbers for the detective. Usually, she hated this sort of thing, killing time on a platform that only made you feel left out and less popular. Something about the social media medium left Eliza feeling like a terrible wife, mother, and friend. She hated it but couldn't stop. It was an addiction she hadn't been able to kick yet.

She looked up when she heard Millie finally connect with the detective.

"Yes. This is Camille Givens. I am returning a call from Detective Gilmer."

Eliza nodded at Millie, who was not looking to her, trying to calm her nerves as she listened to the detective explain something over the earpiece.

"Yes, I was at the party. I have worked for the station for years, and it was a celebration of our ratings."

Millie went silent again, listening.

"Yes, I saw him a few times. We chatted. Last time I saw him was when he gave his speech thanking everyone." Millie looked again at Eliza.

Eliza mouthed "you got this" toward her.

"No. I don't know much about the business side or his personal life, so I wouldn't know if someone was after him," Millie said.

Eliza nodded at her friend and went back to her aimless scrolling as in the background she heard Millie tell the story they had cultivated.

"My friend?" Millie repeated, sounding nervous and looking toward Eliza. "Eliza Kingfield."

Eliza raised her head at the mention of her name.

"Yes, she was my plus one, so that's why she wouldn't have been on the initial list." Millie kept eye contact with Eliza.

Eliza realized that was why the cops hadn't called her yet—they didn't even know she was there, which struck her as odd since they must have shown up in the video footage or pictures of the evening.

"Yes, sir, *that* Kingfield." Millie rolled her eyes at Eliza, Eliza knowing that the detective had asked about Rhett.

When Millie's conversation with the cop went back to the station and her role there, she went back to her phone. Facebook-worthy shots of people she barely cared about flashed across the screen, rending a pit in her stomach. But then she realized she had something these perfect people didn't have, a purpose. She had done something that would make the world a better place for her daughters. She had solved a problem that seemed to be spreading through the headlines every day, only growing bigger, more invasive. She had single-handedly taken a stand against the male power dynamic and the misogyny blanketing our society.

And almost as if on cue, she saw it. Another headline of men thinking only with their dicks. Except this time, it was the headline she had braced for since talking to Nina Parks.

There, reposted by her friend Tracy Nichols, was article from the *Central Circadian*: "Dirty Dixon: Sex, Drugs, Shock & Payroll." Her eyes immediately widened as she reread the headline, almost shocked to finally see it in print.

Just as she was focusing enough to read it, she heard a clicking noise and looked up to see Millie snapping at her, still on the phone. She mouthed "What's wrong?" obviously having watched Eliza's face register sudden shock.

Eliza got up, walked over to the couch, and sat down next to her friend, who was still answering what seemed like mundane questions from the detective. Eliza placed her hand on Millie's thigh and held her phone out for her to see.

She watched Millie squint, her hand still pressing the phone to her ear, and scan the headline. Her mouth dropped open and the phone started slipping from her ear, Millie catching it at the last minute. She looked at Eliza, who just shook her head slightly and lifted her eyebrows as to signify that it was what she had told them all along. Now there was proof.

"Yes, detective, I will let you know if I hear anything," Millie said, turning away from Eliza's phone.

"Yes, Eliza's number is . . ." Millie said, giving the cop Eliza's number so she could be questioned next.

"Yes. Thank you." Millie finally pulled the phone from her ear and turned back to Eliza.

"Well, good news is that there are going to be a hell of a lot more women who will look way guiltier than us." Millie smiled at Eliza as the story cleared from Eliza's phone, replaced by the number of the police department. She was up. Lights, camera, action.

CHAPTER 83

CAMILLE

"HELLO," ELIZA COOED AS SHE answered the phone next to Camille. "Yes, this is Eliza Kingfield."

As Eliza went into her dissertation of the same story that Camille and just laid out for Detective Gilmer, Camille looked again at her phone screen, which was now lit up with a slew of texts.

Many different forms of the same question: "Did you see this?"

Seems over the last few minutes, the news of Connor's infidelity and sexual abuse had spread like wildfire across the internet. Camille was sure that the network was in full-out panic right now, first a missing president and now one accused of forcing himself on women and using company money for drugs.

Ignoring the texts, she clicked on the link. She had to commend Deacon on his headline. It was clever and kitschy, drawing you in immediately, something she knew a thing or two about. A well-executed headline could make or break a story. Not that this story wouldn't make the rounds on its own, but the headline made it even juicier.

"Connor Dixon is a man of means. A man of power. A man with a plan. A man with a wife. A man with an empire. A man with a problem. A man with many problems," the article started. Camille felt her body settle back into the soft couch cushions, ready to find out who exactly was the man they had murdered. And then as if the cop on Eliza's phone could hear her inner thoughts,

Camille looked over at Eliza, who smiled, winked, and kept on lying through her beautifully straight teeth.

"This, of course, isn't the first time we have heard of a man in power using blackmail, force, coercion, money, and status to get his way. This is, however, the first of this magnitude. The lengths Connor went to cover up his actions were beyond comprehension. It took me two years and countless interviews to piece the web together. He thought he would never get caught, but when you spin a web, eventually you get up stuck in the middle."

The last sentence made Camille's mouth dry a little. They were in the midst of their own web. The question was how far they were from getting caught in it themselves?

The article was written of course by Deacon Hunter, an acquaintance of Camille's in the industry. He was known for no-nonsense journalism with a thirst for the bloodiest of stories. Recently he had been pretty quiet on the news front, writing a lot of puff pieces usually surrounding politics. Camille had wondered a time or two in the last year what had happened to his hunger, but it now turned out that he was working on the story of the decade.

It began with an anonymous source, a news tip in the form of a slip during a cocktail conversation one evening. One too many cups of courage later, and the story was beginning to unfold, Deacon lapping it all up. The source never said it was "off the record," so he ran with it.

As the article went on to explain, untangling a web this intricate was near impossible. Some parts weakened easier than others, most being paid well enough to keep the web secure.

Then, he got Emery Hall to tell her story. The blockbuster Hollywood beauty had just finished her first big-budget superhero film for the network, becoming the breakout star of the franchise. A fresh face for a new generation of comic lovers. She had gone into a meeting with Connor in his office in Santa Barbara, alone at his request. Though she wasn't thrilled at the idea, she went anyway, knowing it would be good for her career. A young, thin, redhead with a short skirt and knee high boots walked into that office a woman on the rise, and walked out a damaged young lady who wouldn't work again in Hollywood for years to come.

All the women who opened up after Emery's story told the same tale, but the ones who didn't speak had a much more fairy tale ending.

It always began with a closed-door meeting, an invite to his hotel room, or a dinner at a restaurant with a large, VIP-blocked area. His demeanor started off complimentary, leaning toward fatherly pride, trying to ease their comfort around him. Insert joke here, flattery there. Talk a little about his extensive power and her amazing potential. And once she was feeling pretty good about herself, maybe even good enough to take a risk, he would proposition her. His hand on her thigh, his words asking for her to meet him in the middle. You do this for me and I'll do things for you. If not, I will kill your career. Except this time, Camille had killed his.

CHAPTER 84

VERA

VERA WATCHED ALL THE COLOR drain from Melia's face, her eyes begin to roll back in her head, and every muscle in her body go limp. She knew what was happening and yet was so in shock herself she couldn't do anything to stop it. Melia's head landed squarely in her lap.

"Melia? Melia?" Vera called, tapping the side of her cheek lightly, but firm enough to wake her. Detective Goodwin shoved her chair back and quietly was at Vera's side, concerned for Melia, as well. Vincelli sat there, seemingly unmoved by the display.

She wasn't out long, her eyelashes fluttering before her eyes shot open wide. She woke with a look on her face that Vera couldn't immediately register. Shock? Wrath? Disgust?

She shot up, looking back at the Sergeant Vincelli across the table, not even registering the paper still lying in front of them. As she entered a stare down with him, no one else in the room spoke, neither sure what to say.

Goodwin rose back to her feet and headed to her chair. Vera locked eyes with her, both women unsure of what their next step should be here.

"Melia," Vera cooed, placing her hand on hers, "are you okay?"

Melia kept staring at Vincelli, looking at him with whatever she was harboring for Connor behind her eyes. Vincelli, for his part, kept his dopey-looking eyes staring right back. Vera was unsure if he was letting her have her moment or if he was challenging her. She wanted to believe he was doing the kind thing, but was fairly certain it was the latter.

"Dash!" Vera called as she turned toward the hallway. "Can you bring in some water please?"

And before Vera had turned back to Melia, Dash came running back into the room, arms full of bottled water.

Vera opened one for Melia, setting it in front of her, willing her to drink it. When she didn't move, Vera squeezed her hand firmly, finally breaking the curse that was holding Melia prisoner.

Vera motioned to the water bottle, and Melia took a few small, ladylike sips. Then Vera nodded slightly at Goodwin to proceed.

"Melia. I know this is all a very upsetting, but we need to know if you knew anything about these allegations?" Goodwin asked while Melia took another tiny sip.

"We can give you a few moments to read the piece if you like before you answer," she finished.

Melia's eyes made their way over to the article on the table. Again, she began to stare, her eyes glazing over with the same darkening agent Vera had seen slip over Eliza's the night before.

"Why don't you give us a minute?" Vera asked, nodding to Goodwin.

"Yes. Of course." Goodwin got up, tapping the back of Vincelli's chair, encouraging him to do the same. He looked inconvenienced by the move, but followed her lead nonetheless.

When the cops had left the room, Vera spun Melia's chair to meet hers, putting them knee to knee again like they had been in the stairwell.

"Melia," she said, putting her hands on her shoulders, "I know this is a lot. I know this is hard. But I am here with you. I am going to get you through this. But you have to do as I say."

Melia didn't speak, just nodded. When she finally made eye contact with Vera, the look in her eyes unsettled her. If Connor wasn't already dead, she was sure Melia would kill him now.

Just as Vera handed Melia one copy of the article, taking the other for herself, she heard Dash's voice at the door.

"Um, Vera."

Vera turned her chair.

"I have Nina Park on the phone."

CHAPTER 85

ELIZA

THE ARTICLE HAD BEEN A much longer and intricate detailing of everything Nina Parks had told Eliza at the party. It was a little unnerving how close it was to what had happened to Millie. Eliza had seen it on her face as she read it, the familiarity of the feeling. The only new part of the story was the drug use that he had been dabbling in.

Apparently, Connor had been quite the fan of cocaine, using several times a week, paying off anyone who saw him partake. "Recreational" wasn't the word one would use for his activity. He was an addict.

Now, as she threw a few more pieces of wood onto the small flame she had pridefully started, Eliza was reflecting on her conversation with the police. All had gone as planned, but when she asked how they didn't already know she was there, they had mentioned something about the lack of video footage at the event.

And after a quick text to Vera, she had found out that "lack of video footage" was code for the fact that Connor disconnected all cameras at his events. He used the fact that people of this status wanted to be able to enjoy some privacy for once in their lives as his excuse. But in light of the article, it seemed it was all part of a much larger plot for him not to get caught.

Luckily for the women, his forethought worked to their advantage. There would be no footage of Millie with Connor, none of them leaving, and none of the aftermath. All because he wanted to force himself on some unsuspecting woman. Eliza had to thank him for his disgusting ways on this one.

Through the warm, amber light of the fire that Eliza was trying to grow, she could see Millie sitting in a ball on one of her blue Adirondack chairs, one arm wrapped around her sweatpants-covered legs, the other holding a glass of Prisoner wine, Eliza's favorite red, strangely fitting for the moment.

Millie had run the gamut of emotions today. Her face looking battled, defeated, and yet somehow relaxed. This was the most at peace Eliza had seen her since she had gotten to NYC. Her cheeks flushed as the heat grew and the fire rose. Eliza loved when Millie looked happy; it was one of the few times in life she felt she could truly breathe. She had worried about her friend every day since that day in the tub, and things hadn't gotten any less worrisome in the last twenty-four hours. But as she brought the glass of wine to her mouth, took a sip, and gave Eliza a crimson stained–lip smile, Eliza felt her entire body ease, if only for a moment.

"I think it is ready," Eliza called through the roaring fire now. "You ready?"

"Born ready," Millie called back as she stood up from her chair, wine still in her hand, and reached down to the pile of fabric at her feet.

Single handedly, Eliza watched Millie first toss in Connor's suit coat, the fire extinguishing a little, then sending up a puff of black smoke, as if eradicating the evil from the garments.

Eliza used a pitchfork to move the material around as the fire began to do its job, incinerating the thousand-dollar fabric in moments. As soon as the jacket was gone, Millie threw his pants, then his shirt, undershirt, socks, and shoes. There was something so oddly satisfying about watching thousands of dollars go up in smoke. Watching their couture dresses sizzle and pop in the fire was the only tragedy in the moment. The lace and silk curling up in dark rolls before crumbling into ash. Lastly, she threw the bed sheet on the fire. Another large puff of smoke, and then the smell of burning continued.

Millie returned to her seat, grabbing the wine from the ground beside her and refilling her now-empty glass. Eliza came over, taking a seat next to her, setting her glass on the armrest of her chair as she continued to move the bits of fabric around the fire, making sure every single thread burned.

When her neuroses ceased, Eliza stuck the pitchfork into the ground next to her, leaned back into the chair next to a permanently smiling Millie, and grabbed her wine glass.

"Everything is going to be okay," Millie said, catching Eliza a little off guard. She wasn't sure if it was a question or a statement, but then she caught sight of Millie's face in the firelight. She was beaming.

"To us," Eliza called, raising her glass in Millie's direction.

"To us," Millie echoed, clinking her glass with Eliza's.

Both women brought their glasses to their lips, taking a sip, and stared back at the fire dancing in front of them. Eliza felt like the flames were dancing in unison with her soul. Something about all of this felt so right to her. And over the next few hours, while the two women sat silently marveling at the power in the fire and in themselves, Eliza realized she enjoyed the smell of evil being burned at the stake.

CHAPTER 86

CAMILLE

IT WAS WELL AFTER MIDNIGHT when Eliza and Camille had finally headed back into the guest house, snuggling up in bed, back to back. The room still smelled of campfire and wine when the morning light glinted in through the windows and Camille's phone began to buzz.

She ignored it the first time, hoping she could fall back asleep after opening one eye enough to see it was only after seven a.m. But when the buzzing happened a second time and then a third, she finally forced herself out of bed, Eliza sitting up in the process.

"What is going on?" Eliza called as Camille headed over to her phone, plugged in across the bedroom.

Camille unplugged the phone as the screen lit up her face.

She felt her breath catch.

"It's the network."

Eliza threw the covers back, got up out of bed, threw on a robe, and called back to Camille as she headed into the kitchen.

"Wait one minute. I will make coffee before you call them back."

Camille loved her friend for this, knowing that she couldn't function without caffeine in her veins, much less her brain. Knowing the phone would likely ring again any moment, she rushed into the bathroom, brushed her teeth, still pink-tinged from the wine the night before. She brushed and threw her hair up into a loose bun, though no one at the network would see her. She came out of the bathroom, hit first by the aromatic smell of life that was coffee in the air, then to a cup in her hand, her phone buzzing yet again.

Camille took a large gulp, ignoring the fact that it was much too hot to drink, and answered the call.

"Hello? Camille Givens," she uttered into the phone, taking another quick sip as she listened to a roomful of people introduce themselves to her one by one over speakerphone.

It was the board of directors, most of whom she had met, none of whom she remembered the names of. Nonetheless, she listened while they listed, trying to mainline her coffee in.

By the time they had gotten through the names, Camille was seated at the breakfast nook table, overlooking Eliza's vast acres. A sea of green and bright yellow coming to life under the early-morning sun. Another day on the horizon.

Eliza came and sat across from her, sipping her coffee, scrolling through her phone, punching away, and waiting for Camille's next move.

"Camille, this is Grant Donovan, board VP. Listen, in light of everything that has happened, we feel the best thing for the station is to get some good press out there. Try to drown the dramatics surrounding Connor a little."

Camille nodded before realizing that they couldn't see that and quickly responded, "Yes. Um . . . what did you have in mind?"

"I realize that may have sounded callous." Grant continued, "What I meant was that while we are hopeful for Connor's safe return, we need to do some damage control in regards to this article." He cleared his throat. "I am assuming you have read the article."

"Yes," Camille said, quieter than she wanted.

"Right, well, as a board, we thought the best thing would be for us to announce you as the new lead for the online news division that we are launching. Your numbers are continually on the rise, and people all over the country, especially women, seem to love you, and we just feel that this would be a good PR move to counteract the negative female attention the station is receiving right now."

Grant finished speaking, but before Camille could respond, a woman's voice came over the earpiece,

"Camille. Ivy Collins here. What Grant meant to say was that because of your amazing performance and huge draw, this was a move we were already going to make, but due to Connor's appalling and disgusting actions, we are forced to speed this up. We hope you understand we are not doing this as a PR stunt. You are more than deserving, and we are very excited to see what you will do with this new venture."

Camille smiled at this. Trying not to be too eager, she sat quiet for a moment, letting it digest.

"Oh, and did we mention it comes with a huge pay raise *and* you will be in charge?" Grant threw in.

Camille could swear she heard Ivy mutter something about men and money under her breath.

"Wow," Camille finally spoke, "I am honored and humbled."

She stopped, realizing that what she was about to say next could force them to change their mind. She took a deep breath, closed her eyes, and said, "Thank you for this opportunity, but if I am going to do this, and I really get to call the shots, I want to launch my first post with the truth."

Camille's eyes opened and met Eliza's, who were wide and frightened looking, her mouth slightly open, ready to object.

"I need to tell the world . . ." Camille stopped and took another breath as Eliza scrunched her brow. "That my picture-perfect life isn't as it seems. . . . I am getting a divorce."

Camille could hear Eliza audibly breathe out as she heard Ivy chime in again on the phone.

"Camille, we are so sorry you are going through that. I have been divorced twice and know how difficult it can be. That being said, while I know you are worried about the optics, I want you to know that we aren't. In fact, I think this may just make people even more endeared to you. Life is messy. Things fall apart. But putting ourselves back together after tragedy—that's something everyone can relate to."

Camille smiled, knowing Ivy would never realize just how incredibly true those words were.

CHAPTER 87

VERA

IT WOULD TURN OUT THAT talking to Nina would be a dead end. Not only did it seem like she had little to no recollection of the evening, it also appeared that she had decided to remove herself from any and all connections to Connor after the events of that evening. Vera couldn't explain it, but something told her that Nina had nothing to do with the events of that night.

After hanging up with her, Vera read the entire article, her stomach turning time and again at the vile nature of the man she was about to help run for even more power.

Not feeling as though she was ready to go home, Vera crashed on her office couch, sending Melia and Dash home, promising to return the next morning, since the cops were coming back after letting the article digest.

Bright and early at seven a.m., Dash arrived with coffee and a change of clothes for Vera. Still casual, her skin already feeling too tight.

Later, Melia and the cops followed up after lunch, the police insisting on talking to Melia alone first. She had left Melia alone with the cops in the conference room, Vera keeping an eye on them from outside the glass walls. Melia was stronger than anyone knew, but Vera was beginning to get an odd sense about her.

Walking back into the conference room, a bleary eyed Melia finished reiterating to the cops that while she knew about the drug use and had begged him to quit, trying several times to check him into rehab, she had no idea about the women.

"Every wife of a powerful man hears the stories of other powerful men using their power in negative ways, but Connor wasn't that man. I believed in the good in him," Melia said, tears streaming down her face.

Vera tried to stop her brow from scrunching together. This was a woman whose husband beat her, repeatedly, and now she was claiming she saw the good in him. Either she was one hell of an actress, or she was suffering from some form of Stockholm syndrome.

"Okay," Goodwin said as she rose to her feet, stacking together the papers in her folder, "that's all for now. We will be in touch as we know more. Again, Mrs. Dixon, I am sorry for everything you are going through right now. We are going to do our very best to find your husband."

She walked around the edge of the desk, Vincelli behind her like a good lapdog. Extending her hand to Melia, Vincelli spoke up from behind her, "One more question before we go?"

Melia sniffled and nodded.

"Do you think your husband had any idea he was about to be outted?"

"Excuse me?" Melia asked.

"I am just wondering if he somehow knew this was coming and decided to take off before it hit," Vincelli said.

"Not that I know of." Melia sniffed again.

"I just know that if this shit was coming out about me, I'd get the hell out of dodge," Vincelli said, nodding to himself as he said it.

The two cops exited the conference room and were led out of the office by Dash, who was then on her way to get some dinner for the two women after a long day.

Vera took a seat next to Melia, again turning their chairs to face one another, knee to knee, their signature.

"Melia, I am so sorry about everything. I . . ." Vera was about to go on but Melia wiped her eyes and placed her hands on Vera's knees.

"Don't be," she said, the darkness clouding the edges of her eyes again. "You did everything I hoped you would and more."

Vera couldn't stop her brow from creasing together this time. "What?" she asked.

"When I searched you out, I knew you would be the perfect partner," Melia started.

"You had all the qualities I was looking for. You were bright, tenacious, beautiful, and not to mention very good at your job. I knew Connor would trust you immediately."

Vera sat silently, still not understanding what Melia was getting at.

"I was going to do it all myself until I saw your friend talking to Nina Park. Willa . . . Willa Morgan, right?" Melia smiled, proud she remembered the name.

Vera felt the color drain from her face this time as Melia continued.

"They seemed to be in quite a deep conversation and knowing that there were rumblings about Connor wanting to throw some money Nina's way, I figured it was about Connor's infidelity, especially since I had been feeding the stories to Deacon for years. And knowing that he was close with Nina, I figured he would've spilled the beans."

Vera felt a lump in her throat start to close her airway.

"I snuck behind them, listening for a moment to their conversation, and I could see in Willa's eyes that she was ready. Ready to be a rebel with a cause. I didn't need to be the one to do it; she would do it for me."

Vera tried to catch her breath, tried to remind herself to breathe in and out as Melia continued.

"After I saw Connor take off with your other friend, Camille, I knew that it wouldn't be long until he would repeat his routine, and if I could get Willa to catch him in the act, then the present I left for her in the bathroom might just do the trick."

"The syringe?" Vera croaked out, her mouth almost too dry to speak.

"Yes. 'Black death' they call it. A mix of cocaine and fentanyl. I figured it would be ruled a drug episode gone bad, but then you guys went over and above, didn't you?"

Melia gave Vera a sinister smile, one that unnerved her to her bones.

"What do you mean?" Vera pursed her lips together, trying to get saliva to moisten her mouth again.

"You went full cover-up on it," Melia started. "I saw you sneak the body out of the suite, but after that, I thought it best for me to stay seen at the party, so I headed back in, ditching my umbrella in the dumpster out back."

"So, don't you see . . . we are in this together now." Melia reached for Vera hands, taking them in hers. "I told you mine. Now you tell me yours."

Vera's head was spinning. All along she had thought she was helping this simple, sweet, vulnerable woman escape a monster, but it turned out that she didn't really need her at all; she was just as brave as Vera had seen in her eyes the night they met.

"Wait," Vera interjected before she told her how the rest of the night played out. "The bruises, the bracelet, the flirting, was that all real?" Vera then realized her hands were shaking in Melia's.

"Every single thing I have ever told you or done for you is real. He hurt me every way a man can, and when I saw you in an article, I knew you were my ticket out. My ticket to happiness. My partner." Melia squeezed Vera's hands and pulled her closer. "What we did was a good thing. You have no idea the extent of his evilness. You freed me. We freed a lot of women. We are the heroes no one will know about. But together, together we know what we are and what we did. Together we are unstoppable."

And then she kissed her. A long, slow, passionate kiss. The kind of kiss Vera had waited her whole life for, the kind of kiss you form a life around.

And when their lips finally separated, Melia placed her hand on Vera's cheek and said, "We aren't murderers. We are martyrs."

EPILOGUE

ELIZA

THREE MONTHS HAD PASSED since Eliza's life had gone from mundane to meaningful. She carried herself with a little more pride and now secretly enjoyed her time on social media, looking for more stories of men doing wrong, igniting in her ideas of ending their reign of terror. She hadn't done it yet, offed yet another man throwing his dick around, but she thought about it every day, the feeling sitting warm in the bottom of her stomach, gurgling, waiting.

The police and media attention around Connor's disappearance had died down. There had been no leads and no evidence of foul play, so at this point the cops had all but assumed he ran off to avoid the wrath of his transgressions coming to light, or just ended it all off a cliff. The internet was full of rumors and stories, people guessing what happened, others stating that they wish they could kill him themselves to make him pay for his actions. Eliza loved reading every one of them, bringing even more validation to her secret.

Vera had done one hell of a job making Melia seem like the sad, lost, "assumed widow" in the media. People had begun to root for her in ways they never saw coming. Even Nina Park had reached out, wanting to talk about Melia running for some sort office. Women in power was the new men behaving badly, and Eliza, for one, was loving all of it. One of the narratives people rooted for the most involved the idea of Vera, one of the most powerful lesbians in DC, and Melia, the sweet, abandoned wife learning to find her way, getting together in the end. Of course, Eliza already knew that story was written; the two women had fallen head over heels for each other in private, waiting until the right time to go public. The last time they had come to dinner with Eliza and Rhett, there was even talk of adoption, a thought that had warmed Eliza's heart.

And then there was Millie. She had done exactly as she had said she would, launched her online news brand by coming out about the impending divorce, and just as Ivy had predicted, the support had been overwhelming. There were the trolls, too. There always would be, but for the first time in her life, Eliza had watched her friend and had not been worried about her every day. Noel moved out, and Camille had moved on. She had settled into her new career and was thriving on a new medium. She was a trailblazer, just like Eliza knew she could be.

Eventually, she would tell the world she was one of Connor's victims. Not the time or entire story, but she would share the deep secret of being a survivor in a world where survivors were supposed to stay silent. But it was going to be on her time, and maybe a little on Vera's, since she knew when it was best to pull the Band-Aid off and let the world in on the truly big news.

The three women had become even more bonded that night than they had been before. Vera had recognized that Millie and Eliza shared something she would never be privy to, but for the first time in her life, she was truly okay with that. The women had gone to war and survived the aftermath, all three of them changed for the better. Chauvinism had tried to bury them, but it didn't know they were the seeds.

And as Eliza kneeled in the dry dirt of her garden, pulling up the last of her vegetables in the crisp, fall air, she sprinkled a white dust in the holes where the plants once were. In the spring she would plant more seeds there, and the circle of life would continue. But for now, the ground would be filled with bits and dust of the teeth she had finally found in the pig pen. She had checked for weeks and weeks, finally catching a glint of yellowish white through the mud after one of her early-morning runs. She had pulled them from the mud, taken them out to a rock along one of the back trails, and with her pink-handled hammer, smashed them into tiny pieces.

As Eliza used her crème, floral-gloved hands to pile dirt back over the holes, she took a moment, staring at a spider web in the corner of the garden gate. The beautiful silk glowed orange in the autumn sun. Behind it, the leaves on the trees began to turn colors and drop. She couldn't help but think it oddly comforting how autumn was so beautiful, yet everything was dying.

Acknowledgements

I never went to school for writing. Never knew my innate creativity would lend itself to imaging stories that had yet to be told. That being said, in order for me to get from imagination to novel it took a lot of people who aided me, kept me sane, kept me going, and gave me opportunities I wasn't always sure I deserved.

A huge thank you to **Sarah Fader** who saw something in me and gave me the chance to share my stories with the world, and agreed to be my publisher. Thank you for taking a chance on my brand of crazy.

Thank you to the team at **Eliezer Tristan Publishing** who helped mold and shape my words into a story ready to share.

I am incredibly grateful to **Erin Servais** who took my messy manuscript and help develop it into a work of art.

To **Lala** who dealt with my continuous anxieties and constant questions about the book industry and publishing in general. You are a wonderful friend.

To my **family and friends** who have taken the time to check in on me, support me, read my unedited crap that after much editing would actually become literate, and love my through this pipe dream of mine I am forever grateful.

Addie and Lyla, the reason I fought so hard to pursue my dream. I hope you saw in your mother the perseverance and drive to make anything possible. You have the ability to become anything and everything you want if you work hard enough. You are my reason for being. I am so grateful to be your mother.

Glen. You have loved me through my crazy, supported, and encouraged me when I wanted to quit. I know being married to me isn't always easy, and my constant need for words of affirmation must drive you nuts but I am so thankful for your patience and strength when I needed both. I love you.

Last but not least, the person who above all encouraged me, cheered me on, begged to be involved in every mundane step, dropped everything to help me, and showered me with constant positive reinforcement ~ **Anna**. To say I am thankful for you would fail to come close to how integral you were in me becoming an author. You believed in me when I couldn't. You went over and above. Your help was immeasurable and your support needed. Without you this book would not exist.

CPSIA information can be obtained
at www.ICGtesting.com
Printed in the USA
LVHW030303240919
631985LV00003B/64/P